CITY
of
THIEVES

Tobias knew he was running from himself. If he stopped to think, he'd be lost. Only once before in his life had he been this frightened.

Voices screamed in his head: Mum, Moleglass, Zebediah, Ambrose, Windlass. And as he crossed a patch of open ground, he heard Charlie call his name: 'Tobias! Tobias!'

Her voice echoed through the night like a silver bell and dragged him to a halt. He stood, shivering with terror, then turned slowly around. His eyes flew up the Castle walls to the rooftops where he had so nearly died all those months ago.

She was there. He saw her plainly in the moonlight, leaning forward over the parapet, staring down at him. Her face was as clear as if she were standing in front of him. He saw the disbelief, the horror in her eyes. They looked at each other for long, painful heartbeats, and Tobias felt the breeze blow cold on his wet face. He shook his head, turned, and ran into the dark...

CITY
of
THIEVES

ELLEN RENNER

ORCHARD BOOKS

ORCHARD BOOKS
338 Euston Road, London NW1 3BH
Orchard Books Australia
Level 17/207 Kent Street, Sydney, NSW 2000

First published in 2010 by Orchard Books

A Paperback Original

ISBN 978 1 40830 446 4

Text © Ellen Renner 2010

A CIP catalogue record for this book is available from the British Library.

10 9 8 7 6 5 4 3 2 1

Printed in the UK

Orchard Books is a division of Hachette Children's Books,
an Hachette UK company.

www.hachette.co.uk

For my parents

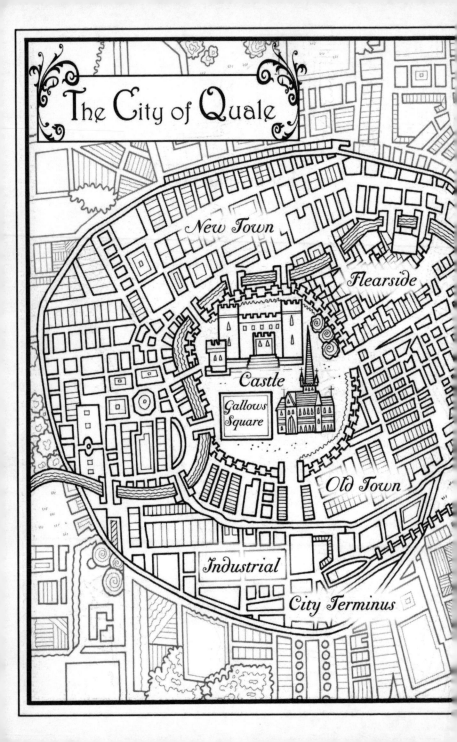

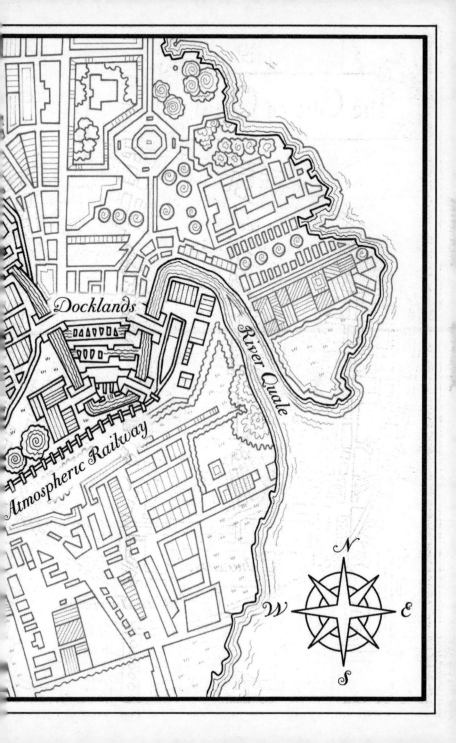

Prologue

Over a thousand souls had gathered in Gibbet Square when Tobias arrived to watch his father hang. They were not eager to let him pass, having arrived early to win the best vantage points, but Tobias hardly felt the cuffs and kicks as he pushed his way through the crowd.

He squeezed between a fat man and a family, husband and wife each with a child pick-a-back, and found he had reached the front. Beyond was a line of photographers, setting up tripods, readying plates. Beyond these stood a row of constables, facing the crowd, batons drawn. Trouble was expected. The prisoner had been kept in the Castle dungeons, instead of prison, for fear of lynching.

Black and square-shouldered, the gibbet towered over the round-hatted constables. It stood on four stiff legs on its stone hill, and Tobias saw the ladder that hangman, prisoner and priest would mount each in their turn. For a moment his head swam and he thought he might faint.

'How long?' he asked the fat man on his right.

'Two hours yet, lad. They always give the condemned a hearty breakfast. They ought to hang 'em at dawn, like the old days. Food'll do him no good, where he's going.'

The man reached into his satchel and pulled out an

enormous sausage. Holding it in one hand, he began carving slices off with a knife and stuffing them in his mouth. 'I brought me own breakfast.' His voice was thick with sausage. 'Don't see why I should go hungry waiting to see a scoundrel hanged. Want a bit?' He speared a slice with the tip of the knife and held it under Tobias's nose.

Bile surged up Tobias's throat and he just managed to swallow it down. Feeling green, he shook his head.

'Suit yourself.' The man shrugged and shoved the slice into his own mouth.

Tobias eased himself onto the damp pavement. The rain had stopped at dawn. Now a freshening wind shredded the last of the clouds and blew them north.

Two hours. He put his pounding head on his knees and hoped the sick feeling in the pit of his stomach would go soon. How long he sat like that, not asleep but not quite awake, he didn't know. The voice of the crowd surged about him: laughter, shouts, wails of children, thousands of feet shuffling and shifting. The tang of sweat, of onions and beer, mingled with the sounds and became part of the same restless sea.

'I won't go with you!'

Even as he said it he knew it was no use. His mother just stood there. The disappointment in her eyes hurt, but it was the fear that threatened to defeat him.

'You'll just get upset, Mum! He ain't worth it. The sooner he's dead the better.'

'He was my husband, Toby. I loved him once.'

'He threw you away! You weren't good enough for him.'

She flushed but held his gaze, her brown eyes on a level with his. He was as tall as she was now. Soon he would be big enough to look after her properly. If only she'd let him.

'I'll be going by myself, then.' Rose Petch turned away and gathered her shawl from the peg by the front door. She pulled it over her shoulders, wrapped the ends around her waist and tied them. Her hands were shaking. That did it.

'I'll go,' he said.

They didn't speak on the way to the Castle. Tobias travelled these streets six mornings out of seven, but the familiarity of the route made this journey all the stranger.

The wind was picking up. It blew in from the coast, raw and damp, promising another wet February evening. They shivered and hurried along the cobbled streets. It was only three in the afternoon, but the sun seemed to have given up and the narrow lanes of the Old Town were gloomy.

Tobias found he kept thinking of Charlie and how she would hate it if she found out about this visit. Not Charlie...Queen Charlotte, he corrected himself. He was going to the coronation. *Him*, Tobias Petch, the gardener's boy, sitting in Quale Cathedral alongside all those lords and ladies. He shook his head at the thought. But that was next week. He had to get through today first. And then...

Tomorrow. They were all waiting for it. Him, Charlie and Nell. Charlie's mum. Lord Topplesham and the whole of Parliament. Newspapers and shopkeepers. Greengrocers and flower sellers and the rag-and-bone man with his cart piled high with rubbish. It was all anyone talked of, from gents in coffee houses to ragged boys sweeping street crossings. The whole country was waiting.

Tomorrow would see a man dead. At the precise moment the Cathedral bells chimed ten o'clock, the former Prime Minister of Quale would hang by his neck. It would be a fitting end to the man who had betrayed his country, who had driven Charlie's mother away all those years ago and driven the King mad before killing him. It would be the end of the man who had ruined Rose Petch's life and his own. The end of Alistair Windlass...his father.

All too soon, they reached the Castle. His mother's hand felt cold and clammy as he helped her down the slippery steps to the dungeons. She was breathing fast, as though she'd been running. A guard unbolted a thick oak door, stepped aside to let them pass, and then – for the first time in his life – Tobias found himself standing in a room with both his parents. He stopped just inside the door and listened to the bolts shoot home behind him. The smell of rot settled at the back of his throat. Age-old damp sweated from the stone walls, and the dungeons stank of it.

'Good evening, Rose. And Tobias. I had not expected a second visit from you.'

Without hurry, his father rolled off the narrow bunk that served him for a bed and unfolded to his full height, watching them through the bars that separated prisoner from visitor.

Tobias had not seen him since the week of his capture. Alistair Windlass had been famous, not just for being the youngest Prime Minister in history, but for the fastidious elegance that had made him a darling of the fashion pages. Tobias despised him for a dandy, but seeing him now, he couldn't help but be shocked.

The man in the inner cell stood as tall and straight as ever, but his clothes were crumpled and stained. His fair hair hung in lank strands over his forehead. Stubble shaded his chin and his eyes shone paler than ever from bruised sockets. Windlass's mouth twisted into a smile.

'Don't worry, son,' he said. 'I'm to have a bath and fresh clothes this evening. And a barber. They'll want me looking my best for the hanging.'

Rose gave a strangled gasp and began to cry. Tobias shot his father a look of contempt. 'Come on, Mum,' he said. 'Let me take you home. There's nothing you can do here.'

'Find your mother a chair, Tobias, and stop ordering her about. She's capable of making her own decisions.'

'Don't you tell me what to do!' He'd sworn to keep calm, but the hated voice shredded his self-control in an instant. 'We're nothing to do with you! You scraped us off the bottom of your boots before I was even born!'

'Enough, Toby!' Rose said, wiping her eyes. 'Your father's right. I'd like a chair, please.' Tobias stood, uncertain. Then he went to the door and pounded on it.

'What's all the fuss about?' The spy hole snapped open and Tobias found himself staring at a pair of scowling eyes. 'Want out, do you?'

'No,' he said. 'A chair. For me mum. Please.' His voice came out in a series of jerks. When the chair arrived, he took it to his mother and retreated to the door, where he leant against the damp stone wall and studied the floor.

'I've come to say goodbye, Alistair,' his mother said, 'although I know it means nothing to you. I'd not rest easy with myself otherwise.'

He couldn't help himself: he glanced up. She sat, small and neat, hands clinging together, worrying the handkerchief threaded through her fingers. Windlass watched her beneath slightly lowered eyelids. 'You undervalue yourself, Rose, as always. I'm glad you've come. Tobias was right when he said you owe me nothing. However, it might be argued that I owe the two of you a great deal.'

Tobias's head jerked up. What was the villain up to?

'I abandoned you for personal advancement,' Windlass continued. 'It was a calculated decision and, in the same circumstances, I might make the same choice. But it was done, believe it or not, with a certain amount of regret. I have amassed considerable personal wealth over the years. Legally, Tobias, so you can take that look off your face.

'I shall obviously have no need of the money after tomorrow, and I see no reason to let the Exchequer take all of it. The authorities have been kind enough to allow me to draw up a will. I have named Tobias as my heir. A fund will be set up, and you will both be able to live on the interest from my estate until he is twenty-one. After which, I'm sure I can trust him to look after you, as I have not.'

Rose Petch's hands fell into her lap. The handkerchief fluttered to the floor. She stared at her former husband, speechless.

'*No!*' Tobias shouted the word, threw it like a stone at a snake. 'We won't touch a penny that comes from you. Even if it were clean money, and it ain't, no matter what you say.'

'The money's coming to you whether you like it or not.'
Windlass's expression and voice were as calm as ever but
he began to pace back and forth, striding from one side
of his cell to the other in three swift steps. He came to an
abrupt halt and his eyes blazed at Tobias. 'Show a bit of
sense, boy. Think of your mother. This will give her a life
of ease and comfort; little enough to make up for the last
thirteen years, I know, but allow me that at least. And it
might help to turn you from a dirt-encrusted illiterate into
a gentleman, as befits my son.'

'I'd sooner grub in the earth for the rest of me days than
have ought to do with you!' Tobias struggled for control
and lost. 'And just so you know, I'm not illiterate. Mr
Moleglass did your job for you: he taught me to read and
write. He may be a butler, but he's more of a gentleman
than you'll ever be. You're a thief, a traitor and a murderer,
and tomorrow I'll be there to see you hang!'

'Tobias!' His mother stared at him in horror. 'Don't
you dare say such a thing. You make me ashamed of you.
Look at the two of you,' she cried. 'As like as two peas in
a pod with your pride and stubbornness! Say goodbye to
your father, Toby. Make peace before it's too late.'

His mother's words hit him like a punch to the heart.
That she, of all people, could think there was anything of
that villain in him! He looked at her, his throat clogged
with bitterness.

'Toby!' she cried. 'I didn't mean—'

'*I'm not like him!* And I'm not stopping in here with

that murderer. We're leaving! Now!' He glared at her. 'Are you coming?'

'I can't.' Her eyes were huge with anxiety, red with spilt tears. 'Not yet. Wait with me, Toby, please.'

But he stumbled to the door and hammered on it until the guard rushed up cursing and fumbled open the spy hole. 'What is it now?'

'Let me out!'

'Toby, please stay!' his mother cried. Windlass was silent. The door creaked open and Tobias pushed through.

'Here, boy! What about your mother?' the guard called after him.

'Let her out when she asks. It's nothing to do with me!' As soon as he rounded the corner, Tobias began to run. He didn't stop until he was out of the dungeons, out of the Castle, and had lost himself in the twisting lanes of the City.

Two

When Charlie woke, the first thought in her mind was: *Tomorrow Windlass dies.* Her second was: *I want to be there.* Of course, they wouldn't let her. The Queen of Quale did not attend the hanging of a common felon, even one who had killed her father.

Pain rose in her throat like vomit, and she pressed her hand over her mouth until it faded. She had sworn Windlass would never make her cry again. Best to be up and doing. She flung herself out of bed and began to pull on her clothes: a heavy black dress trimmed with satin ribbons, black stockings, black boots. Even her petticoats were black.

She dressed quickly. Mother would already be eating breakfast. If she didn't hurry she would miss her. Caroline, Dowager Queen of Quale, had only returned to the Castle a few weeks before, after an absence of nearly six years. Charlie still felt awkward in her company, but she felt worse when she was not with her. It was all too easy to imagine that her mother had disappeared again.

But when she burst into the lesser dining room, making the footman stumble over himself leaping to open the door, her mother was not there.

'Has the Dowager been in yet...Wilkes?' All the servants who had worked for the former housekeeper, Mrs O'Dair, had been replaced, and there were so many new faces in the Castle that Charlie struggled to remember names.

'Watts, ma'am,' the footman replied, hitching himself even taller. He seemed irritated, although she couldn't imagine why. 'And Her Majesty, the Queen Dowager, has not yet appeared.' He repositioned himself beside the door and stiffened into immobility.

Charlie pushed a surge of unease to the back of her mind. Her mother had merely forgotten breakfast. It had happened before and she knew where to find her. She quickly buttered half a dozen slices of toast, wrapped them in a napkin under the scandalised gaze of the footman, and ran out of the dining room to clamber up five flights of stairs to the north attics and her mother's laboratory.

Charlie pushed open the door and saw her mother seated at her desk, her golden hair the brightest spot of colour in the room. The laboratory was long and narrow, well lit, even on a gloomy February morning, by a row of large skylights in the ceiling. Tables held beakers, scales, burners and microscopes. Against the walls stood cupboards full of chemicals and crystals. In the middle of the room was a large electric generator, all shiny brass and glass valves.

Almost from the day of her return the Dowager had

spent every spare moment working. Now she was writing at great speed with one hand, while with the other she struggled to capture an escaped curl with a hairpin. The hairpin slipped and fell onto the floor with a ping.

'Drat!' said the Dowager, stabbing her pen into the inkwell and bending to scrabble under her chair.

'You should cut it short, Mother, like me. It isn't worth the effort.'

'Charlie!' Her mother jumped out of her chair and stood, tall and shadow-thin in her black dress, looking vaguely guilty. 'I didn't know you were there.' Another hairpin plunged floorwards.

'You missed breakfast again,' said Charlie, glancing at the papers on the desk. As she did so, her mother covered them with a piece of blotting paper.

'Did I? Sorry.' The Dowager pulled her chair around to face Charlie and sank into it with a tired groan. 'I forgot the time. I just wanted to finish writing up a bit of research.'

Charlie shrugged and held out the napkin. 'I brought some toast.'

'Excellent!' Caroline smiled, but Charlie noticed dark shadows beneath her mother's eyes and signs that, not long ago, the Dowager had been crying. Windlass again! Each day that brought his execution closer seemed to cause her mother more anxiety. Neither of them would feel safe until he was dead.

Caroline took the napkin and unfolded it. 'If you bring

a second chair,' she said, 'we can have a picnic.' They sat munching toast and licking butter from their fingers.

'Have you even been to bed?' Charlie asked, when they had run out of toast.

'Of course.' The Dowager tucked a stray curl behind her ear. A faint vertical line grew between her eyebrows. Charlie recognised the signs. Her mother was not telling the strict truth. If she had slept, it had only been for a few hours.

'Do you want to make yourself ill?' Charlie scolded. Years of living hand to mouth, years of fear and strain, had damaged her mother's health. 'If you go on like this you'll kill yourself! And I've only just got you back.'

'What a little worry wart!' her mother chided. 'But then, you've had good reason. All that is over now. I've come back to look after you, not the other way round.'

She gathered Charlie in her arms and held tight. For a moment it felt odd and difficult, and then Charlie relaxed. She pressed her face into her mother's neck and caught the faint scent of roses. A memory flickered to life: that of being held like this in a time before fear. It faded as her mother's arms loosened. Caroline held her by the shoulders and smiled. 'You won't lose me,' she said. 'But now I need to work.'

Charlie's eyes returned to the desk. 'What is it? You never seem to want to talk about your science.'

When Charlie was six, her mother had discovered a powerful new weapon. She had destroyed her research and disappeared without trace rather than let it fall into Alistair Windlass's hands. Surely she wouldn't be recreating that research? But what else would keep her at her work day and night?

Charlie reached past her mother and lifted the blotting paper. But before she could read what was underneath, the Dowager scooped up the papers, snapped open a filing cabinet and shoved them inside. She turned to Charlie. 'My work is private. You do not have a right to read it without my permission.'

'Are you working on the weapon Windlass wanted? You can't, Mother! It's too dangerous.'

'Tomorrow morning Alistair Windlass will die.' The Dowager's face was pale, her voice barely a whisper. 'He is no longer a threat, but the Esceanians are. His arrest and execution will buy us time. The Emperor will try to discover how much we know about their plans, and whether or not the weapon Alistair promised them exists. But they will not hold off forever. We are on the brink of war, Charlie. My job as a scientist is to help Quale face that threat. And that is the end of this discussion. Now, I have work to do, and I cannot do it with an audience.'

It must be all right. Charlie stood uncertainly, trying to read the truth in her mother's face. She *couldn't* be duplicating her research. That would mean that everything that had happened – the years of separation, the years of loneliness and Mrs O'Dair, her father's death – it would all have been for nothing. No. It wasn't true.

As Charlie clattered back down the long, twisting stairwell towards the lower floors, she tried to ignore the feeling that she was running away.

Three

Tobias ran until he couldn't run any more. He stumbled into a walk, breathing deeply. The stitch in his side faded, his stride lengthened and he walked on, not minding where he was going. Night fell and brought drizzle. It soaked through his jacket and set him shivering.

It was fully dark. Dusk never lasted more than minutes in the narrow streets of the old City, and this part was older and darker than most. He had wandered into Flearside. The houses were collapsing with age and neglect: timbers sagging, bricks crumbling, top stories bulging over the narrow streets. The people lounging in the doorways were as grimy and neglected as the houses. They stared at him as he shuffled past, his jacket collar turned up and shoulders hunched against the cold.

Flearside was the most notorious slum in the City. Tobias spared a moment from shivering to wish that his feet had taken him in a different direction. But at least the weather had succeeded where the police had failed and cleared the streets of the gangs of mug-hunters and dippers. Not that anyone would be likely to mistake him for rich pickings.

The drizzle paused for breath, then turned into

drenching rain. Doors slammed, shutters clattered, and he was left alone in the downpour. A light glimmered at the end of the street. He blinked rain from his eyes and saw that it was a pub lantern. A Flearside pub. He barely hesitated before making for it. Yesterday, he would have sooner climbed to the top of one of the Cathedral spires than gone into a Flearside pub alone at night. Now, it didn't seem to matter.

He pushed through the door into a fug of tobacco smoke, kerosene fumes, stale beer, damp wool and sweat. He stood for several minutes, stunned by the heat and stench, deafened by the muttering roar, and dripped onto the sawdust floor. When his teeth had stopped clattering, he threaded between bodies to a narrow bench in a corner, squeezed into a gap and leant his head back against the wall. He was aware of his clothes beginning to steam gently in the heat as his eyes closed and he drifted off to sleep.

He woke to roars of laughter and a mouthful of sawdust. He was face down on the floor. Tobias tried to scramble up but got no further than his knees. A foot rammed into the small of his back and squashed him into the sawdust. It flipped him over and found a new resting place on his breastbone.

'This ain't no dosshouse, boy!' The foot's owner was a ratty looking man in a greasy apron. He was holding a tray of empty beer glasses. He nudged Tobias's chest for emphasis. 'Buy a drink or get out!' The foot withdrew and Tobias sat up, coughing sawdust.

'Which is it?' asked the landlord. 'Drink or door?'

'Give 'im the boot!' shouted someone behind him, to howls of approval. Tobias jumped up.

'You want my money or not?' He stared at the ratty man, trying to look like buying drinks in a Flearside pub was something he did every night. 'It's as good as any of theirs.'

The landlord's smile was as thin as his hair. 'Show me.'

Tobias dug in his trouser pocket, praying he'd remembered correctly. His fingers closed around a coin. A shaky grin spread across his face as he flashed it at the landlord. The laughter and comments died away as he followed him to the bar. The man slammed the tray down. 'What'll it be?'

'What've you got?' Tobias asked without much hope. He hadn't eaten for hours and had no desire to spend his only bit of money on strong drink.

'We got beer,' said the man. 'Or gin. What'll it be?'

'Beer,' said Tobias. 'Only a half,' he added quickly.

The man grabbed a pint mug off the tray and began to fill it at a spigot.

'I wanted a half.'

'Don't do halves.' The man slid the beer onto the counter in front of him. 'That'll be a tanner.'

'Sixpence? A pint of beer ain't half that!'

'Not for men, no. It is for snotty brats like you.' The ratty man smirked. 'Pay up,' he said. 'Or it'll be the boot.'

Tobias slapped his money on the bar, grabbed the beer

and carried it into a different corner of the pub. He sat holding the mug. His head ached. The sour smell of the beer made him nauseous, and he tucked it beneath his stool. His sixpence had bought him half an hour at most. Before then he would duck out of the door and hope the rain had stopped. Rain or no, he'd be a fool to stay longer.

He didn't know where he'd go after that. Not home. Mum would be in a state, and he was sorry. It felt wrong to be causing worry when he'd always done his best to protect her from it. But he couldn't face her. Not yet. If it wasn't raining he'd walk the night out. If it was – well, there were always bridges to huddle under. It was only hours now. And then it'd be over. Windlass would be dead.

He had to be at the hanging. He owed it to himself and most of all he owed it to Charlie. She didn't hold his blood against him, but he did. Windlass had killed her dad. There was a debt to be paid, and he would be at Gibbet Square to watch his father pay it.

Afterwards, maybe he could think about other things, about the future, about whether or not to go to school like Charlie wanted. But first, he had to get through tomorrow. He'd seen dead men before. He'd seen Windlass kill Peter Majorian, the Resistance leader. He'd shot at men himself. But that had been in a fight. A hanging was different. Despite the heat of the coal fire and the sweating men pressing round him, he shivered.

The crowd shifted as a massive figure shoved through

and halted in front of him. Startled, Tobias looked up into a broad hairy face and a pair of speckled eyes the colour of seaweed: green and brown and rusty red. 'I know who you are,' the man said, and his voice growled deep and rich.

Tobias gazed at him in shock, wondering how this man knew that he was the son of the most notorious criminal of the century. Wondering if his secret would cost him a beating – or worse.

'I said, I know who you are, boy.' The hairy face parted to show a row of tobacco-stained teeth. 'You're Barty's boy. You're Toby Petch. Don't look so frit, boy. I'm your uncle Zebediah. Don't tell me you never heard of Zebediah Petch!'

Zebediah Petch? The relief that he wasn't about to get beaten up drained away. For thirteen years his mother had made sure to keep him away from his uncle, and now he'd undone all her hard work simply by walking into a Flearside pub.

Running into Petch was bad enough, let alone here, on his own territory. But tonight of all nights…

Zebediah's grin faded. His black eyebrows knotted in a scowl. 'Don't look too pleased to see me, boy,' he growled. 'Think you're too grand for your ol' dad's family, do you?'

'It ain't that.' Tobias quickly stretched his mouth in a smile. 'I'm not allowed to be here, see. If Mum came to hear of it…'

Thunder faded from Zebediah's face, and he winked a speckled eye. 'What she don't know won't hurt her, eh? Well I ain't gonna tell, if that's what's worrying you. Budge over, lad,' he said, pulling up a chair and squashing into the last inches of space beside Tobias. 'Time we got to know each other. Your mum treats you like the crown jewels. Never lets your dad's kin near you. As if we was nothing but a parcel of thieves.'

Since Zebediah Petch was head of the biggest criminal gang in the City, Tobias only gave a weak grin in answer. His uncle put his head back and roared with laughter. He thumped Tobias on the back with such force that he nearly found himself on the floor for the second time that night.

'Here!' Zebediah's voice rolled across the room. 'Landlord! More beer. Make it seven. We got us a Petch family reunion!'

They had grown an audience. Tobias looked up into a circle of faces. The men stared back at him. He did not doubt for a moment that these were more Petches, but the look on their faces was not welcoming. Tobias wished even more fervently that his feet had taken him anywhere but Flearside.

Another mug of beer was shoved into his hands, and he gazed down at it miserably. He didn't think much of Flearside beer: the smell of it made him want to spew. 'Drink up, boy!' shouted Zebediah. 'Here's to family, eh?' Tobias took a mouthful and swallowed quickly. To his relief, it seemed to settle his stomach. He took another sip.

'That's more like it,' Zebediah said approvingly. 'Now, Toby. What're you doing in Flearside? Tell it straight and honest, boy. That's the way to keep on the good side of Zebediah Petch.' The man beamed at him, but the pebbly eyes missed nothing.

His mum had always warned him to keep clear of the Petches. He had heard it so often he ignored it, like her reminders to keep his feet dry, wear a muffler round his throat in cold weather and watch out for hansom cabs bowling along looking for boys to run over. Zebediah Petch had been the bogeyman of his childhood, and Tobias had almost stopped believing in him.

The man sitting next to him, so big and solid he seemed to squeeze the air from the room, was only too real. Tobias knew he ought to be careful, but a flood of anger came out of nowhere. He was angry with so much: his mum, his bad luck and, above all, Windlass. Trying to lay claim to him, just like this man.

'I had a row with me mum!' he snapped. 'Not that it's any of your business!' His uncle's smile faded and Tobias's anger vanished even faster. That had been a mistake.

One of the circle of men growled but Zebediah stilled him with a look. 'That's where you're wrong, Toby. You're a Petch, boy. That makes you my business. Barty was me only brother and you're his son. I been keeping an eye on you since Barty was killed, biding my time till you was old enough. A rare thing finding you here tonight. Almost like it were fate. I reckon you be thirteen-year-old now. Good age for an apprentice.'

Tobias spilt half his beer. He let it drip and then carefully put the mug down on the floor. He noticed his hand was shaking.

Bartholomew Petch had been a fond stepfather, larger than life in a shabby, thieving way. He'd loved Tobias's mum fiercely, and when he was sober he'd been proud of his wife, who was seamstress at the Castle. But he was oftener drunk than sober, and when he was drunk, Barty Petch beat his wife and stepson. When he'd been murdered and tipped into a canal, Tobias had felt a terrifying mixture of grief and joy.

He gazed up at the men surrounding him. A lanky ginger-haired man gave him a quick, sympathetic smile. All the other faces were hard. His leg muscles tensed, but there was nowhere to run. He would have to talk his way out of this. He looked up at his stepfather's brother and lied. 'That's more'n kind of you, Uncle. I never hoped for such.'

Zebediah's speckled eyes warmed and the ring of men shifted and relaxed.

'It being,' Tobias continued, with a careful note of regret in his voice, 'that I weren't Dad's blood, but only adopted. I never thought you'd want much to do with me.' Zebediah beamed genially at him, and Tobias's heart sank: he'd played his only card and lost. His uncle didn't seem to mind that he wasn't a real Petch.

'Barty adopted you legal and clear,' Zebediah said. 'That's enough for me. Your dad never stopped talking of you, Toby. Going on about how clever you was. Said you took to the tools quicker than anyone he'd ever seen. A born thief. Clever hands you got, Toby Petch. I reckon it's time to see just how clever you be. So you can come along home with me. You'll be living with me from now on. Time you got to know your cousins.'

Zebediah rose to his feet. Tobias must not have been quick enough to hide his dismay, because with one nod of Petch's head, two men stepped forward and lifted Tobias off his stool. They stood either side of him, gripping his arms and pushing him forward, towards the door. Panic swept over him. 'Uncle Zebediah, wait!' he called to the massive back surging through the crowd in front.

Petch turned. 'What?' His eyes were like stones.

'I'll come to you tomorrow, Uncle, and gladly,' Tobias lied. 'But let me stop with me mum tonight and say goodbye. We had a fierce row earlier and I couldn't rest easy leaving her so. Please, Uncle Zebediah.'

The pebbly eyes watched him for a minute, considering. Then the teeth glared through the whiskers once more. 'Your dad always was soft on that woman. Runs in the family, I guess. All right, Toby. But mind.' The grin vanished, and Tobias found himself facing a force of will as mountainous as the man. 'You be here, in this pub, by six tomorrow evening. If you're not, lad, I'll make sure you regret it when I find you. And I *will* find you.'

Zebediah looked at the men holding Tobias and they let go. He turned and drove through the crowd and out of the door, the other Petches following in his wake.

A stranger shoved Tobias to one side. Someone else trod on his foot. But all he noticed was that the pub felt surprisingly empty. He shivered with relief as the tension left his body. He'd see Windlass hang tomorrow and then get back to the Castle and hole up there for a while. With any luck, his uncle would soon forget about him.

Four

Every morning after breakfast Charlie had three hours of lessons with her tutor, Professor Meadowsweet. But she had hardly sat down at her desk with its yellow, shiny varnish and looked up at the professor with his pink, shiny head and fringe of white hair, when a footman knocked on the schoolroom door and announced that she was required in the lesser parlour.

Blast and botheration! Mr Moleglass had hired another lady's maid. This would make the fourth, and Charlie was getting tired of inventing new ways to get rid of them. She was used to living alone in her attic and looking after herself, and the last thing she wanted was a maid nagging about washing behind ears or clean fingernails. It was bad enough being Queen when you were barely twelve without all that. Well, she would send this one packing, too!

The footman bowed her through the parlour door.

'Heavens, Charlie! What's got into you? You look cross as spit.'

'Nell!' Charlie skidded to a stop in the doorway. Nell Sorrell stood in the middle of the parlour. She looked very grown up in a blue serge dress and straw hat, but it was the same old Nell, with her brown eyes and curly dark hair.

Nell was Tobias's stepcousin and had helped fight Windlass in the days when she was spying for the Resistance as a Castle maid. Charlie raced across the room to hug her.

'What are you doing here? Have you come for a visit?' Charlie looked up into the older girl's face and saw that Nell had been crying. Her nose was red and her eyes puffy and swollen. 'What's wrong?' Charlie asked.

Nell stepped back and made a face that was half a smile and half a grimace. 'I'm your new lady's maid, ma'am,' she said, and curtseyed.

For a moment, Charlie was furious. If Mr Moleglass thought he would get round her this way... But the look on Nell's face killed her anger at once. She grabbed her by the wrist and pulled her across to the armchair beside the fireplace, where a coal fire burned in the grate. Nell looked cold as well as miserable.

'Sit here,' Charlie ordered, 'and tell me what's happened.'

'The Family have kicked me out.' Nell took a deep breath, obviously struggling not to start crying again. 'I haven't got anywhere else to go, Charlie. I got to earn my keep for real.'

'But why did your family make you leave?' Charlie frowned at Nell. 'Is it your work?' Now that Windlass was defeated, the Resistance had transformed itself into a political party called The People's Alliance, and

Nell was helping run their election campaign.

'No. They don't care.' Her voice was hard. 'Nothing matters to the Petches except thieving.'

'But…'

'Uncle Zebediah ordered me to work in the warehouses, and I said no. So Mum's thrown me out. She…she said I'm not welcome at home. And I'm not to see Lizzy or Will again. Not ever!'

Charlie stared at her, open-mouthed with shock.

'Lizzy was crying when I left, fit to bust.' Nell's voice wobbled. 'Mum threatened to belt her. After that, I didn't stay to argue. I just… Oh, Charlie, I miss them so much already. Lizzy and Will and Dad. I don't think I can bear it!' Nell burst into tears.

Charlie knelt beside the chair and put a tentative hand on her arm. She couldn't imagine what it was like to have a little brother or sister, but she knew what it felt like to lose someone you loved and know you would never see them again.

'I'm sorry,' she said. 'But surely your father won't allow that. He's not a Petch.'

'No, but he was fool enough to marry one!' Nell's voice was bitter. 'His soul ain't his own now. The Family owns him, and he won't dare go against Zebediah. Not even for me.'

'But…' Charlie hardly dared ask the question. 'If you knew what would happen why not just work in the warehouses?'

Nell gave Charlie a look of such scorn that Charlie found her face growing hot. 'I might've been born into a family of low, thieving scoundrels, but that don't mean I got to be like them. I want to do something with my life! Something I can look back on, when I'm old, and feel proud about. I won't do that minding stolen goods in one of Uncle Zebediah's warehouses. It's all right for you!' Nell added. 'Always knowing you'd be Queen some day.'

Charlie jumped to her feet and turned away. She walked to the window and stared out. 'No one ever asked me if I wanted to be Queen.' Her fists were clenched and her voice tight and scratchy.

'So? You think you got it bad? Kids in the workhouse scrub and clean and tote all day from the age of five, and they're the lucky ones. They've got clothes to wear and food in their bellies. I can show you things in this City that'll make you right pleased to scuttle back to your Castle. So you ain't been asked...well, I wasn't asked if I wanted to be a Petch!'

Charlie whirled around. 'Yes,' she cried, 'I have clothes to wear and food to eat and I live in a castle. *My father's still dead!* Is it supposed to hurt less because I'm Queen of Quale? I'm going to spend my whole life being a thing rather than a person. It's like being in prison! You can choose to be a Petch or not. You said so yourself. I haven't got a choice.'

The scornful look on Nell's face faded. 'I'm sorry. I know things aren't easy for you right now.' The sudden kindness in her voice made Charlie even more miserable. Nell didn't really understand.

'I shouldn't have said them things,' Nell continued. 'It weren't fair. Friends?'

'Queens don't have friends!' The words burst out before she could stop them.

Nell flushed and stood up. 'Have it your way.' She walked to the door. 'I'll be off to the servants' quarters then. When will you be wanting me again, ma'am?'

'Nell…I didn't mean—'

'I'll report back when I've unpacked, shall I, ma'am?' And with that, Nell Sorrell turned and left the room.

Charlie stared at the door. Why couldn't she ever say the right thing? Today was turning out to be horrible. She thought of her mother, shut up in her laboratory. She thought of Alistair Windlass, imprisoned deep in the dungeons beneath her feet, and shivered.

She wished Tobias were here. He was the one person who understood how she felt about being Queen, the one person she could talk to about Windlass. But he was at home, looking after his own mother. None of them, she thought, would get much sleep tonight.

Five

Tobias had been awake all night. At least eight hours shivering under a bridge had wiped any worries about Zebediah Petch from his mind.

Now it was past nine in the morning; he was in Gibbet Square, and his only worry was staying well long enough to see his father hang. As he sat at the front of the crowd, shivering in the February wind, the knowledge that he was sickening for something was forced upon him. But he couldn't let a touch of fever stop him. Not now, when the time had nearly come.

'Citizens of Quale!' The voice of the town crier belled across Gibbet Square and pulled Tobias to his feet, heart pounding. He looked to see a familiar figure being led in chains onto the stone hill. Instead, he saw a dozen officials in uniform. Soldiers in cockaded hats marching in to face the crowd, rifles on shoulders. And the town crier mounting the scaffold, scarlet coat-tails flapping in the breeze.

'Here!' cried the fat man. 'Something's up!' The crowd gave a puzzled, grumbling bellow that muttered and swelled and faded away completely when the crier reached the top of the scaffold and turned to face them.

'Citizens of Quale!' roared the town crier. In the absolute silence his voice cracked across the square, over the heads of the nearly two thousand souls squashed into the space, anxiously awaiting the day's entertainment. 'I regret to inform you that the execution scheduled for this morning will not take place!'

Tobias felt the scream of the crowd break over him. His mind had frozen. What was happening? The town crier stood motionless and silent, waiting. The soldiers grasped their rifles, waiting. Silence ebbed back across the square.

'Citizens of Quale! I regret to inform you that the traitor, Windlass, did last night escape from the Castle dungeons and is presently at large!'

This time, the roar of the crowd made Tobias stagger. It surged forward. Back. Forward, back, waves in a human sea. The line of soldiers took their rifles from their shoulders and aimed them over the heads of the crowd. The waves steadied, slowed, stopped.

'Citizens of Quale! Her Majesty's government is making all possible effort to secure the fugitive and assures you that he will soon be in custody. A reward of one thousand guineas is offered for his capture, dead or alive. You will now disperse and return to your homes!'

An ominous mutter rose from the crowd, grew more threatening. A solitary cloud passed overhead. Raindrops sharp as pins drove earthward, and the noise stuttered. Then, as the line of soldiers stepped forward, the crowd broke apart and drifted away.

Tobias stood as though turned to stone and watched the soldiers shouldering their rifles, the officials relaxing, the photographers shaking their heads and packing away their equipment, the town crier swaying on the ladder. Soldiers and constables advanced through the remnants of the crowd, hurrying stragglers on their way.

A soldier paused in front of him, peered into his face. 'You all right, lad?' Tobias nodded. He wasn't all right. He was shaking so he could hardly stand. His head had gone strange and swimmy. 'Get off home with you, then.' The soldier reached a hand to Tobias's shoulder, turned him round and gave him a gentle push.

Tobias stumbled into a walk, then a run. Fear gave him strength. He caught the tail end of the crowd and twisted through it without breaking stride. He ran faster, tearing down the cobbled streets, pushing past bodies, not hearing the curses thrown after him.

White-hot fear chased him and he ran for his life. He spun into his narrow street, past the bakers, the fruit stall. The flower seller called to him but he was running too fast to hear her words. Terror caught him the moment he saw his house and burned through him at once: the door was open.

He knew what he would find before he stepped inside. The little house was empty. She wasn't there. He looked in the lean-to kitchen and saw the remains of a slice of bread on a plate, a half-drunk cup of tea. That told him. She never left the house without washing up.

It was only five minutes' run to the Castle. He knew every pothole, every cobble, every building, ditch and drain along the way. The guard at the gate waved him through as though it were an ordinary day.

He raced for the main entrance. No time for the familiar route through the kitchen and a chat with Maria. As he neared the guards' hut, the man on duty stepped out. It was Davis. His face was puzzled. 'What do you want, Toby?'

Tobias climbed onto the lowest step. 'I need to go in.'

'You know better'n to come this way. Round back with you.'

'No!' Fear made him shout. He took a deep breath. 'It's important. The Queen wants to see me,' he lied. 'Ask Moleglass if you can't take my word.' Davis frowned at him, wanting to chase him away and not quite daring. 'Please,' Tobias said. He could see the man calculating where trouble lay thickest.

'All right, Toby,' he said at last. 'Stop there while I check.'

Tobias stood on the step, shaking worse than ever, and waited. After a few minutes the door swung open. 'In you go, then.'

Moleglass waited for him on the threshold. The look on the butler's face almost unnerved him, and he gasped as fear burned his stomach. 'Mr M…' he began and stopped.

'Tobias, I think you should come with me now and have something to eat and some rest. You've had a dreadful shock. So has Charlie. It isn't a good time—'

'She's got to see me!' He hadn't meant to shout. He wiped damp hair away from his eyes. He was sweating. 'Please, Mr M,' he said. 'She's got to see me.'

Moleglass shook his head. 'It would be better to wait but I cannot stop you if you insist.' With a sigh, he turned and ushered Tobias inside.

Their footsteps rang in the silence as he followed Moleglass down the marble hall. All traces of the hubbub and activity of the past weeks had vanished. The Castle seemed deserted. Moleglass bowed him through a door. The three people standing in the room turned and looked at him.

One was Lord Topplesham, the acting Prime Minister. Topplesham was a fat old man in a white wig and old-fashioned knee breeches. Tobias had met him once, when Charlie was staying at Topplesham's house in the days following her father's death. The other was a large man in a dark blue suit. He was a stranger, but Tobias knew a policeman when he saw one.

The last person was Charlie. Queen Charlotte Augusta Joanna Hortense. He had known Charlie half his life. Had feuded with her when she was a scrawny ragamuffin running wild in the Castle, become her friend during her struggle to free her father from Windlass's power, helped her defeat his own father and put him behind bars. And now Windlass had escaped...

She was dressed in mourning. Her red hair curled

above the black silk like a flame. Her face was white, her blue-green eyes as cold as the sea, and she looked old. He was shocked at how old she looked: a changeling, a weirdling, and not a girl of twelve at all.

He felt Moleglass approach and put a hand on his shoulder. That shocked him, too. Ancel Moleglass was the most circumspect and rigorous of butlers. The friendship between the three of them was kept strictly out of the public eye. 'Tobias has heard the news, ma'am,' Moleglass said. 'He is deeply shocked and has come to offer his sympathies to yourself and Her Majesty, the Queen Dowager.'

'I haven't!' Tobias shrugged off Moleglass's hand. 'I mean, I have, of course. You know that, Charlie... Your Majesty. I was there...waiting...' He stopped. His head had gone swimmy again. He shook it irritably. 'But I'm here for my mother. You've arrested her, haven't you?' He was shouting now. He tried to stop but it was no use. 'How could you, Charlie? Why would she help him? The one person that's hurt her more'n any other? She didn't do it!'

Charlie looked at him, her face whiter than ever. Then she turned and, moving like an old woman, walked to a chair and sat down. 'Tell him,' she said.

The policeman stepped forward. 'Superintendent Blundell,' he said. 'I'm sorry, son, but your mother aided and abetted the convicted felon, Alistair Windlass, in escaping custody. She made a second visit to her former husband last night, during which she drugged the guard's drink, stole the keys and—'

'No!' roared Tobias. 'She wouldn't do that!'

'She's confessed, son,' said the policeman.

And Tobias found he had known all along. Since the moment the town crier had told them Windlass had escaped. He, Tobias, had left his mother with that man, and Windlass had got round her. Manipulated her as he had manipulated so many others stronger and cleverer than Rose Petch. She'd done it. And now she would hang, instead of his father. And it was his fault. The room spun and tilted him into darkness.

Six

For the fifth time in the past hour, Charlie eased out of the chair where she sat trying very hard not to cry, and crept across the thick carpet to stand beside her mother's bed.

The Queen Dowager, Caroline of Quale, lay on her back, hands folded on top of the eiderdown. She was fathoms deep in sleep, like a princess entangled in spells of enchantment. The doctor had given her tincture of opium. He had been with her since the early morning, since the captain of the Castle Guard had interrupted them as they sat not eating breakfast.

Moustaches quivering, the captain had saluted and stood to attention while he informed them of Windlass's escape. Terrified for himself, of course, stupid man. Stammering excuses while Charlie watched her mother rise from her chair and stand white and silent as though carved from a block of salt.

Charlie looked at the clock on the mantel. Nearly eleven. The doctor must have finished with Tobias by now. When would they come and tell her? When he had turned greenish-white and crumpled onto the floor, she had thought, for a horrible moment, that he was dead.

It was all Rose's fault. The police were still questioning

her. Of course, Windlass had tricked her. He was a devil! But what Rose had done was unforgiveable. How could she have set that murderer free? Charlie hated her for it. Rose had committed treason and the penalty for treason was death.

She shivered. She wanted Rose punished for what she had done, but she knew too well what it was like to lose your mother. If she did that to Tobias he would never forgive her.

The attic stairs creaked and Charlie was at the door in a second. Maria's fist rapped on thin air. 'Give me a heart attack you will, Charlie!' the cook snapped.

'Never mind that! How is he? Is he going to be all right? What did the doctor say?'

'Go talk to Mr Moleglass yourself. Go on, I'll stay and watch your mum.'

Charlie cast a quick look at her mother then scrambled down the stairs. Moleglass was waiting in the corridor. He wasn't pacing, she was pleased to see. Not pacing and not wringing his hands. Tobias couldn't be too ill. 'Is he better?' She ran to Moleglass and clung to his black-suited arm. 'Is he awake? Can I see him?'

'Careful, child!' Mr Moleglass plucked her hand from his sleeve and smoothed the fabric. He turned his mournful seal's eyes on her and captured the removed hand in both of his own. 'The answers to your questions are: no. No. And best not.'

'What?' she cried, a fresh pang of fear gripping her.

'What's wrong with him? Why isn't he awake?'

'Listen, Charlie. Tobias is very ill. He has a high fever. The doctor was worried at first that it was diphtheria, but he thinks it's only influenza. Combined with shock and exposure. According to Rose, Tobias didn't go home yesterday. He must have been out all night in that rain.'

'Influenza! But you can die from that!'

'Yes. But Tobias is young and strong. The doctor thinks he will pull through. Maria is an excellent nurse. She and I will tend him between us.'

'I want to see him.'

'He won't know you, Charlie. He is delirious. You'll only upset yourself.'

She tugged her hand away. 'I will see him! You can't stop me.'

His mouth thinned with disapproval beneath his neatly curled moustache, but she didn't care. 'Very well,' he said. 'But you are not to go near the bed. Influenza is contagious. You will stand just inside the door, with me, and you will leave after one minute.'

Moleglass had been right: she should not have come. Tobias was tossing and turning on the bed, moaning and muttering. His eyes were half-open but they looked at things she couldn't see. Before her minute was up, Charlie fled.

She ran all the way to her attic, flung open the window and scrambled out onto the roofs. A stiff breeze billowed the skirt of her dress, flapping it round her legs like crow's wings. Drat the thing! She grabbed two fistfuls of fabric and tied the skirt around her middle, knotting the ends.

The wind blew off the sea, bowling through the sooty haze over the City and bringing the tang of salt and seaweed. Charlie squinted past the Cathedral spire at the jumbled rooftops of Old Town. Then she turned to gaze north across the river towards New Town and the suburbs beyond.

Somewhere, out there in the City, Alistair Windlass roamed free. Any one of those rooftops might be hiding him. The thought made her stomach churn. Surely the police would find him soon. Even the army had been called out. Shoot on sight. He wouldn't get far…not even Windlass…but it had been hours now, an entire night and half a day and no sign of him. Had he escaped the City?

She didn't believe it. He wanted her mother's science. He had betrayed his country and killed his King for it. He wouldn't give up. She shuddered as the wind blew stronger, whipping her hair back from her forehead.

Charlie turned her back on the City and began to climb. She should be downstairs now meeting Topplesham and Blundell. They wanted to discuss Rose Petch. Charlie didn't want to think about Rose and how they were going to punish her.

She slid from one stretch of slate and lead to another, skidded down a gentle slope of slates, landing on her feet as lightly as a cat – and froze. She hadn't meant to come this way. To the place Watch had nearly caught them, nearly killed them, had died himself.

A few feet in front of her, a ridge of lead crossed the top of a roof, like a narrow bridge across a canyon. The ridge was ten feet long and six inches wide, and there was nothing on either side of it but steeply sloping slates and death. For years she had walked across it. Six inches had seemed as wide as a road.

Charlie looked at the ridge and saw Watch pointing his pistol at her head. She saw Tobias, lying unconscious at her feet. She felt the gust of wind, saw the night watchman stagger, saw him fall, heard his scream.

She took a step backward, then another. She was shaking. Something cold and slimy circled in her belly.

Fifteen minutes later, she scuffed towards the audience chamber, listening to her footsteps scrape along the cold marble. She was very late. Moleglass was waiting outside the door. His eyebrows raised when he saw her, and she knew she would have a lecture on manners before the end of the day, but she didn't care.

'Have they caught him?' She never said Windlass's name if she could help it.

Moleglass shook his head. 'You might at least have bothered to wash your hands.'

Charlie saw that her hands were grubby with coal dust from the roof slates and her dress crumpled and stained. She should have washed, but it was too late now. 'I didn't have time. It's only Topplesham and Blundell.'

His mouth thinned, but he opened the door and

ushered her inside. Charlie frowned at the two men, who stood as she entered, then felt ashamed and tried to smile. She was fond of Topplesham, for all that he was a bit of a fool. He had been one of her father's oldest friends.

'Sorry I'm late,' she said.

'Not at all, Your Majesty.' Topplesham ducked his white-wigged head.

The Superintendent merely bowed politely. He was annoyed, she could see. A busy man who knew his own importance and expected other people to know it, even a twelve-year-old queen. She sighed and flopped into a chair. She had been dreading this meeting all day.

'Please sit down,' she said. 'And I need Mr Moleglass to stay.' She turned and looked at the butler, who was in the act of bowing himself out of the room. He straightened and frowned at her.

'I don't think that would be appropriate.'

'I don't care about "appropriate"! I need your advice.'

'I've no objections,' Topplesham said. 'In fact, considering your knowledge of the persons concerned, I was going to suggest it myself.' The inspector nodded his agreement, and Moleglass shrugged.

'If I can be of help, obviously.' He must have seen Charlie's distress, for his brown eyes softened, and she knew she was forgiven. Some of the queasiness in her stomach faded. Until she realised, after long seconds of silence, that they were waiting for her to begin. Her mouth went dry.

'Well?' she snapped. 'We have to decide what to do with her, don't we? I need to know what the law says, Superintendent, and I need to know what the politicians think, Lord Topplesham, and then...' She felt sick and stopped.

'Treason, ma'am,' said Blundell. He was quite old, well over forty, dark-haired and square-faced, with a mind that seemed as neat and sharp-cornered as his face. She didn't like him very much. 'Treason and felony. If things progress in the normal order, she'll hang.

'I'm sorry,' he said, looking at Charlie, although she'd said nothing. She couldn't have spoken. 'I know you're acquainted with the prisoner and her son, but she's committed a capital offence. Of course, this isn't the normal order of things. Mrs Petch is not the normal order of criminal. There might be a question of coercion. Whether or not she could be said to be in her right mind when she did it. There might be room for legal council to manoeuvre, but not much. If she goes to trial, odds are, she'll hang.'

Charlie's breath whooshed out in a gasp. She hadn't realised that she had been holding it. Feeling sick, she turned to Topplesham.

'The Privy Council wants it buried, ma'am.' He pulled an enormous handkerchief from his pocket and patted at his sweating face. 'No trial, no leaks. News of Windlass's escape is all over the City. There have been outbreaks of unrest and rioting. We need to catch him and kill him quick. Hung or shot, it makes no difference as long as the man is dead and *seen* to be dead, with photographs of his corpse on the front page of every newspaper in the land. We can't risk Windlass being built up into some sort of legend. Three-quarters of the country think he's the devil incarnate, but t'other quarter is wondering if he ain't some sort of Republican hero. If we were to hang his pretty little wife for helping him escape, well...a can of worms ain't in it, ma'am.'

'A crime has been committed,' Blundell said. 'The state can't just ignore that.'

'It must!' Topplesham spluttered and rubbed his nose. His face was tomato-red beneath his powdered wig. 'As Prime Minister, ma'am, I advise you to grant Mrs Petch a royal pardon. Get her out of the country and her son with her. If folks were to find out who they were, their lives wouldn't be worth a sparrow's ransom. And I believe you're fond of the boy.'

Charlie stared at the floor. It was all a miserable muddle – as bad as could be. She didn't want Rose Petch to hang, but she had set Windlass free. Charlie could never forgive her for that – for the fear that haunted her mother's face and her own dreams.

She gnawed her thumbnail and listened to the silence grow. She didn't know what to do.

'Perhaps,' Mr Moleglass said, 'I might suggest a third option.'

Seven

Barty Petch had been beating him again. Every inch of his body ached, even his bones. He groaned and tried to push the bed clothes off so he could get up and help his mother. Petch always started in on her. She would be hurt, needing him.

Tobias fought the covers away and sat up. A large, cold hand clapped onto his forehead and pushed him back. 'No you don't, my boy. You're burning up with fever. You lie still and sweat it out. Do as you're told, Toby Petch!' The hands buried him up to his neck in blankets, tucked tight, heavy as the sod on a grave.

'Maria?' he croaked.

Maria floated above him, suspended in gloom like a long grey heron. 'Drink this,' she said, lifting his head and pouring something warm and bitter down his throat. 'Yarrow, elderflower and peppermint. Best thing for fevers.'

'Mum,' he groaned. 'She's hurt, Maria. Help her!'

'Your mum's fine, boy. She's not hurt.'

Why was Maria lying? Was Mum dead? Had Petch gone too far this time? Tobias struggled and fought, but the covers won. He sank beneath them and lay still.

*

When he woke he was lying on a long, white bed. He felt like a cobnut after the weevil had finished with it: hollowed out and brittle. He had stopped hurting and knew he had been ill. The thought made him bad-tempered, prickly as a hedgepig. He wanted out of this bed, but knew if he stood he'd fall on his face. He tried to shout, but the croak that came out of his throat embarrassed him. He would have to wait for someone to come.

He didn't know this room. It was too big, the window too far away. He could barely see the sky, and nothing at all else. Rotten luck, being ill in a room like this. Why wasn't he home, in his own bed, with Mum looking after him? And then he remembered.

Moleglass opened the door fifteen minutes later and nearly trod on him. 'What...? Are you mad, boy?' Tobias hadn't the strength to answer. He lay in a limp straggle, listening to the amazing fact of Mr M in a fluster: 'Maria! Maria! The crazy boy's crawling on the floor! Help me get him into bed!'

Maria took his head and shoulders and Moleglass his feet, and in a matter of seconds they undid all his hard work. He felt like crying. He shoved away Maria's hands, with their smoothing and tucking. 'Leave me be! Where's Mum?' Moleglass was standing near. Tobias clutched the sleeve of his jacket. 'What's happened? How long have I been ill?'

Maria left. Moleglass unlatched his fingers, brought

a chair from the distant window and sat beside Tobias. 'You've been delirious for over a week.'

Tobias struggled to sit up but Moleglass put a hand on his shoulder and pushed him back onto the pillows. 'Don't be a fool! Lie still! Nothing has happened, Tobias. Your mother is well. She is being looked after—'

'In prison?' His voice came out like a squeaking mouse, and he thumped the bed in frustration. 'I know how they look after folks in prison—'

'She is not in prison, Tobias. I promise; she's fine. Quiet, son, or you'll make yourself worse.'

'Not in...' He stared up at Moleglass. Took deep breaths. Waited for the burn of anger to cool. But without anger to keep it at bay, weakness flooded back, and he felt tears prick behind his eyes. He clenched his fists and blinked. 'Where is she?'

'She is here. In the Castle.'

'Not in the—'

'Of course not in the dungeons. She has a large attic room in which to live and work.'

'Work? I don't understand.'

'There is no shortage of sewing, Tobias. Nearly every curtain in the Castle needs mending or replacing. As do the bed hangings, household linens—'

'But...she's under arrest.'

'She is detained at Her Majesty's pleasure. The Privy Council advised Charlie that it would be best for the public not to find out about your mother's role in Windlass's escape. It would serve no purpose and only incite further riots.'

'Riots?!'

'A few. Windlass is much hated. Most of the populace wants to see him hang. Were they to find out about your mother, some might feel she should hang in his place.'

'Then she won't? She won't h-hang?' He gasped the word out.

Mr Moleglass shuddered. 'Thank God, no. Charlie has granted your mother a royal pardon, on the condition that Rose remain confined in the Castle and work without pay as seamstress for a period of five years. After which your mother will be at liberty to live wherever she wishes.'

Tobias closed his eyes. Fear loosened, and a great weariness grew in its place. She would not hang. Tears squeezed between his eyelids, trickled down his face, sticky and slow.

After a few moments, Moleglass spoke, his voice low and hesitant. 'Your mother would like to see you, Tobias. Do you feel strong enough?'

A minute ago he had been desperate. 'No...I can't.' He loved her so much but...*stupid, stupid woman!* How could she have done it? To Charlie? *To him?* How could she choose that villain over him? He couldn't bear the thought of seeing her.

He heard Moleglass sigh. The butler stood and walked to the window. He drew the curtains and moved towards the door. 'You need to rest now, Tobias. I know it's difficult, but try not to worry.'

'Wait!' He had to know. Moleglass was reaching for the doorknob, his back more egg-shaped than ever in the dim light. The butler turned around.

'Have they found him?'

'No,' said Moleglass. 'I'm sorry, son.' He turned and left the room.

Tobias's eyes watched the door shut, but his mind saw Gibbet Square. This time he watched his father mount the scaffold, saw the noose fastened round his neck, heard the thud as the trapdoor opened, watched the body plummet. It should have been over. It all should have been finished. And now... Exhaustion flooded up and swept him towards unconsciousness, and he went willingly. He had never felt so alone.

Eight

Charlie stood in the audience chamber, stamping the rare ninth-century Tokian rug into fragments as she raged at her Chief of Police: 'What *exactly* have you been doing? How can a man simply disappear? Do you even know if he's still in the country?'

'I do wish you'd sit down, Your Majesty.' Lord Topplesham pulled a giant handkerchief from his pocket and mopped his glowing forehead. 'My gout's playing me up something fierce.'

'Bother your gout!' snapped Charlie. But she plopped into one of the chairs that had been set out for them. With a groan of relief, Topplesham subsided into another, and Blundell lowered himself stiffly onto the third. He cleared his voice.

'Windlass's bank accounts were frozen at the time of his arrest.'

'Those you know about,' she said. 'There are bound to be ones you don't. He'll have plenty of money stashed away under false names. Have the banks been given his description? Been ordered to report any movement of large sums of money? Particularly between here and Esceania?'

'Of course! Give me credit, ma'am, for knowing my job!'

'This isn't about you, Superintendent, it's about Windlass. I want him found. It's been days. He should have been picked up within hours! What makes you think he's still in the City?'

Blundell sighed. 'We've been through this, ma'am.'

'Tell me again, Superintendent. Please.' She smiled at him, but there was steel in her smile and in her eyes. He flushed a darker russet.

'There have been blockades on all roads leading out of the City since the morning of Windlass's escape—'

'But his escape went undiscovered for several hours,' Charlie said. 'He could have fled the City in that time.'

'Unlikely, ma'am. His escape was opportunistic. He would have had had no time to organise funds or transport. I do not believe the man would have fled the City as a penniless vagrant.'

'Alistair Windlass, a penniless vagrant?' Topplesham snorted. 'He'd have stayed to be hung sooner than that, the dandified popinjay!'

'If he's trying to get out of the City he'll head for Esceania,' Charlie said. 'What about the ports?'

'We have police patrolling the wharves, ma'am, and a man in every major shipping office with a photograph and full description.'

'What about the minor shipping lines? The independents? The privateers?'

'There are not enough policemen in the City to watch every ship on the Great East Docks, ma'am.'

'Then he might have gone! You don't know, do you? You don't have a clue where Alistair Windlass is!'

Superintendent Blundell straightened his back and looked at her with ill-disguised dislike. 'Put like that, no, ma'am. I don't.'

Charlie stared back at him, despair flooding through her. This man would never find Windlass. It would be comforting to think that the enemy had run away to Esceania, but she didn't believe it. He was hiding in her City. Waiting.

She tripped over a cobblestone and unease began to curl into the edges of her mind. Was she lost? She walked faster, reached a crossroads, but it was too dark to read the street signs. Fear stalked her, scuttling on crab feet. She began to run.

The house must be here, it must! But all the houses looked the same: tall, narrow rectangles pasted on a black sky. The doors were made from playing cards: ace of diamonds, seven of spades, three of clubs. She needed the queen of hearts and it wasn't here. There were hundreds of them, thousands. She ran and the dark chased her. She was too late. Where was Mr Moleglass? Tobias? They were supposed to help her.

Then she saw it: the queen of hearts. She stumbled to the door, pushed it open, raced up rickety stairs to a corridor of empty rooms. Bare floorboards rang with her footsteps and echoed with the sound of her voice as she screamed for her mother.

Charlie pushed away the bedcovers and lurched upright. She groped for the packet of safety matches on the bedside table, then swore as her shaking hands scattered matches across the eiderdown. One left in the box. There was a smell of sulphur; the match spluttered to life. The candle caught at once, creating a circle of yellow light, but this time her panic didn't fade.

The nightmares had started after Windlass escaped. Every night now, for over a week. The fear was always the same: how did she know her mother was safe in her bedroom, all those floors below? Windlass might have broken in, spirited her away in order to torture her secrets from her. Charlie's breath shuddered in and out, faster and faster.

Don't be an idiot, she told the panic. The Castle is surrounded by armed men. The hounds are out. Even Windlass can't get past the hounds. Panic wasn't listening. She was shivering so hard the bed shook with her.

Tonight, fear won: Charlie left the candle to gutter out and scrabbled down the stairs in the dark all the way to her mother's bedchamber. There she paused, gasping, with her ear pressed against the door. Silence. Her fingers grasped the doorknob and twisted. Locked. Her mother must be safe inside. But how did she know?

She knocked. Softly at first. When there was no answer she began to bang on the door with her fist. Shame and relief replaced panic as candlelight rayed beneath the door. Footsteps approached.

'Who is it?' Her mother's voice was strained.

'Charlie.'

A key jangled in the lock and the door swung open to reveal the Dowager standing in the doorway, a dressing gown flung over her nightdress and a revolving pistol in her hand.

'Mother!'

'Don't worry, I know how to use it, and I'm quite a good shot. Now, what's wrong? Has something happened?'

'No, I just...' Charlie bit her lip in dismay. Her fears seemed so childish.

'Come inside. It's freezing.' Her mother took her by the arm and led her to the large four poster bed. 'Jump in. We can talk in bed.' She placed the pistol on the bedside table next to the candlestick and climbed into bed, pulling up the eiderdown to cover them. 'Brrr. That's better. February has turned cold and grumpy. Now, why don't you tell me what's bothering you?' She put an arm around Charlie's shoulders and pulled her close. Slowly, Charlie began to get warm.

'I had a dream. It woke me, and then...I couldn't sleep.'

'A dream. What sort of dream?'

'I can't remember.' It was a lie.

Her mother must have felt her shiver. Her arm tightened. 'Was it a nightmare?'

'Yes.'

'About Alistair Windlass?'

She couldn't speak.

'I know you don't want to talk about him. I haven't insisted and that may have been a mistake. Fears don't go away unless we confront them. Alistair will be caught. Until then, he cannot reach us here. We are too well protected.'

'Then why do you have that pistol?'

Her mother gave a shaky laugh. 'Because I'm not as rational as I pretend.'

'Would you use it? Would you shoot him?'

Now it was her mother who shuddered. The Dowager was silent. Then: 'I think none of us knows whether or not we could kill until the moment of decision comes. I believe I would kill to protect you. But otherwise? The idea of taking a life fills me with horror.'

'Even his?'

'Even Alistair's. I cannot forget that once we were friends. I keep remembering the young man I used to know: intelligent, witty, ambitious…even visionary at times.'

'He killed Father!'

'He is responsible for his death, yes.'

'*I* would shoot him.' Hatred boiled up, hard and shiny.

'I told him that night that I would kill him, and I will!'

Her mother hugged her tight. 'Shhh.' She stroked Charlie's hair. Slowly, the anger faded. As Charlie drifted towards sleep, she felt her mother's body gently shaking, as though she were weeping.

Charlie woke inside a tent of green and gold brocade. Sunlight drew a shimmering white line in front of her eyes, where the edges of the fabric gaped. It took her a moment to realise that she was lying in her mother's bed with the hangings pulled.

She wriggled out of the bed. A fire burned in the grate, sunshine streamed through the window, and there was no sign of her mother. The pistol had vanished along with the Dowager. The mantel clock said twenty-three minutes past ten; doubtless her mother was hard at work in her laboratory.

Should she go and check? Her stomach growled in argument. There might still be breakfast to be scrounged in the dining room. She dressed as quickly as possible and went in search of food. But as she reached the ground floor, Charlie heard a series of distant crashes and thumps. Then the sound of Mr Moleglass shouting. Mr Moleglass *never* shouted. What was going on?

She followed the noise, which seemed to be coming from the ministerial wing. By the time she arrived in the main corridor, the crashes and thumps had stopped. So had the swearing and shouting. But the door to her father's old office – *Windlass's* old office – stood wide open.

She had not been in that room since the night of her father's death. The sick feeling in her stomach dissolved into amazement as she stepped inside. Three large men in overalls stood in a corner. The men were watching Mr Moleglass crawl about the floor on his hands and knees, muttering and swearing over a large dent and several deep gouges in the floor. The object which must have done the damage, a large oily-looking metal safe, stood in the centre of the room, squat, ugly and totally out of place.

'What,' Charlie's voice hissed like steam from a broken pipe, 'are you doing in here? *With that?!*'

The three large men turned their heads and stared at her. Mr Moleglass jumped to his feet with a yelp of surprise. 'Char— Your Highness! Your mother said you were asleep.'

'I gave orders that this room should remain locked. Why have you brought a safe in here?' She crossed her arms and glared. Mr Moleglass hesitated, glanced at the men. Two shifted uneasily. One grinned.

'Ma'am,' said Mr Moleglass. 'Surely this can wait until the men have finish—'

'No. It can't.'

Moleglass sighed. 'Very well. Her Majesty, the Queen Dowager requested—'

'*My mother ordered this? Why?*'

'I'm afraid I couldn't say, ma'am.' Moleglass drew himself up, carefully avoiding her gaze. 'If I might suggest, you should enquire of Her Majesty.' He gave a small bow and stood silently, every inch the butler. The three large men stared.

Defeated, Charlie turned and walked from the room. Once she was out of hearing, she began to run.

She raced up the attic stairs and burst through the laboratory door. Her mother turned in her chair, smiling in welcome. 'Hello! Awake at—'

'Why are you having a safe put in Father's old office?' Charlie came to a halt, puffing and out of breath. 'I ordered that room to be kept locked.'

'I know, but—'

'You knew I didn't want the room used, and you still had that safe put there? Why?' she cried.

'Because it's too heavy to carry upstairs, of course. Please don't get in such a state.'

'I'm *not* in a state! Am I Queen or aren't I?'

'Yes. And I am your mother.'

'That has nothing to do with it! That room belonged to Father when he was King. It's mine now.' She took a deep breath, trying to calm down. 'And I choose not to use it. There are plenty of other places in the Castle to store a safe if you need one so much. The worst thing is you didn't even bother to ask me. No – that's wrong. The worst thing is that you made Mr Moleglass lie to me!'

Her mother frowned. 'Now you're just being silly.'

'He was trying to get the safe moved while I was asleep because he knew I wouldn't like it. That's a form of lying. And you made him do it!'

The Dowager opened her mouth, shut it again. 'You're right. I should have talked to you about it and asked your permission to use the room. I apologise. But what's done is done. The room will stay locked, I promise. The only difference is that now there is one more object in it.'

'What do you want a safe for, anyway?'

'To keep valuables in, of course. Now, come and give me a kiss. You haven't even said good morning.' The Dowager smiled at her. Charlie didn't smile back. Her mother was lying. She didn't know why, but she intended to find out.

After lunch, Charlie visited the library and then staggered along the Castle corridors beneath a tower of books. She had overheard Maria telling Mr Moleglass that Tobias was well enough for visitors, and she intended to be the first.

But when she knocked and eased open the door, she saw that Nell Sorrell had beaten her to it. The two of them turned to look at her. Nell had been crying again, but Charlie barely noticed. She stared at the occupant of the bed. Instead of the brown, freckle-faced boy she knew, a stranger looked back at her. His face was pale and thin. Lank brown hair fell across his forehead, above silver-blue eyes. Except for the hair, the boy in the bed might have been a younger version of Alistair Windlass. Charlie looked at him, her face blank with dismay.

'You ain't supposed to be here, Charlie.' Tobias's voice sounded funny. It had gone deep and buzzy. 'You might catch something. Best go.' He hunched himself up and frowned at her, his cheeks flushing faint red.

'I brought you some books.' Such a clever thing to say. But they might have been strangers, the way he and Nell stared at her. 'And Mr Moleglass said you could have visitors now. Anyway, she's here.' She pointed with her chin.

'Yeah,' Tobias said. 'Well, she ain't…um… You can put the books on that table. Thanks.'

Her arms were aching so Charlie dumped the books. Then she advanced on the bed. 'She isn't what? The Queen?'

'Well you are, ain't you?'

'So it's all right if Nell gets ill, but not me?'

'Don't twist it. You know right well what I mean. It's kind of you to bring the books, but I think you should go now.' He looked miserable. Suddenly she understood.

'It isn't your fault, Tobias. It's nothing to do with you.'

He wouldn't look at her. 'I'm tired, Charlie. Could you leave, please?'

She turned and walked out the door, shutting it carefully behind her. It was a good thing she'd sworn never to cry again, because otherwise tears would have been streaming down her face.

Nine

He had grown long and bony during his illness. Even his hair and fingernails needed cutting. Maria worked round his head with the scissors, snipping furiously.

'Ow! Blast it, Maria, that's twice you've nicked that ear. Leave off now. You've done enough.'

'Right scarecrow you'd look with half your hair hanging in your face. Hold still and you won't get cut.'

'Leave off! I'll bleed to death at this rate. Why can't I have a proper barber?'

'And who's to pay for that? With your mum not earning and you nobbut a schoolboy?'

'I'm not!'

'Argue with Her Majesty, not me. Right, you intolerable fidget! If you must have a proper barber I'll go and fetch one. Sit you there and don't move, or it'll be the worse for you when I get back!' She stamped out, clacking the scissors.

He poked a snippet of hair with his toe, wondering how long it would take her to find a barber. Hair had sifted down the back of his nightshirt and set up a fierce itch. It almost made him look forward to getting into the tin bath steaming beside the fire.

The door opened and he glanced up, surprised that she'd been so quick. But it wasn't Maria standing there holding the scissors. It was his mother.

He had not seen her for a fortnight, and he caught his breath at the sight. The pretty, neatly dressed, young-looking woman had disappeared. Her face was pale, her clothes shapeless. She was like a jenny wren at the end of winter, thin and draggle-feathered.

'I'll leave if you'd rather,' she said. 'Only I always did use to cut your hair.' Her voice was hesitant, her eyes pleading. He found he couldn't bear to hurt her.

'It needs cutting,' he said.

She gave a little laugh, like a gasp. 'That it does.'

She cut hair nearly as well as she sewed, and he relaxed beneath the familiar touch. Her fingers were light and swift in his hair. Clever fingers. He had got them from her. 'You've grown, Toby,' she said at last. 'I hardly know you.'

'I hardly know you,' he shot back, before he could stop himself.

Her fingers faltered, then began again, slower. 'There,' she said. 'It's done.'

She turned to go, and he caught one of her hands. Stood, and found to his amazement that he had to look down to meet her eyes: he had finally grown taller than his mother. But the milestone he had looked forward to for years gave him no pleasure. He might be big enough to look after her now, but it was too late to keep her safe.

 71

She and Windlass together had seen to that. The dull ache in his chest deepened into pain. His throat was swollen with it, but he squeezed the words out.

'Why did you do it, Mum?'

She gave him look for look. Her face went calm, and her brown eyes were steady. 'When you've grown old enough to have seen your fill of pain and suffering, Tobias – you'll know that death isn't the answer to death.'

'So you just let him loose, to go on hurting and killing?'

'No. He's finished with that. He promised me.'

'And you believed him? Are you that *stupid?*' He shouted it. Saw her flinch, blush, fade paler than ever. He had a sudden vision of Barty Petch, fist raised. He felt sick. 'I shouldn't have said that.'

'Say what you feel, Toby. Get it out, or it'll sit inside and fester. I know you think I'm a fool, and weak. I know I've hurt you – caused problems between you and your friends. Maybe you're right, and Alistair was lying to me. I'm not clever like you and him, Toby. The one thing I knew was that the father of my son was going to die if I didn't help him. He'd already lost everything he ever cared about, and he didn't have the power to hurt anyone any more. It didn't seem to me that him dying would make anything better.'

Tobias shook his head. 'He's evil through and through, that man. He should have hung. I went to see him hang!'

'I know you did, son. I stopped that at least. Now,

I brought along some new clothes. Maria was saying you needed them. I'll wait for you to visit me...when you're ready. I can't be sorry I married Alistair – he gave you to me. But there's no denying he's been a bad father. Poor Barty were little better, but at least he loved you. I'm sorry, Toby. I've made a bad job of choosing the men in our lives.'

What could he do? He couldn't stop loving her; couldn't punish her for being what she was: good, gentle, trusting. The pain in his chest and throat grew until he thought he would choke. He put his arms around his mother while she clung to him and wept. He held her for a long time, and with each passing second, his hatred of Alistair Windlass hardened into something colder than ice.

He wasn't given to looking in mirrors, but he wanted to look decent when he said goodbye to Charlie and Mr Moleglass. Mum had dressed him as a schoolboy: grey trousers, waistcoat, natty little black jacket and a white shirt. He had struggled to button the stiff collar onto the neck of the shirt, struggled even more with the tie, but he'd managed in the end.

The boy in the mirror didn't look like him. His hair was plastered neat and smooth. His face seemed to have grown longer, and he hadn't got used to the thin scar on his left cheekbone: the scar he'd got escaping with Charlie over the Castle roofs. His face was paler too, so that his hair looked almost dark above it. And as for his eyes...he'd never liked his eyes. Windlass's eyes: pale blue, almost silver. He remembered eyes like those looking at him above the mouth of a pistol. Eyes cold as time and death. He shuddered and turned away. If he didn't go now, he'd be late.

Moleglass was waiting for him outside the parlour. 'What on earth...?' The butler whirled him round and wrinkled his nose as if at a bad smell. '...do you call that thing under your chin?'

'You mean my tie?'

'Tie? I thought perhaps you had mistaken your neck for a parcel and knotted it with string. Who taught you to tie a tie like that, Tobias?'

'I figured it out. Now let go. You'll make me late.'

But Moleglass didn't let go. He grabbed hold of the tie and proceeded to strangle Tobias. 'Better to be late than appear so before ladies. Hold still!'

Tobias could not move for fear of asphyxiation, so he stood and suffered as the butler attacked the tie, muttering subdued and intricate curses.

'There!' Moleglass stepped back at last and inspected him with critical eyes. 'Much improved. You have quite the refined air these days, my young friend. It must be the loss of that inch of garden soil you used to carry around on your skin!' He flashed a wicked grin, then, his face a study of butlering rectitude, swept the door open and ushered Tobias inside.

Charlie was standing in the window, her back to him.

She turned round and studied him without smiling. 'I like your old clothes better,' she said. 'You look ridiculous like that.'

The knot of nerves in Tobias's stomach untied. She couldn't be angry about the other day if she was insulting him. Relief made him grin.

'Charlie! That was rude.' The Queen Dowager rose from her chair, and his nerves flooded back double strength. She was one of the most beautiful women he had ever seen: tall, with a long oval face – the sort of face you saw on statues of angels in the Cathedral. Her eyes seemed to look right through his skull and read what was written in his brain. Alistair Windlass had killed her husband. Each time she looked at him, he was sure she saw his father.

Now she put her hands on his shoulders and kissed him on the cheek. He just managed not to jerk away. 'We're happy to see you well, Tobias. Charlie has been very worried about you. Do come and sit down; you're still looking slightly pale. Mr Moleglass, will you see to coffee?'

'Certainly, ma'am.' The butler bowed himself out of the room.

Tobias sat on the edge of a chair and blushed at the toes of his boots. He dared a glance at Charlie. She was still glaring at him, and the familiarity of her frown made him feel slightly better. 'Your Majesty—' he began, and her almost-smile dissolved.

'Since when have you called me "Your Majesty"? Don't you dare start that nonsense!'

'Look, you're the Queen now. I'm the gardener's boy. What's it gonna look like if I go round calling you by your first name?'

'Call me Charlie in private. And you're not the gardener's boy any more.'

'Yeah, well that's one of the things I need to talk to you about.' He swallowed and wished Moleglass would come back.

'Yes?' Charlie's blue-green eyes flashed, and Tobias knew he had a fight on his hands. It was never going to be easy.

'I know you want me to start at this fancy school—'

'You are starting. In two weeks. It's all arranged.'

'Well...' He cleared his throat. 'I reckon you'd better un-arrange it.'

'What?'

'I can't do it, Charlie. I'm real grateful – don't think I'm not. Maybe when I get back—'

She jumped to her feet. 'Back? Back from where? What are you talking about, Tobias? The only place you're going is school. It's all settled!'

'Charlie!' said the Dowager. 'Calm down. Let Tobias explain.'

The door opened and a trolley appeared, laden with sandwiches, cakes and coffee, with Mr Moleglass at the end of it. He paused, taking in the scene before him. 'Oh dear,' he said. 'Refreshment first, I think, to give tempers time to cool. Please be seated, Charlie.'

The room was silent except for the tinkle of china as the butler poured coffee and handed round plates. Tobias devoured an egg-and-cress sandwich, polished off three more, then five cakes, one after the other. He had been starving ever since waking from the fever, and Moleglass had kindly piled his plate high. He looked up to see the Dowager and Charlie watching him and froze in mid-bite, blushing furiously.

'Didn't you have any breakfast?' Charlie asked, a look of blank amazement on her face.

Tobias choked, coughed, blushed even harder.

'Boys of thirteen are always hungry, my dear,' the Dowager said with a smile.

Moleglass cleared away the remains. 'Now,' he said. 'From the beginning, if you please.'

Tobias looked at the three people watching him and almost wished himself back on his sickbed. Best do it quick and get it over. 'I've come for two reasons. The first is to thank you, Charlie, and you, ma'am, for your kindness to me mum.'

Charlie's face went stiff. He took a deep breath and ploughed on. 'You would have been within rights to lock her in prison. Even...I feared...' He stopped and waited for his breath to wheeze back. 'But it weren't just her. You were wrong what you said the other day, Charlie. It *is* my fault Windlass escaped. I left Mum alone with him...I

couldn't stick being in the same…anyway, I run off.
That's when he got round her. She needed me to stay –
she begged me.' He was shaking now. The room was
silent, and he glanced up at Charlie, who was glaring at
him as though he'd just said something incredibly thick.

'That's just stupid! You're not responsible for what
Windlass did, or your mother.'

'Charlie is right,' Moleglass said. 'I feared something
like this was preying on your mind.'

'It ain't,' Tobias said. 'It's just a fact, that's all. But
everything's changed now for me, and that's another fact.
I can't stay here and go to this fancy school of yours,
Charlie. I'm sorry, but I'll be leaving tomorrow.'

'To go where?' Moleglass's voice was stiff with
disapproval.

'I can't tell you that,' Tobias said. 'Sorry. And I don't
know when I'll be back. I just wanted to thank you
properly and ask you to look after Mum while I'm gone.
She's bound to worry.'

'But you can't…' Charlie began. She stared at Tobias,
a look of horror growing on her face. 'No!' she cried.
'You're not to do it. Absolutely not! The police will find
Windlass. Or the army. Or bounty hunters. *You* can't—'

'Charlie, don't be absurd. Tobias wouldn't be so
foolhardy as to go looking for his father.' The Dowager
looked at him for confirmation, but he avoided her eyes.

'I-I best be going.' He stood up.

'Sit down!' Moleglass snapped. 'You're not going

anywhere, my lad. Is Charlie right? Are you crazy enough to go chasing after the most dangerous man in the country? Unthinkable at any time, let alone fresh out of the sickbed! My God,' he said, when Tobias didn't answer. 'I think the boy's gone mad. Well, you're not doing it! Put it out of your head! And I asked you to sit down!'

Tobias remained on his feet. After his mother, Ancel Moleglass was the person he loved best in all the world, and it hurt to disobey him. 'I'm sorry, Mr M,' he said slowly, 'but I don't reckon you can stop me.'

'Well, I can!' Charlie had jumped to her feet as well. Two spots, red as her hair, burned on either cheek. 'I am Queen, Tobias. I forbid this. You will stay here and go to school as I have ordered.'

He struggled to control the jumble of emotions bouncing through his head. 'You may be Queen, Charlie,' he said, speaking carefully, 'but you were never the boss of me when we were little, and you're not now. Don't come over all grand. Not about this. It's too important. I helped you when you needed it and, as I recollect, that were more'n a touch dangerous.' He tried to grin, willing her to understand. 'Watch nearly shot my head off. To say nothing of my blessed father. Come on, Charlie. You should know, better'n anyone.'

'That was different!' Charlie shouted. 'Nobody's life is at stake now.'

'No? I wouldn't take any bets on that, if I was you.' He

noticed the Dowager shudder. 'Sorry, ma'am. You're bound to be safe here, don't fret.' Now he just wanted to be gone. 'Goodbye, Charlie, Mr M, ma'am.'

'Tobias!' Charlie's eyes burned blue-green. 'You are not to leave the Castle! Don't try, because the Guard will stop you.'

She hadn't understood. For some reason, that made him angriest of all, and he felt his temper, chancy since his illness, snap. 'Under arrest now, am I?' His voice was icy.

'That's up to you.'

Tobias glared at her for a long moment. He would have to lie. Well, serve her right for thinking she owned him. He gathered back his self-control and shrugged. 'I'm too tired to fight you, Charlie. You win. But I'd rather carry on working with ol' Fossy in the gardens than go off to that posh school of yours.'

'Perhaps we could discuss that another time,' said Moleglass. 'The Dowager is fatigued.' Tobias saw that Charlie's mother had gone white and silent. Charlie ran to her and took her hand, a strained look on her face that he had never seen before. Although he was sorry for it, it gave him the distraction he needed.

He was out of the door and upstairs before they noticed. Charlie and Mr M would be busy with the Dowager for a while. And he could only hope he had fooled Moleglass, though he doubted it. He had an hour, maybe two.

He had no clothes other than the ones on his back. These were about as useful as a foot full of bunions, but he could pawn them in the City and buy proper clothes. From his bedroom he collected the flat cap that matched the jacket, toothpowder and brush, and his lockpicks. He'd write Mum a letter tomorrow, once he was safe away. Now he had to get out of the Castle, get home and off again before Mr M sent the Guard after him. It was a shame to cause his friends worry, but he had no choice.

He owed it to Charlie. Windlass had killed her dad, and his mum had set the villain free. He didn't believe what he'd said to the Dowager. Sure as snakes wriggle on their bellies, Windlass would be after her again.

It was up to him to fix the mess he'd made. He would track Windlass down. He wasn't totally clear about what would happen at that point. Find the police if he could. But it would be as well to get a gun. Any pawn shop in Flearside would have an old duelling pistol going cheap. A muzzle-loader was next to useless – plus he'd have to carry powder and shot – but he'd never be able to afford a fancy revolver. And Windlass had a reputation as a marksman. One shot was all he'd get.

Tobias travelled the back stairs down to the kitchen. Maria was at the sink. He paused for a moment, watching her narrow shoulders twitch as she peeled parsnips. It felt strange to sneak off without saying goodbye, but she'd try to stop him, same as the others. He turned and crept silently out the scullery door, through the yard and into the grounds. As he ran past the high brick walls of the kitchen garden, he heard Foss shouting at the new boy. Almost, he wished it was him. But soon he was pushing through the curtain of ivy hiding the ancient door in the Castle wall he'd discovered years before, had picked the lock, and was loping down the alley towards home.

Before he was halfway there, he was gasping and his legs had gone to rubber. He slowed to a walk. Curse this weakness! He gritted his teeth and forced himself to walk faster. It would be lunchtime in two hours, and Moleglass would be sure to miss him. He couldn't afford to hang about.

The Cathedral bells were chiming eleven when Tobias let himself in the front door of his house. It was locked, but locked doors hadn't stopped him since his stepfather had started him on the tools. What a row there'd been when Mum found out. He'd never seen her so angry. Even Barty had been cowed. He smiled at the memory.

The house was dark and musty inside. Everything was just as he had left it weeks ago. This was probably the last time he would come here – the house would be sold, or let, perhaps. He pushed back a surge of misery and ran up the stairs. A house was a house. And time was running out.

He went into his mother's bedroom, pulled up the loose floorboard, lifted out the tin, dumped the contents on her bed. Over two pound. More'n enough for new togs and a pistol. And a bed for a few nights, if he weren't too fussy. He swept the coins back into the tin and headed towards the stairs to the kitchen and whatever supplies he could find.

Tobias clattered to a stop halfway down the stairs. Two men stood below, staring up at him. After the first surge of panic, he saw they weren't in uniform. Not the Guard, then. But something about them seemed familiar. 'What d'you want?' he said. To his annoyance, his voice, untrustworthy since the fever, cracked on the last word. One of the men grinned.

'You, Toby-boy. You missed an appointment.' The man was tall and ginger-haired, with a long nose. Finally, Tobias recognised him. Flearside. The pub. Zebediah. Oh God. He'd completely forgotten about Zebediah Petch.

Ten

Despite nearly fainting during Tobias's visit, the Dowager refused to rest. Charlie trailed after her mother as Caroline strode through the east wing to her study, sat at her desk and began to write a letter. Charlie perched on the window seat.

'You'll be very bored if you intend to sit there until lunchtime,' her mother said over the sound of a quill scratching on paper. I've sent for my secretary. She and I must spend the rest of the morning rearranging my diary. The police have advised me to cancel all my appointments in the City until Windlass is caught. And after lunch Moleglass and I will be interviewing housekeepers.

'I don't want a housekeeper!'

'You may not, but Mr Moleglass cannot be expected to carry on doing a housekeeper's work as well as his own. The point is, I'm very busy today, and you have your own studies to attend to. I'm perfectly well. You don't need to watch over me.'

'I wish you'd let me send for the doctor.'

Her mother sighed and looked up. 'I won't pretend that Alistair's escape hasn't scared me. But I'm not about to die of fright.'

'Don't call him Alistair.'

'That is his name. And he used to be one of my dearest friends.'

'Mother!'

'Or, I thought he was. Obviously, I never really knew him. I don't suppose anyone does, even Rose, poor woman.'

'And please don't talk about her.'

'Not talking about things doesn't make them go away. One thing you're not is a coward, Charlie. We have to face the things we don't like, and especially the things we fear. I'm afraid of Alistair. I have been for nearly six years. It's a hard habit to break, even when I know he can't really be a threat now.'

'No,' Charlie said. She dropped her eyes and looked at the floor, wishing she could really believe that Windlass was gone forever. It would be comforting to think that he had fled the City. But the man she knew would never give up.

She felt a chill crawl down her back and tried to suppress a shiver. She couldn't let her mother see how frightened she was. After all, clever though he was, Windlass was only one man, hunted and alone. Topplesham had promised that every policeman, soldier and spy in the City was looking for him. 'They'll catch him,' she said, trying her best to believe it. 'It can't be long now. And then he'll be dead and in Hell where he belongs.'

'Charlie!' Her mother's eyes were full of misgiving.

'Hating isn't the answer, my darling.'

'He killed Father!'

Her mother shut her eyes. For a moment she looked like she might faint again. 'I am so sorry. I miss him too.'

And then Charlie said what she had never meant to. What she didn't allow herself even to think: 'Then why did you leave us? You ran away and left us alone with that monster – and now Father's dead!'

She gasped and clapped her hand over her mouth. Her mother's blue eyes stared out of an ashen face. The colour had gone even from her lips. Charlie stood up and backed away. The room was silent. She wasn't even sure her mother was breathing. She turned and ran, tearing open the door and nearly bowling over her mother's new secretary.

She escaped to the only place that seemed to belong to her now.

The weather had calmed. There was no gusting wind, only a steady breeze that bowled across the sky. She scrambled aimlessly over the slopes and gullies of the Castle roofs. Almost without thinking about it, she was heading towards the ridge.

It glinted dull grey, the lead basking in the chilly sunshine, like the spine of a dragon's back. If she touched it, it would be warm beneath her fingers. Alive. She could almost see it rise and fall with each slow breath.

She sat at the edge of the roof, feet dangling in space.

86

She was scared. A great fat yellow coward. Her feet swung in the breeze, kicking against the slates that spilled into the long slide to death. The slide Watch had taken. Twice now, she had nearly died here. The dragon wanted to kill her.

At last she stood up. She had to do it. She couldn't lose the roofs too. Her heart was trying to hammer out of her chest. She took a deep breath and stepped onto the ridge.

It was going to be all right. She glanced up and saw clouds tumbling out of the sky into the sea. She had nearly reached the middle when it happened. She, Charlie – who loved the roofs, the high places; loved scrambling to the topmost ridge and fronting the wind like a bird taking wing – she froze. She stared down at the sliding slates and a wave of dizziness slammed into her head. She was going to fall.

Charlie threw her eyes across the chasm and flung herself after. The top of her body crashed onto the opposite roof but her legs swung in space. There was a moment of balance, and then she slipped backwards. She slid off the roof, slowly at first, then faster and faster. There was nothing to hold onto. Her fingers scratched and scrabbled at the lead, dug into a seam at the very edge and clung on.

She stopped with a jerk that threatened to pull her arms out of their sockets. For a second or two she hung, panting with the effort of holding herself. She didn't waste breath shouting for help – no one would hear. She hung there for an age, thinking about her mother and how she would have to live the rest of her life believing that her daughter had died hating her.

She began to swing her legs sideways, gently, then faster. Her fingers burned as she dug them into the lead; her arms shook with effort. And…now! Her right leg swung up, her foot hooked onto the roof, slid forward, her knee found the top. She inched her hand further up and in. And then she pushed, rolled, and felt the solid roof hold her and give her back her life.

'Where have you been?' Moleglass whirled round as she ran down the stairs to the great hall.

'I can't find Mother!' She had gone looking for Caroline as soon as she was off the roofs, searching her mother's study, the library, the drawing room, even her bedroom. With every passing moment, she had grown more frantic, remembering the stricken look on her mother's face. What if the shock had killed her?

'You've missed lunch,' Moleglass said. 'You've worried everyone! Half the staff are searching the attics for you!' His face was red, his moustache spiky, and Charlie knew that something was very wrong.

'Mother!' she cried. 'Where is she?'

'Your mother is fine,' he snapped. 'Answer my question!'

She had never seen Mr Moleglass so furious. Not with her. He couldn't have found out about the roofs, could he? She had crawled back into her bedroom to discover that her dress was filthy and her stockings ripped. Her hands were scraped raw. She had taken the time to change and wash. Now she hid her hands behind her back and lied. 'I was reading. In the attics. Sorry. I lost track of time. *I'm sorry!*'

Moleglass must have noticed her terror at last, because his face softened. He reached out and hugged her tight. This was so extraordinary that Charlie gawped at him open-mouthed. 'What is it?' she cried. 'Tell me where Mother is!'

'The kitchen. Come, let us go find her.'

Her mother never went to the kitchen. What was going on?

Moleglass didn't speak again. He held her hand tightly and pulled her along corridors and down stairs until they reached the kitchen door. She winced as the raw places on her palm were squeezed. He pushed through the door and pulled her after. An amazing sight met her eyes.

Rose Petch was sobbing in her mother's arms. Nell sat at the table, watching her aunt, her face grim. Maria, her own eyes red and streaming, stood beside them holding her enormous brown teapot. She looked up as they entered, turned without a word, slammed two more cups onto the table, and began pouring out tea.

Charlie stared at the women, then yanked her hand from Moleglass and backed away, glaring at the butler in accusation. 'Where is he?' she shouted. 'Where's Tobias?'

Eleven

Tobias grabbed the banister rail to steady himself as he stared at Zebediah's men. This couldn't be happening! Not now! Petch wouldn't care about catching Windlass. Worse than that: he'd heard enough from Nell to know that once his uncle got hold of him, he'd be forced to turn thief whether he wanted to or no. Life as Zebediah's apprentice would be little better than slavery.

'We been waiting for you to show your face for two weeks, boy,' said the second man. He was shorter than Ginger, with curly dark hair and a sour face. Tobias recognised him from the pub too.

'I been ill.'

The man grinned nastily. 'You'll be sicker yet when Zebediah's finished with you. You had an agreement.'

'You don't understand. I—'

'Tell it to Zebediah. Come on down those stairs, boy, or we'll have to get personal.'

Tobias's heart began to thud. His mouth went dry at the thought of what lay ahead: a beating for sure. But that was only the beginning. Zebediah wouldn't trust him after this. He might not get a chance to escape for weeks. By then there'd be no hope of tracking Windlass down.

No, he'd have to run for it.

'OK,' he said. 'I don't want no trouble.' He clutched the tin box in his right hand and started down the stairs. The second man moved forward to meet him, and Tobias took his chance. He bowled the box clean at the man's head, as hard as he could throw. It hit him between the eyes and burst open, spilling coins everywhere. The man yelled and slumped to his knees, his face in his hands. Tobias jumped over the banister and sprinted for the door, but Ginger was already coming for him.

Tobias swerved, but Ginger reached out a long leg and hooked his feet from under him. He crashed to the floor and, before he could move, his hands were yanked behind him and tied together.

'No! Get off!' He tried to twist away, swearing a blue streak as fury and panic took over. He struggled to his knees, but someone pushed him down again.

'Lie still, Toby. Lest you want a beating. I'd rather not have to do that.'

The slow, quiet voice cut through his panic, and he stopped struggling. He lay panting for a moment, then rolled over and glared at Ginger, who studied him with a measuring eye and smiled when he saw that Tobias made no further effort to get up. 'Good lad,' he said.

The other man was sitting on the floor, holding his forehead and uttering a stream of curses. 'Brat needs a kicking,' he growled.

'None of that, Perce. Dad wants him in one piece. Go get the carriage.'

Perce threw Tobias a foul look, but stood and walked out of the door. Ginger reached down and hauled Tobias to his feet. He held him by the arm and gave him a gentle shake. 'Now listen good, Toby. Don't try nothing else, understand? I'll only have to hurt you. I'm your cousin Ezra, by the way.'

Horse's hooves clattered on the cobbles outside. Ezra yanked Tobias out of the door. A small, shabby brougham stood at the kerb. Perce glared down from the driver's seat, a lump the size of a hen's egg sprouting on his forehead. As Ezra reached out to open the carriage door, his grip slackened. Knowing it was his last chance for freedom, Tobias flung himself sideways and fought in grim silence, kicking at Ezra's long legs. It was no use: his cousin might be a beanpole, but he was terrifically strong. He picked Tobias up by the scruff of his jacket, threw him into the carriage and climbed in after. There was a smack of reins and the brougham lurched forward. Tobias crouched in the corner where he'd landed and stared up at Ezra, waiting for the punch or kick he'd just earned. His cousin peered down his long nose at him and shook his head.

'You'd best not try that sort of thing around Dad,' he said. 'Tain't wise. He gets riled when folks go agin him. Specially Family.' He reached down and lifted Tobias onto the seat.

Tobias leant back and closed his eyes. He was trapped. For the first time in weeks, Alistair Windlass faded from his thoughts. Instead, the image of Barty Petch floated before him and an old, familiar sickness filled the pit of his stomach: a sickness he thought had died for good with his stepfather.

Zebediah Petch was waiting for them. Ezra pushed Tobias through the door of an old brick warehouse on the fringe of Flearside, a depot for freshly stolen goods, he guessed. Petch turned from the group of men he'd been talking to and strode towards them.

He had forgotten how huge his uncle was. As the man approached, Tobias began to sweat. He had to force himself to stand still. Zebediah looked at him with his speckled eyes. There was a flicker of satisfaction – and something less pleasant. His eyes travelled from Perce's swollen forehead to Tobias's bound hands. 'Give you trouble, did he?'

'Startled him a bit, Dad. Wasn't expecting us. Lad's been ill.'

'Has he now?' Zebediah towered over them, even the lanky Ezra. Tobias made himself look up into his uncle's eyes. He was furious to find that he was shaking. He clenched his jaw and glared at Zebediah Petch.

'You got no right treating me this way, Uncle.' His voice was shaking too, but at least he hadn't squeaked. 'I been ill with fever for the last fortnight. I'd have come soon as I could.'

'You're up and walking now, boy, so I guess you were on your way to find me when Ezra and Perce gave you a lift?'

'No, I wasn't, and you know it. I got family matters I got to deal with first.'

'Like where your mum's got to?' Zebediah's eyes never left his. 'Curious that. She disappeared the same time you did. Now, maybe I got a nasty, suspicious mind, but you and her vanishing the day after we had our little meeting seems a trifle convenient. You scarpered, the pair of you. Don't deny it, boy! Your mum never wanted you to have anything to do with us Petches.'

'It weren't like that! I took ill next day with fever and didn't get out of bed till yesterday. To be honest, Uncle, I been so poorly I clean forgot our appointment.'

'Maybe.' Zebediah turned and walked towards a lantern hanging from the ceiling. 'Bring the boy into the light.' Ezra pushed Tobias into the yellow glow of the oil lamp. Zebediah's seaweed eyes studied him. 'All right. You been ill. Anyone can see that. You may just have let yourself off a hiding. But I ain't satisfied yet, boy. You might've been ill, but that don't explain where you were, and where your mum's got to.'

'The Castle.' Tobias's eyes darted round the group of men studying him before sticking at Petch's face. He needed to be careful now. 'I was there when I took sick. I was too ill to move. They put me to bed, had the doctor round, and Mum's been looking after me. She's still there. She's living in, there's so much sewing to be done. I was feeling well enough today, I thought I'd come check the house. Make sure it was locked up all right and collect Mum's savings so they wouldn't get stolen.' It was so nearly the truth that Tobias hardly felt he was lying. Surely Zebediah would believe him.

'Think a lot of you up at the Castle, do they?' His uncle's eyes gave nothing away, and the bristling black beard hid the rest of his face.

Tobias shrugged. 'Been working there since I was seven. Got some friends.'

'Friends rich enough to send you off to grammar school, I see.'

Tobias gawped at him. The clothes. He'd forgotten. His mind raced for an explanation. Found nothing.

'Powers of invention failed you, Toby? You look quite the gent. I hardly knew you. Who's so fond of you, Nephew, that they'd pay twenty pound a year to send you to a swanky grammar school?' Zebediah's voice dropped to a dangerous growl. 'You never had no intention of working with the Family, did you? Got a better offer from one of your fancy friends. Come on. I want the truth this time, boy, or I'll beat it out of you!'

Tobias stared at him, aghast. The last thing he needed was for Zebediah to find out about his friendship with Charlie and decide to blackmail the Queen for ransom. His chances of escape were slim enough already. There was only one alternative: 'I-it's Mr Moleglass.'

'Moleglass?' Zebediah frowned. 'Who's he?'

'The butler. He taught me to read and write. And now he wants me to go to a proper school.'

'And why should the blinking butler care whether you're schooled or not? What are you to him, boy?'

'I don't know! He's a good man, Moleglass. We get on. But I don't want to go. A school like that, full of toffs. They'd make my life merry hell. I tried to explain to him, but he's got a bee in his bonnet about schooling. If you must know, I was fixing to run off.' Tobias stared at the floor and scowled. 'That's what I was doing at home today. I knew my mum had some money hid—'

'Stealing from your own mother! Running off from her and your kind friends at the Castle without so much as a goodbye. I'm shocked, boy. You know what that makes you, don't you?' Tobias looked up and saw Zebediah Petch's eyes sparkling wickedly, his teeth grinning through his beard. 'That makes you a Petch, boy! Welcome to the Family!'

Tobias sagged with relief.

'Take the boy home, Ezra. Find him some grub and a bed. He looks done in. Oh, and, Ezra, take care to keep him safe for me. A boy who runs off from one set of relations can't be trusted not to run off from another, can he? And from the look of that bump on Perce's head, Toby, you weren't too keen to come see your old uncle, now, were you?'

The grin disappeared behind the beard, the pebbly eyes

went cold, and Zebediah jerked his head towards the door. Ezra and Perce hauled Tobias out. They didn't untie his hands.

The brougham rattled over a dozen winding Flearside streets. Hopelessness squashed Tobias into a corner of the carriage. Zebediah would not be in a hurry to trust him after this. He stared out of the window. Ezra hunkered beside him, a preying mantis of a man, his long limbs sharply folded, his long face nodding peaceably at each lurch of the carriage.

They slowed in front of a large, old merchant's house, and Tobias realised that they must be near the river. The house was twisted with age and had the same seedy, neglected air as the rest of Flearside, but it had not been cut up into tenements like its neighbours. It had a long, tiled roof and enormous brick chimney. Its top story jetted out over the street and was graced by no less than five large, grimy windows. The huge wooden gate at one end of the ground floor opened as they approached. Someone must have been on the lookout for them.

Perce drove the carriage through into a large, cobbled courtyard behind the house, and Tobias felt his body tense. For years he'd made sure no one could make him feel this way, that no man had the power to hurt him. Now the old feeling of helplessness was back, as strong as if Bartholomew Petch had never died. Sweat oiled the palms of his hands, and he swallowed, trying to ease the dryness in his mouth.

Ezra opened the carriage door and unfolded onto the ground. 'Slide on out, Toby,' he said. Tobias jumped out and froze. People were coming at him from every direction. There were women, children, several men, and a handful of older boys. He lurched backwards, bumping into the brougham and nearly tipping himself in at the open door. Two ginger urchins, twins by the look of them, who had attached themselves to Ezra's long legs, burst into screams of laughter.

'What a silly!' one shrieked in delight, pointing a fat and dirty finger at Tobias.

'Why hasn't he got any hands, Daddy?' cried the other, jumping up and down and pulling on Ezra's baggy trousers with such force that they seemed in danger of descent.

'Yes, Ezra,' said the tall, sandy-haired woman who had led the march. 'Untie the poor boy.' Ezra turned Tobias around and loosened the rope. Tobias was painfully aware of the dozen pairs of eyes on him. As he turned back to face his stepfamily, he knew he had gone bright red. Embarrassment was forgotten the next second as pain boiled into his hands and wrists. He'd never felt pins and needles like it. He bit his lip to keep from crying out and stared at the ground, eyes smarting.

Someone snorted, and he looked up and met the eyes of a beefy, black-haired boy; a boy wider and taller than most men, though he looked to be only fifteen or sixteen. The boy gave him a gibing, sneering grin. 'Aw, he's scared! What a pretty little schoolboy!' He reached out a brawny arm and flipped Tobias's cap off his head.

All the anger and fear he'd been holding back broke free. With a roar of fury, Tobias launched himself at his tormentor. He rammed his head in the boy's stomach. The boy gave a surprised grunt and fell. Tobias jumped on his chest and drew his fist back. He forgot everything except how good it was going to feel to smash his fist into the ugly red face lying on the ground gasping for air like a landed fish.

Someone pulled him off the boy. 'Let go!' he shouted, but his captor kept him pinned with a single arm round his chest as though he were no bigger than the twins – now jumping up and down and screaming with fear and delight.

'Calm down, Toby. There'll be no fighting today.' It was Ezra holding him and, at the sound of his voice, Tobias stopped struggling, shaking as rage drained away and left the familiar hollowness. For a moment, Ezra's arm was the only thing keeping him on his feet.

He felt sick with self-disgust. Stupid to lose his temper. Stupid above all here, when his only hope of escape was to fool the Petches into trusting him.

The boy he had attacked rolled over with a groan and staggered to his feet. His eyes were round marbles of hatred, and his mouth stretched in a grin of rage. 'You

scab! You maggoty piece of tripe! I'll pay you out for that!'
He lumbered towards Tobias, but the tall woman grabbed
the back of his shirt.

'Enough of that, Albert. You earned what you got. If
I catch you tormenting your cousin I'll have a word with
Dad. Now off with you. Go and make yourself useful
helping Wilf.' She released him and, after one last glare at
Tobias, the boy shuffled towards one of the brick
warehouses that formed the other three sides of the
courtyard.

'And as for you, Toby,' she said in her slow, dry voice,
'you need to keep your temper round Bert. Best to ignore
him when he plays the fool. Brains is not his long suit,
and I ought to know, for I'm his mum. I'm Elsie,
Zebediah's wife, and I bid you welcome.'

Ezra released him, and she reached out a long arm and
shook hands with Tobias solemnly. 'I see you met my
eldest already. I'll take over from here, Ezra. Dad'll be
wanting you back at the depot.'

Ezra detached the twins from his legs and handed them
to a small, plump, dark-haired young woman. 'Be seeing
you, Toby,' he said, blinking his large, round eyes. He
clambered up onto the brougham and settled next to
Perce, who reversed the carriage and drove it clattering
out of the gate.

A door beside the gate opened, and a man stepped out
to shut it behind them. A proper gatehouse, just like at
the Castle! This wasn't a house, it was a fortress. Heart

sinking, he turned back to find Elsie watching him. Her narrow face had the same long nose and prominent, cornflower-blue eyes as her eldest son; the same mild but determined expression. She could have been any age from thirty to fifty: the red of her hair so faint that it was difficult to tell pink from grey; her face as washed out as her hair: lips, cheeks, freckles fading into her skin. 'Time enough for introductions all round later, Toby. There's a mort of us, and you look near done in. Food and bed for you. Molly, come here.'

A girl his own age with coppery plaits pushed through the crowd. She eyed Tobias dubiously and sniffed.

'Moll, take your cousin into the kitchen and dish him up some of last night's steak and kidney pudding,' said Elsie. 'Then show him up to his bedroom. Privy's out here, Toby,' she said, pointing to a small brick outbuilding. 'Best use it before you go up for I don't hold with chamber pots.' Tobias blushed, caught the copper girl's eye and blushed redder than ever.

'Well, come on then,' Molly said, slinging her plaits over her shoulder and setting off towards the house.

'Uh...thank you,' Tobias muttered to his aunt before weaving through the ring of Petches and followed the rapidly disappearing plaits.

He sat at a massive scrubbed table that reminded him painfully of Maria's. His body was telling him that he had overdone it. The run from the Castle, the fight at the house, the set-to here – it was all coming home now, and it was as much as Tobias could do not to lay his head down on the table and sink into oblivion.

The kitchen was beautifully warm. A modern range purred in the fireplace, a range that would make Maria's eyes glisten with envy. Big as it was, it was dwarfed by the fireplace, which spread itself across one whole wall of the kitchen, an oak beam as thick round as Zebediah himself holding up the wall above it.

But Maria would not have approved much beyond the range. It was the most cluttered, harum-scarum and downright dirty kitchen Tobias had ever seen. Sunlight oozed through the encrusted windows. Dirty crockery was strewn about the table and piled in the stone sink, and a bucket of peelings and slop leaked onto a stone floor which looked as if it had not been scrubbed or even swept for years.

A greasy white plate plopped in front of him, a knife and fork stabbed into the middle of the lump of steak and kidney pudding humped upon it. Tobias looked at the cold heaviness of the pudding and, hungry as he was, felt a distinct reluctance.

'Go on, then. Eat.' Molly pulled a chair up and sat down opposite him, pinning him with eyes as brilliant and hard as sapphires. As she stared, a slow smile spread the corners of her mouth. 'Don't worry,' she said. 'It's better than it looks. Susan made it, not Ma. Ezra's wife,' she explained. 'Ma can't abide cooking, but Susan likes it. Says she married Ezra to fatten him up. But she's bound for disappointment. He won't fatten – he's a Sweeting, like Ma. Petches be stout and wide, Sweetings tall and thin.'

Tobias hooked a forkful of pudding into his mouth and discovered that Molly was telling the truth. Even cold, the filling was rich and meaty and the suet crust melted on his tongue. He concentrated on filling up the gnawing pit that his stomach had lately turned into and only remembered his audience when he was scraping the last bits onto his knife and fork. He glanced up to see Molly watching his every movement, a look of amused contempt in her sapphire eyes. He felt his face burn scarlet.

'Would you like some more?' He saw her bite her lip to keep from laughing. Pride fought hunger, but the battle was brief.

'Yes,' he said. 'And something to drink, please?' She took his plate into the larder and returned with another wodge of pudding and a mug of small beer. Tobias ate more slowly this time, washing the rich pudding down with the weak, slightly bitter beer. He could feel the food giving him strength, but it also brought a heaviness that weighed on his eyelids and stretched his mouth in yawn after yawn.

'Which are you?' he asked, more in an attempt to keep awake than anything.

'What d'you mean?'

'Petch or Sweeting?'

'Oh,' she said, 'I'm neither. Neither wide nor tall, neither Petch nor Sweeting. Me and Ambrose are the only ones. He's youngest after me. We're the odd ones out.' A bitterness in her voice cut through his daze, and he looked up, startled. Her cheeks were flushed and her blue eyes glittered. Then noticing him looking, she jumped up from the table. 'Come on, if you've finished. I'll show you your room. Oh,' she stopped and looked at him, the mockery back in her eyes and voice, 'best visit the privy first, hadn't you?'

He woke in the smoky forgetfulness of a long, exhausted sleep and stared up at the wooden rafters tenting overhead. They were grey with age, holed with worm, and he was sure he had never seen them before. He became aware of sunlight streaming through a dormer window, a lumpy mattress beneath him, musty smelling sheets and blankets over him, and the eyes of some unseen person watching him.

He turned his head and saw a boy of about nine or ten. The boy had russet-brown hair and a thin white face with blue eyes embedded in thick bronze lashes. He was sitting cross-legged on the other bed in the room and staring solemnly at Tobias, his face as blank as though carved from soap. Tobias's memory fell back into his head with a terrifying thump, and the scariest thing of all was this silent boy.

'Who the blazes are you?'

'You knocked Bert down,' the boy said. 'Can you teach me to do that?' His voice was a whisper of desperate longing. No ghost, Tobias reasoned, would want to head-butt a fifteen-year-old tough. He sat up in bed and discovered he was naked. Vaguely, he remembered clawing his way out of tie and collar, leaving them and the rest of his clothes on the floor where they fell. They were no longer there.

'Where are my clothes?'

'Ma took 'em.'

'Why?'

'To keep you in bed. I'm to tell her when you wakes, and then she'll come and bring you some togs. She don't want you running round till she tells you what's what. You might try and escape and that would be stupid.'

'Why would it be stupid?'

''Cause you can't escape from here without we let you. You'll see. You'd only get a beating from Dad.' The boy's face went pinched and narrow. He stared at Tobias, and Tobias stared back at him.

'Well,' Tobias said when nothing seemed to be happening. 'You'd best go fetch her then. What's your name?'

'Ambrose,' said the boy, refocusing his blue stare on Tobias. 'I'll fetch Mum if you promise to teach me how to knock Bert down.'

'What I did was stupid. You don't want me to teach you that.'

105

'Yes I do. Bert thumps me most days.'

Tobias winced at memories of his stepfather's fists and the damage they had done. Poor kid. 'Yeah, well, picking a fight with someone as big as your brother is just plain dumb.'

'You did it.'

'I told you: I was stupid. You try something like that with Bert and he'll hit you twice as hard. You gotta be cleverer than him. Think of another way to get him to stop thumping you. Anyway, I done you that favour already. The only person your brother is likely to want to hit for a while is me.'

The wizened look faded and the child beamed at Tobias: a blazing smile that transformed his thin face. 'I'll fetch Mum,' he said and bolted from the room.

Tobias had a long wait but he hardly noticed. Ambrose's room was one of the oddest places he had ever been. Boxes lined the walls, boxes piled on boxes. More crowded under the beds, on the windowsill, in every available square foot of space. They seemed to be filled with junk: scraps of metal, broken tools, bits of machinery, wire, nuts and bolts. A workbench stood beneath the window. It was covered with metal constructions: parts of machines possibly, though they looked like nothing he recognised. A rack of polished tools stood on one side of the bench, and on the other stood a small bookshelf crammed with books and pamphlets.

But strangest of all were the walls: every inch was

papered over with drawings – the oddest drawings he had ever seen. Cobwebby lines mapped the paper, searching, testing, tracing, then solidifying into cogs and wheels, bridges, pulleys, levers, machines simple and complex. He knew some of them: a steam engine, a hoist, a lift. Many he did not. Some looked more like insects or spindly animals made of metal than machines.

He crawled out of bed and went to look at the largest drawing, the one above the workbench. It was of a machine with what must surely be wings. A machine for flying. He shook his head, unable to believe that Ambrose had thought of such an amazing thing.

His eyes lost themselves in the maze of silvered lines, and he hardly noticed the footsteps on the stairs until they stopped outside the door. Tobias gave a yelp and flung himself beneath the bed clothes just in time. Elsie Petch knocked and opened the door, a bundle of clothes in her arms. He pulled the blankets up to his chin.

'Well now, Toby,' she said, standing at the foot of his bed, tall and thin, wisps of ginger-pink hair floating about her face. 'You'll be feeling better. Slept the clock clear round.'

'What?! You mean it's Wednesday?'

'Past noon.'

He closed his eyes in dismay. Mum would be in a state. He'd meant to get a letter to her before now. Charlie and Mr Moleglass would know he'd run off to find Windlass, but no one would think of looking for him here.

Elsie put the clothes on the foot of his bed. 'In a minute you can put these on and I'll take you over to Wilf in the warehouses,' she said. 'Dad said you can read and write and figure, so you can help with the lists today. Tomorrow you'll join Ezra and the other boys. Ezra's the best kidsman in the business.' Her mouth curled in a proud smile. 'Dad says so, and he's sparing with praise, so it must be true.'

'Kidsman?'

'Someone who trains up you young'uns for the trade: puts you on the tools, teaches you the ropes. Barty already trained you up some, though, didn't he?'

He nodded, his heart sinking still further.

'He did always talk about you, Toby. I'm right pleased you've come. I was awful fond of Barty. So was Zebediah. Your dad was his only brother, and Zebediah sets a store by family. That's what I wanted to talk to you about. Ezra reckons you ain't happy to be here. He says you'll be off first chance you get. Now tell me honest, Toby, 'cause I'm after helping you, for your daddy's sake. Is that right now? Do you plan on scarpering?'

She stood tall and straight beside his bed, her round blue eyes staring solemnly into his, her hands folded as if she was in church. Her face was so peaceful, a stranger might take her for a simpleton, but he knew, looking up at her, that she was no more a fool than Ezra. If he answered her question, he would be the fool.

He frowned at the foot of the bed. 'They was fixing to

put me in grammar school, back at the Castle. I don't fancy that.'

'Well then,' she said. 'Wouldn't you rather come into the Family? You'll be like one of my own, Toby. Ezra's took to you already, and as for Zebediah…well, I might as well tell you straight. He means to have you, Toby. First because you're Barty's boy, and Barty always wanted you to join the Family. Second, because Barty said you took to the tools quicker than anyone he ever seen.

'Best you understand this, Toby: if Zebediah Petch means to have you, he will. He gets what he sets out after. I never known him be turned aside. So put any notion of running off out of your head. If you try, you'll be caught, and you'll only rile him. He'll have you, one way or another. Take my advice and go the easy way.' She gazed down at him, her face as mild as milk, and his blood chilled.

'Something's bothering you, boy. What is it?'

'My mum,' he said. He would tell her that much truth and none of the rest. He'd figured out years ago that it paid to be honest with your lying and lie with what you left out rather than what you said.

It didn't take much effort to let his face show some of the worry he was feeling about his mother. 'She don't know what's happened to me,' he said. 'It'll make her ill, not knowing if I'm alive or dead. I'm all she's got.' The thought of his mother's distress made him clench his mouth tight and stare at a drawing on the wall opposite, not seeing it. She had lost everything now, and this last was his fault. Somehow – anyhow – he had to get word to her.

Something brushed his head, and he looked up to see Elsie draw her hand back. Her face was solemn, her eyes larger than ever. 'I'll see what I can do, Toby. Now, get dressed and pop down to the kitchen for a bite before you start work.'

He glanced at the bundle of clothes. 'Those aren't mine,' he said.

'Them clothes wasn't suitable. They've gone to be sold. These are some of Ezra's old things when he was a boy. Should fit you well enough with a bit of turning up. Bert's too wide, I reckon. His old things would fall right off.'

'You sold my clothes? Without asking? My mum made those for me!' He hadn't liked the new clothes, had planned on selling them himself, but the outrage was real.

'The clothes wasn't suitable,' Elsie explained again, her voice slow and patient.

'They were mine!'

'And you belong to us now, Toby.'

The final shock of it hit home. The Petches were thieves. They hadn't just stolen his clothes: they had stolen him.

Twelve

'We thought you had gone with him. Both of you had disappeared, and we thought you'd gone together, like you did when you were looking for me.'

Charlie stared at her mother. 'Well, I didn't,' she said. The Dowager had her arm around Rose's shoulders. Rose huddled on a chair, a cup of tea untouched in front of her, her face in her hands, sobbing helplessly. Charlie felt something clutch at her heart with needle-sharp claws. 'He never asked me.'

Nell, who had been sitting silently at the table, glanced up at Charlie, irritation and sympathy flitting across her face. 'Scant comfort,' she snapped. 'But at least it shows the boy's not a complete idiot!'

'You had just threatened him with house arrest, Charlie,' Moleglass said. 'Do you think it likely he'd tell you? He didn't tell any of us. I should have checked on him earlier. He gave in too quickly – I knew it. But I simply couldn't believe he would do such a stupid thing! When I catch up with that boy…' He waved away the cup of tea Maria held out to him and began to pace, wringing his hands in their snow-white gloves.

Charlie shook her head. 'He can't have gone just like

that! Not without saying goodbye. Not without...' She stopped before she said it: not without taking me with him. She longed to be free, out of the Castle, tracking down Windlass. She could have helped – she was clever! He hadn't trusted her to help him – hadn't wanted her. Because she was a girl. But even as she thought it, she knew it wasn't true. Not because she was a girl – because she was Queen.

Queen! It was like having a deformity so dreadful people could never relax, never be normal. She wasn't allowed to be Charlie any more – she was Queen Charlotte – and she hated it. And now it had lost her Tobias.

She hadn't felt like this since her father's death. She couldn't bear it. She felt cold, and drew herself up straight and stiff. When she spoke, her voice was stiff too. 'The Guard,' she said. 'Send them after him. And the police. I want him back.'

'Want shall be your master then, missy!' Maria glared at her from behind the teapot, her nose bright red and dripping. 'Mr Moleglass already sent the Guard after him. He were at Rose's house but he's long gone. He's made clean off and we'll not catch him now. Not till he wants us to. So you can stop standing there acting like he's a toy someone's snatched off you! He's his own master, always has been. You don't own him!'

It felt like being slapped. Charlie stared at Maria and tears of shock began sliding down her face.

'No.' The soft voice pulled her eyes. Rose had lifted her head. 'You're wrong, Maria. Charlie is Tobias's friend.

He's hurt her feelings by going off like this, without a word. He didn't take none of us into his confidence. Knew we'd stop him – and he's that stubborn! Perhaps he's been a bit selfish but he's only a boy. He don't realise...' And she dissolved into tears again.

Charlie's own tears evaporated. 'It's your fault.' Her voice was dry as grit. 'You set Windlass free. Tobias has gone after that murderer to try and fix what you did. If he dies, you'll have killed him!'

Silence fell into the kitchen like a stone dropped from the heavens. Charlie was aware of the frozen figures of Maria, Moleglass and her mother, of Nell's sharp intake of breath. Misery fogged Rose's eyes and Charlie felt a savage satisfaction. Then she cried out as someone stepped forward and slapped her across the face.

Charlie stood for a moment, staring at her mother, then fled the kitchen and raced up the helter-skelter of twisting, wooden servants' stairs, her lungs aching and her breath screeching in her ears. She ran from the dislike in her mother's eyes and the disappointment she had glimpsed in Mr Moleglass's face – the disappointment that comes when someone you love and trust has let you down.

She couldn't escape to the roofs any more, so she ran to the library. It welcomed her with the smell of ancient leather and crumbling paper and memories of all the times over the years that Tobias had stolen or blackmailed books from her. She wandered between the tall shelves, looking for one of his favourites to read. She was still searching when Nell found her.

'I don't want you here.' Charlie turned away, trailing her fingers over the leather spines.

'Do you want to get Toby back or not?'

'Of course I do!' Charlie fought off a wave of helplessness and frustration. She glared at Nell. 'But Maria was right, blast her! He'll come back when he wants and not before. If…if…'

'If Windlass don't kill him.' Nell's eyes were bright and hard. 'That man would sacrifice anybody; I know that. And so does everyone who used to be in the Resistance. None of us have forgotten Peter. Tobias wasn't the only one waiting in Gibbet Square to see that man hang. Listen, Charlie. Toby's a fool to think he can tackle Windlass on his own.'

'I know that!' Charlie clenched her fists. She wanted to hit something. 'He should have taken me with him. You could have come too,' she added, as an afterthought. The longing surged back, stronger than ever. She needed to be *doing* something! Windlass had turned the tables: he had escaped and locked her inside the Castle. Rot him! And now Tobias had gone after him without her. But she could follow…

'It isn't too late, Nell! We could sneak out tonight, the two of us! We could use the freight tunnel.' Excitement bubbled up, pushing out anger and fear. 'I've still got the boy's clothes Tobias gave me. Your old friends in the Resistance could help, couldn't they?' The look on Nell's face shrivelled her words. 'Why not?'

'You know why not. Your daddy sacrificed himself for you, Charlie. How d'you think he'd feel if you was to go off and get yourself killed?'

She saw her father again in the last moments of his life. He was looking at her, his eyes full of love. She watched him leap into space. Her father had imprisoned her with his final act and she would never be free. Still she struggled: 'Tobias has gone after him!'

'Toby's a fool. When I get my hands on that boy, I'll box his ears till his head rings!' Tears spurted from Nell's eyes and she wiped them angrily. 'He and his mum's the only family I got left.' She sniffed and shrugged. 'So, will you help me or not?'

'How?' Even to her ears, her voice sounded sullen.

Nell ignored it. 'I want a meeting with Topplesham and the police. The Resistance can get our spy network set up again in a matter of hours. If his people work with us, we got twice as much chance of catching Windlass. Once we have him, Toby will come home.'

'What if Tobias finds him first?'

The look in Nell's eyes chilled her: 'We better hope that don't happen.'

Charlie watched Nell disappear out the library door, off to find her old contacts from the Resistance. She turned and began to trail once more along the rows of shelves, her footsteps loud on the creaking floor. Restlessness was on her like an itch.

Her mother's science lay behind everything, like a stain that wouldn't wash out. It had stolen Caroline for five years and killed her father. Now she had lost Tobias. Charlie hesitated. It seemed wrong to spy on her own mother, but Caroline had refused to answer her questions. As she walked towards the library door, she was still undecided, but by the time it closed behind her, her mind was made up and she was running. She would take a chance and go now. With any luck, her mother would still be comforting Rose.

The laboratory door was open. But it only took a moment at her mother's desk to discover that the Dowager must have locked her important papers in her filing cabinet. All that remained was a few scribbled notes and sketches that Charlie couldn't make head nor tail of. She sighed and leant back in the chair.

'And exactly what were you hoping to find?'

Charlie jumped up and whirled around. Her mother stood in the doorway. She looked tired; her face almost white with fatigue against the black dress, the bun at the back of her neck threatening to tumble to pieces at any moment.

'You won't tell me what you're doing, so I came here to find out – to make sure that you're not writing down all the research you destroyed before you ran away.'

Her mother closed her eyes for a second. But when she opened them she merely said: 'My work is not your concern.'

'*My father died for your science!*' Charlie tried to keep calm, but her voice shook with anger and frustration. 'That makes it my business! Promise me you're not recreating that research. Windlass is out there. He killed the leader of the Resistance for your science. He would have tortured your friend Bettina for it. He would have killed me, you, Tobias – anyone – in order to get it. Don't you understand? While that man is free, it isn't safe!'

'Do you think I don't know that?' Her mother's face was even paler, her eyes had taken on a haunted expression. 'I can think of little else. I sacrificed everything I loved – *everything!* – to keep my discovery out of Alistair's hands! Do you really imagine I would risk letting him have it now?

'He can't get near us or my work, Charlie. We are safe here. And if he stays in Quale he must eventually be caught. Try to be logical. I know that you are still angry because I slapped you when you were unkind to Rose. I apologise: I should not have hit you.' Tears began to trickle down her face. 'Damnation!' The Dowager tugged a handkerchief from her sleeve and blew her nose. 'I loathe crying.' Her mother paused, took a deep breath. 'I know it's difficult for you to trust me. You hate me, and I can't blame you. I often hate myself.'

Something thick and bitter burned the back of Charlie's throat. 'You abandoned us.'

'Do you think it was easy for me to leave you? Do you think I wanted to?'

She heard the pain in her mother's voice, but she turned her head away.

'It was the hardest thing I've ever done. I love you, Charlie. I loved your father. I loved him very much, but—'

'You ran away!'

She looked at last, and her mother's beauty hurt her. Even with a red nose and dripping eyes, her mother was beautiful. She looked like the Renaissance angel in the painting in the long gallery. It was hateful, that beauty. Nothing could fracture it – not a husband's death nor a child's unhappiness. It was as immutable as crystal. For the first time in her life, Charlie was glad she looked like her father – had inherited his red hair and blue-green eyes, his thin face and long nose.

'You didn't love us enough to stay and fight for us. You didn't even love us enough to take us with you. You ran away from Alistair Windlass – and my father is dead!'

'It isn't as simple as that. You don't understand what was at stake.'

'Yes I do!' she spat. 'Windlass told me himself. He told me he was going to kill Father and he told me why. Because of you! Because of your work! You discovered something he wanted. And then you ran away to keep him from getting it. You had to save your precious science!'

She was shouting now, spewing out bitterness and spit. 'You saved your science but you left us! We didn't matter!

You let him have us, didn't you? And now you can hit me again for telling the truth! Both of you – you and Rose! Both of you! I hate you!'

Her mother seemed to draw into herself, grow thinner, translucent. The sound of Charlie's heartbeats vibrated inside her head, ticking off the seconds as her mother stood silently, looking at her, before turning and walking from the room.

Thirteen

Elsie had given him corduroy trousers, a striped cotton shirt, brown waistcoat and jacket, boots and cap. Everything was inches too long, and he rolled up the legs and sleeves. The boots were a bit big, but comfortable enough. He thumped down the stairs into the kitchen, where Elsie was sitting with Ezra's wife, mending clothes. The twins rolled out from beneath the table and stampeded him, grabbing his knees. He thought the one on the left might be a boy, though it was hard to tell beneath the shaggy ginger hair, grimy pinafores and grimier faces.

'You're our cousin Toby,' said the left-hand one.

'Are you going to live here now?' said the other.

'Looks like it,' Tobias said, keeping his voice light and not looking towards the women. 'Who're you, then?'

'I'm Elizabeth,' said the one on the left. 'I'm Thomas,' said the other. He'd got it wrong.

'Leave Toby to eat his dinner,' Elsie said. 'He can't be playing all day like you two; he's got work to do. Come and sit, Toby. It's only bread and cheese, but you'll get a hot meal this evening.' Susan smiled up at him as he sat down, causing him to blush, but otherwise the two women worked on as though he was not there, chatting amongst themselves.

The bread was fresh and well buttered, the cheese sliced thick. He ate slowly to make it last, listening to the murmur of the women's voices, the purr of the range as it chewed coal, the bumps and giggles of the children playing beneath the table. He watched the women's needles flash through fabric like silver swifts darting in and out of a building. It brought his mother's hands to mind, and he looked away.

He swallowed the last crumb and wished for more, but was too embarrassed to ask. Instead, he drained the mug of small beer. The moment he put it empty on the table, Elsie pushed her needle into a pincushion and stood. 'This way,' she said.

In silence, he followed her across the courtyard, surprised again at the size of the place, the large cobbled yard, the long brick warehouses that formed three sides of the square. It really was a fortress: narrow barred windows, thick oak doors, and it would take a ladder to get onto the roofs. He turned and glanced at the gate: shut. In the window above it he fancied he saw a movement. The guard was on duty. Doubtless the gate was kept locked when not in use. Ambrose had been right: escaping this place would not be easy.

He followed Elsie into the central warehouse. The heavy door groaned shut behind him and he stood, eyes adjusting to the filtering light that fell from the row of skylights to break upon the rafters; nose twitching at a dozen new smells: musty, rich, sharp, acrid, mellow, each demanding attention. Bales, cartons, boxes, crates marched across the stone floor and in the midst of them moved a tiny, white-haired man, bent as a shepherd's crook. In the centre of the room, Molly perched on a tall wooden stool at a clerk's desk, writing in a ledger. When the door groaned, they both turned and stared at him.

'Here we are,' Elsie said, pushing him forward into a puddle of dusty light. 'He's woken at last. Toby, this is your great-uncle Wilf. You do your best for him this afternoon. Moll, I'll have you in the kitchen now. You can help Susan get supper.' The girl wrinkled her nose, but jumped down and followed her mother without a word, passing Tobias as though he were invisible.

'Well, boy,' said Wilf, peering up at him sideways because of his crooked back, 'let's see if you can use that block of wood atop your neck. Sit at the desk!' When Tobias had climbed onto the stool, Wilf came and stood beside him. His head barely reached the desktop. His eyes glinted up at Tobias. 'So you claim you can write?'

'Yes!' Tobias glared at the old man, who glared back and poked the ledger with a gnarled finger.

'Then you ought to be able to read. Look there, at what Molly's wrote. See that? Six columns set out neat as ninepins. Read 'em off to me.'

Tobias read out the headings: 'Clothes and Linens;

Foodstuffs and Drink; Money and Banknotes; Silver and Jewels; Furnishings; Livestock.'

'You *can* read, after all. Now see how she's written down the entries: what it is, what it's worth, date it was brought in, where it's going, date it leaves. Got that?'

'Yes,' he muttered.

'How old d'you reckon I am, boy?' Wilf said. Tobias shrugged. 'I'm seventy-seven. When you talk to me you say "sir". Got that?'

'Yes...sir.' Tobias frowned at the ledger. This old man was worse than Fossy. He was a gnarled-up piece of cantankerousness.

Wilf grinned at him, baring a handful of worn stumps for teeth. 'Let's see if you can write as well as you can read. And work quick, boy; I wasted enough time on you already.' He began to move along the lines of crates and boxes, pausing at each one, calling out descriptions, values, dates and destinations. Tobias scribbled for all he was worth. The old man barely gave him time to write down one entry before he was on to the next. Barely time to dip the pen in the inkwell, again and again.

After an hour, his fingers began to ache. Another hour, and they were numb. He wrote on grimly, his lips pressed in a thin line. Dip, scratch, dip, scratch. Sweat beaded on his forehead, and he began to make mistakes. Misspellings. Blots. His fingers were trembling when Wilf's voice, thin and rusty as an old iron knife, finally stopped. Tobias put the pen down and stuck his right hand in his armpit to ease the pain in his fingers.

'Five blots, boy. I won't have blots in my ledger. Use that penknife to scratch 'em out and mind you don't tear the paper.'

Only when the last blot was scratched away and the last misspelling corrected did Wilf allow Tobias to go in search of his supper.

The courtyard, empty a few hours before, was crowded with people and activity. A dog cart and the brougham stood in a corner. Horses whickered from a small stable at the far end of the yard where boys were unharnessing and brushing them. Men and boys traversed the courtyard on unknown business.

Tobias stood in the gathering dusk, watching, studying the to and fro, looking to see if the gate was still guarded. Yes: the gate was shut, the watchman visible in the window above. He swore under his breath. No way out there. Frustration battled with exhaustion as he headed for the kitchen and the promised food: his stomach was clamouring as loudly as the twins.

Something rammed into his back, and Tobias pitched forward onto the cobbles, catching himself with his hands, rolling over and up into a crouch. The boot that had been aiming for his side missed and skidded off his knee. It hurt.

'You maggot! I'll get you yet!' Albert drew back his foot for another kick, but Tobias didn't wait for it. There was no chance of winning this fight. Albert was a head taller and twice as wide. Tobias sprinted for the kitchen, but the kick had done something. He felt the knee give and he fell hard, rolling over and over. Before he could get up a boot slammed into his ribs. He yelled and twisted up, waiting for the next kick.

It didn't come. Painfully, Tobias rolled onto hands and knees. He looked up and saw Zebediah Petch. Petch was staring at Albert, who was backing away, his face yellow with fear. 'I told you.' Petch's voice rumbled through the yard, which had grown suddenly quiet, 'to leave the boy alone. I told you what would happen if I caught you at him.'

'I-it weren't my fault, Dad,' stammered Albert. 'He started it!'

'Boy, if you're gonna lie to me you'd best do a better job than that.' Petch's voice was as cold as a granite gravestone. 'Get yourself to your room. I'm sick of the sight of you. Be in my office at nine o'clock. Now go!'

Albert hesitated. 'But I ain't had no supper yet.'

'Then you'll do without. Get outta my sight!'

Albert ran. Tobias froze as Petch turned and stared down at him. The man's face was blank, his seaweed eyes unreadable. Tobias levered himself onto his feet, praying he wouldn't topple over.

His uncle studied him. 'Did he break anything?'

'No.' His knee and ribs ached, but he'd known worse.

'Get on into supper then. Wilf can tell me how you got on. After supper you and I'll be having a little chat.'

The courtyard hummed with noise and movement again, but as he hobbled towards the kitchen, Tobias was aware of dozens of eyes watching him.

He counted twenty-eight people squeezed around the enormous trestle table in the dining room. He was squashed onto a bench between Ezra and Ambrose. Great-uncle Wilf sat up beside Zebediah, and his rusty voice buzzed above the general din like the whine of a wasp. Elsie sat quietly at the other end of the table, directing the girls bringing the dishes of food in and out of the kitchen.

The food was good, and there was plenty: stewed shin of beef, boiled potatoes and spring greens, followed by apple dumplings. Hunger kept him busy for the first half-hour, but then the ache in his knee and ribs grew bothersome, and he felt the first wave of the old tiredness sweep down and set his head throbbing until his brain felt as thick and heavy as cold porridge. The voices of the men rumbled in his ears, and he had nearly dozed off where he sat when the sound of his own name lifted his head with a jerk. Every eye was fastened on him. He felt his face glow red.

'I said, Tobias, that Uncle Wilf's given you a good report.' Zebediah's voice rolled down the table. His black beard cracked in a grin. 'But it looks to me like he's overworked you. You're near to falling face-first in your apple dumpling, boy! I'd best see you now, so you can get on to bed. Ezra, take him into the office. I'll be along shortly.'

The walk to the other end of the house helped to clear his head, as did the flicker of fear in the pit of his stomach. What did Zebediah want? He followed Ezra into a wood-panelled room where the fire in the big stone fireplace had fallen into red coals and embers. 'Stoke up the fire, Toby, whilst I light the lamps,' said Ezra.

Tobias knelt, fed the fire with wood and piled coal on top. Flames licked upwards, and in their glow, and the light from the kerosene lanterns, he saw a heavy wooden over-mantel decorated with the carved figures of Adam and Eve, round-eyed in surprise at their own nakedness. An enormous desk and chair crouched in the middle of the room, but there was not a stick of furniture else, and the wooden walls were empty of pictures. Ezra leant against the wall, his lanky arms crossed and his head poking between the thick beams holding up the ceiling.

'Why does Uncle Zebediah want to see me?' Tobias asked. The jittering in his stomach was growing worse.

Ezra smiled from between the beams. 'He'll tell you himself soon enough. No need for you to worry. Just do what Dad tells you and you'll be fine.'

'Good advice.' Petch loomed in the doorway and the room shrank to a quarter of its size. He sat in his chair. 'Front and centre, Toby.'

Tobias got up from the hearth reluctantly. He forced his feet to carry him to stand in front of Zebediah's desk.

Whatever was going to happen now, he wasn't going to like it, but he couldn't let his uncle see that. Or Ezra. He stood between them, his eyes unable to break away from Zebediah's face, but aware of his cousin, leaning behind him, watching his every movement.

'Welcome to the Family, Toby.' Zebediah's pebbly eyes studied him, and Tobias kept his face empty. 'I won't keep you long but there's a few things you need to know. Ezra's my kidsman. He's good. He'll train you right and he'll train you quick. When he's done with you, you'll be joining the housebreakers. Perce is in charge of them, and he's good too. The rules here is simple: do as you're told, do it quick and do it right. One other thing you need to know. Don't try and run off.'

Tobias stared into seaweed eyes and listened to the mantel clock count the seconds. He struggled to keep his face blank, aware that his breathing had quickened, his muscles tensed.

It seemed hours before Zebediah continued. 'Even if you manage it, I'll always find you.' His certainty rolled across the desk and struck Tobias like an ocean wave. 'You can't get away, Toby. You're Family now. Settle to it.'

His fists clenched without his permission. He forced his fingers to loosen while his mind leapt through the maze of possibilities, searching for the one which would give him the best chance. As always, he felt the pull of the truth. But only those fragments of truth which would show Zebediah the false picture Tobias needed him to see.

'Can I speak plain, Uncle?' His voice cracked. He could almost hear Ezra smiling behind him and, to his disgust, felt his face grow hot.

Zebediah had the grace to pretend not to notice. 'I never yet killed a man for speaking his mind.' This might have been meant as a joke, but it did little to ease Tobias's nerves. He swallowed. He needed to get this right.

'I never liked working for ol' Foss at the Castle,' he began. 'And I told you I don't want to go to no blistering grammar school. I can read and write and figure and that'll do me. Working in the Family might suit me well enough, and when you offered at the pub, I was flattered you'd want me. But...' He drew a deep breath. 'You got no rights over me! I been earning my keep since I was seven. Looking after myself and my mum. And I don't reckon you nor anybody else has any right to take me over. Not without I agree to it, and you ain't asked! I ain't your son. Barty's dead and...' He paused, swallowed his anger. 'No man's got a hold on me!' He was shaking. He'd gone further than he'd meant to, said more than was wise, but he didn't care. Even if it got him a beating.

Ezra shifted restlessly behind him, but it was Zebediah he watched. The man hadn't liked it. Red flushed from the beard and turned the seaweed eyes to green marbles. Then it faded, and his uncle studied him without a word. He opened a drawer in the desk, took out a long clay pipe, filled it from a tobacco pouch, tapped the tobacco down with a thick finger, struck a match, and lit the pipe.

A wisp of smoke curled snakelike from the bowl. Zebediah put the pipe stem in his mouth and sucked on it. His eyes were thoughtful. 'Thank you, boy. I said speak your mind and you done it. Not one boy in twenty would have been brave enough. Now I'll speak my mind, and there's a difference here, 'cause it's my mind that matters, Toby. Don't make no mistake about that. I heard what you said, and you're right: you ain't got no father. But I'm your uncle. Since Barty's dead, I got charge of you and—'

'My mother's got charge of me!'

'Your mother ain't around, boy. And don't interrupt me again!' The threat in the voice, the eyes, flashed cold and real. 'It may be that I handled you the wrong way. But I ain't used to asking. I'm a thief and a damned good one. I take what I want. As it happens, you belong to me anyway. Barty adopted you. He was your legal dad and he promised you to me. Dead or alive, I'm holding him to that promise.'

Tobias set his teeth to keep from yelling.

Zebediah paused, studied him. 'You're like me, boy. I feel for you. You don't like having anyone over you. And I daresay, when you're a man, you won't. If you're clever enough. But you ain't a man yet – you're a boy. *My* boy. And you'll do exactly what I tell you, or you'll regret it. Ezra's taking charge of you tomorrow. I expect you to work harder than you ever done in your life. I expect a lot of you, boy. I want good reports from your cousin. Understood?'

This was the moment. Tobias struggled for breath. He had to do it, no matter how much he wanted to shout and rage. They had to believe they had won. He looked at the floor and nodded – a reluctant, submissive, giving-in sort of nod.

Zebediah's voice softened. 'Good boy. Only a fool carries on fighting when they can't win, and we both know you're no fool. Which is why there'll be someone watching you every minute of the day and night from now on.'

Tobias's head jerked up, and he saw his uncle's beard part in a slow grin. 'I learnt years ago to read men as easy as you read words on a page, boy. Otherwise, I'd have been dead in the canal years ago, like poor old Barty. You're one of the best damn liars I ever met, and you're gonna be watched for as long as it takes me to be sure of you.'

Fourteen

The next day Charlie gathered Nell, Topplesham and Superintendant Blundell together. There was still no news of Tobias.

'I need you to find him!' The audience chamber was a draughty, echoing room, but suddenly it felt hot and stuffy. Charlie grabbed the arms of her chair to keep from leaping up and screaming with frustration. Nell, at least, looked like she cared. 'Surely it can't be that hard to find one thirteen-year-old boy!' She glared at the policeman. He had one of those reddish faces that large, irritable men get. Now it was brick coloured.

Lord Topplesham sprawled in his chair, surveying his gouty foot with displeasure. He looked up at her outburst. 'The City is full of boys, Your Majesty, and your friend obviously doesn't want to be found. To be blunt, ma'am, we can't afford to waste any more police resources on a runaway lad. It's his father we have to find.'

'Find one and you find the other! That's why I've asked Nell here. I want you to give her and her friends all the support you can.'

'The young lady from the Resistance.' Topplesham smiled genially at Nell, who sat upright in her chair, wearing her best blue serge skirt and jacket and a smart straw hat. She looked nervous but determined. 'My people have quite a dossier on you. You've been remarkably active for a young lady not yet seventeen years of age. Going into politics now, I gather.'

'It ain't illegal.' Nell gave Topplesham look for look.

'Not at all, Miss Sorrell. As long as you and your associates stay within the law: no bombs, no assassinations.'

'I wasn't planning to assassinate anyone this week, Lord Topplesham. Except Windlass. I take it you'd have no objection if we was to kill him?'

'Delighted, miss.' Topplesham inclined his head. 'Any leads?'

'Not yet. I do have a plan, however, which seems more'n you have. You're wrong: you need to put every man you've got on the lookout for Toby Petch. Find the boy and we find Windlass. Toby's been missing nearly a week now. He'd never leave his mum to worry so long. If he'd been able, he'd have got a letter to her days ago. Which means he's found his father.'

Charlie stared at Nell as her stomach fell into a hollow pit. A cold, sick feeling followed and she thought she might vomit. She swallowed convulsively. There must be another explanation. Another reason why he hadn't been in touch. But Nell was right: Tobias would never leave his mother to worry. He had found Windlass: it was the only thing that made sense. Which meant…

'Either Windlass has kidnapped Toby or he's…'

Nell shot her a quick glance then continued. '...he's killed him.'

Charlie clenched her fists until her nails bit into her palms and stared straight ahead. They had rowed, the last time she had seen him. He'd been furious with her. Tears burned behind her eyes and she scowled and blinked them away. No! She wouldn't let Tobias be dead! Nell's voice filtered into her head again.

'A man on his own ain't so easy to find. But a man holding a prisoner – that's different. He'd need a safe house. Somewhere he can keep Toby under lock and key.'

'And if the boy's been killed, which seems more likely?' Blundell's voice grated in Charlie's ears.

'Search the ditches, the canals, drag the river. If you find a body, I'll...' For the first time, Nell's voice faltered. 'I'll tell you if it's Toby or not. And there still might be a clue – where the body was dumped, how it was killed, a witness.' She paused. 'Dead or alive, we've got to find Toby Petch. It's our best hope of finding his daddy.'

'I shall watch your political career with interest, Miss Sorrell,' Topplesham said. 'For now, however, I will put you in touch with the head of my spy network.'

'And you, Mr Blundell?' Nell asked.

Her body seemed to have turned to wood, but Charlie made herself move her head to look at the policeman. Blundell sat in his chair as though he was on parade, back straight, legs bent at ninety degrees. 'If Her Majesty and His Lordship so order, then I must pull my men off their normal duties to look for the boy. But I do it under protest.'

'So.' Even to her own ears, Charlie's voice sounded odd. Three heads swivelled towards her. She looked at the policeman. 'Do you know where Alistair Windlass is?'

'We have no leads at present, ma'am,' he said, his face several shades paler.

'Then you have your orders.'

That night, when she finally fell asleep, Tobias was waiting for her in her dreams.

'Charlie! She ain't here. She's flitted.'

The bedroom of the abandoned house was dark. Charlie gripped the handle of her lantern tighter and whirled to face him. 'I have to find her or he'll kill my father!'

Tobias shook his head. In the flickering light, the pupils of his eyes were huge with fear. 'We gotta get out of here! He'll be coming for us.'

'Wait! There must be a clue.' She ran to the fireplace. The grate was full of ash and cinders. Perhaps something was hidden beneath them. She knelt, began to scrabble. It had to be here!

Tobias's hand gripped her shoulder, pulled her to her feet.

'Let go!' she shouted.

But the hand gripped tighter. Charlie turned and saw...

'You will come with me,' said Alistair Windlass.

'Where's Tobias?!' she screamed. 'What have you done with him?'

'I have killed him.' Windlass smiled. 'Like I killed your father. As I shall kill your mother, once I have her secrets safe. You will be left quite alone. And then I shall kill you too.'

Charlie lurched upright. Shudders tore through her, shaking her bed until its wire frame groaned. The shivers grew worse. Her heart was pounding in her head, faster and faster. Darkness pressed upon her, making the air too thick to breathe.

Tobias dead. She wouldn't believe it! But what if he had managed to track Windlass down? If so…she shuddered at the images racing through her brain: Windlass holding her father at gunpoint; aiming his pistol at Tobias's head; plunging his sword into Peter's heart; shooting Mrs O'Dair. If Tobias was alive, he was almost certainly Windlass's prisoner. The darkness was smothering her. What could she do? How could she stop that monster before he took not only Tobias, but her mother too?

Suddenly, she didn't care that her mother had abandoned her when she was six, that she might be lying to her about her science – she needed to know that Caroline was safe. Once more, she stumbled through the Castle's dark corridors and stairwells to her mother's door. She turned the handle, expecting it to be locked, but the door swung wide.

'Mother?' Charlie stumbled across to the bed. It was empty: there was no dark shape beneath the eiderdown, no sound of breathing.

Windlass had taken her mother! Charlie was frozen; her terror too great for movement or sound. Then she collapsed, grabbing onto the bedside table to hold herself up. And slowly it seeped into her brain...the candlestick was gone...and the pistol.

She gulped air, ignored the pounding in her head and forced her brain to work. If Windlass had kidnapped her mother he wouldn't need candle or gun. The Dowager had left the room herself, taking them with her. *Windlass didn't have her!* Caroline must have been unable to sleep and had gone to her laboratory to work. Relief did what fear couldn't and felled Charlie. The grey-shadowed night-time of her mother's bedroom broke apart and Charlie slid into a sea of black sparks.

Some unknown time later, she woke to find herself lying face down on her mother's bed, stiff-necked and freezing. It was still dark and she was alone in the room. Charlie grappled for the bedclothes and tugged them up to cover her. Slowly, beneath their weight, she warmed. The shivering stopped. Still, her mother did not return. When she felt well enough, Charlie pushed out of the bed and climbed, haltingly, to her own room, where she collapsed into an exhausted sleep.

Fifteen

On the first morning of his new life as an apprentice thief, Tobias was woken at dawn by hammering.

'What the...?' He pushed up onto his elbow. Ambrose sat at his workbench, outlined in dusty light from the window over his head, tapping away at something with a tinsmith's hammer. Pieces of wire and metal littered the floor. The boy hunched over his work, barefoot and still wearing his nightshirt, even though the room was freezing. Tobias shivered and tugged his blankets up round his neck. 'Why the devil are you making such a racket?' he groaned either side of a jaw-splitting yawn. 'It ain't time to get up.'

Ambrose hunched a shoulder in reply, the rhythm of his hammering never faltering. 'Sorry, Tobe!' he sang out cheerfully. 'I only get to work mornings afore breakfast. Wanna come see?'

Tobias drew breath to explain, in his most inventive language, another use for the hammer, but stopped himself just in time. Ambrose was near enough to being a friend, and he needed as many of those as he could get in this place. The boy might prove useful.

'I can't wait,' he called, over the clattering. With

a groan, he rolled out of bed and began pulling on his clothes. He spent the next eternity holding bits of wire and metal, and sucking whichever of his fingers got in the way of the hammer, while he listened to Ambrose explain, in elaborate detail, the many and marvellous machines he intended to invent. He couldn't decide whether his fingers or his head ached more when, at last, the jangling of the dinner bell called them to breakfast.

Tobias stroked the largest lockpick. It was a fine set: six shiny picks, with their heads of different shapes and sizes. The sight of them made his fingers tingle. Brought back memories of Barty. Hours they'd spent together, working the locks. Barty had started him as soon as he could hold a pick. It had been their special game, their secret from Mum.

Tobias stared at the heap of locks on his table. Dozens. Padlocks, wardlocks. All waiting for him to open them. And Ezra waiting too. He felt the man's attention as he moved around the large room over the stables, working with the other boys but always, Tobias knew, always watching him. It was only three hours into the day, and he was near ready to scream with it.

There were seven other boys. Ambrose was one. The others were second and third cousins. They stared at him and said nothing. Ezra gave them little time for talking, but at breakfast Ambrose had whispered over his porridge: 'Albert's had a beating off Dad. He won't be at school today.' The smaller boy smiled secretly into his bowl, but Tobias felt his own appetite fade. Albert had another reason to hate him now. He could only hope that his cousin was scared enough of Zebediah to leave him alone, but he had a strong hunch that Albert was not clever enough to take a hint, however painful.

The morning had been a surprise. One of the two large rooms above the stable block was rigged out as a gymnasium, with climbing ropes, pipes to shinny up, tunnels of boxes and crates and sewer pipes to wriggle through, and a punching bag.

Tobias's strength was coming back rapidly now, but even so, he struggled to keep up with the other boys as they scrambled up ropes, wriggled through pipes, climbed walls of netting. He was puffing and sweating when Ezra took them into the other room and sat them down to a lesson of locks.

'First one to finish will pocket a bob.' Ezra pulled a shilling from his pocket and set it on a windowsill. 'And get an early dinner. Off you go then.'

Tobias was aware of Ambrose, seated at the desk next to him, staring hungrily at the shilling. The boy sighed and set to work on his first lock. Tobias studied his own pile. He could pick these easy. He could do the lot in fifteen minutes. But maybe...if he wasn't so good at lockpicking...just maybe, Zebediah would lose interest in him.

Tobias sighed. Blast Barty. This was his fault. Because of

his blessed boasting. Tobias shut his eyes, wondering again how you could love and hate someone so much – and at the same time.

'Feeling all right, Toby?' Ezra loomed over him. His goggle eyes were assessing, studying, no doubt preparing the report he would make to Zebediah tonight. Tobias found he had made his decision.

'I haven't picked a lock in over five years,' he lied. 'I'm not sure I remember how.'

'Fingers don't forget,' Ezra said with a gentle smile. 'We're not expecting miracles on your first day. Just do your best and everyone'll be happy.'

Happy? Now that the decision was made, he felt a fierce satisfaction, and it was all he could do to keep it from showing in his face. The Petches weren't going to have it all their own way. Zebediah thought he was nobbled but he'd show him. Tobias felt Ezra's eyes following his every movement as he picked out his first lock, a heavy padlock, and chose exactly the wrong pick to open it with.

Thirty minutes later a plump third cousin raised his hand, shouting, 'Done it, Ezra!' Tobias heard Ambrose groan as the boy went to claim his bob before sauntering out of the door to freedom.

'I never win!' Ambrose grumbled, poking at the three unopened locks still on his desk. 'And I need the money more'n any of them.'

'Why?'

The hungry look returned to his cousin's face. 'I need proper tools and engineering books. Dad won't buy 'em for me. Sometimes Molly nicks something outta the warehouse, but it's not near enough.' He scowled at his locks.

'Never mind,' Tobias said. 'You're doing better than me, at any rate.'

Ambrose peered over at Tobias's pile. Nearly half of them remained locked. His eyes widened. 'You're even slower than Albert!'

Tobias shrugged. 'I haven't done this for years. Guess I lost the knack.'

The boy eyed him doubtfully, flicked his eyes towards Ezra, and went back to his own locks. Twenty minutes later, Tobias was the only boy left in the room. Ezra sat across the desk from him, watching, not saying a word, not offering advice. It was unnerving.

Tobias felt his fingers begin to shake. He was on his last lock, going through pick after pick, avoiding the best one as long as possible, making his fingers clumsy, but not too clumsy – he had to look like he was trying. Finally, he let the pick do its work and the lock snapped open. Tobias glanced up at his cousin. Ezra's eyes were wide and unblinking, his long face like a thoughtful sheep's.

'Sorry, Ezra,' he said. 'I've kept you from your dinner.'

'The food'll wait,' Ezra said peaceably. 'How do you think you got on, Toby? With them locks?' His blue eyes goggled.

142

'Not too well.' Tobias frowned down at his hands. 'I can't seem to feel it no more. Will it come back to me?'

'I reckon.' Ezra nodded, a slight smile curving his wide mouth.

Dinner was lamb stew and parsley dumplings. At least the food is good, Tobias thought, as he sat at the kitchen table scooping spoonfuls into his mouth as quickly as he could. The other boys had finished and it felt awkward, being the only one left in the kitchen while Susan and Molly cleared up around him. Ezra had disappeared without eating, to Susan's irritation. 'That man will dwindle down to a skeleton one of these days!' she grumbled, picking a twin up off the floor where it lay screaming for its daddy.

When Tobias wandered out into the yard his eyes automatically flicked to the gate. He visited the privy and washed at the pump, then strolled to a sunny wall and squatted down, leaning against it, wondering if he had fooled Ezra. His eyes kept travelling to the window above the gate, trying to catch another glimpse of the guard.

He had to get out of this place! It felt worse than prison: it was like being locked away in an old trunk in an attic room where no one would ever look. And he knew, with a hot, shameful feeling, that as soon as he managed to escape he'd forget about finding Windlass and head straight for home. If he stayed in the City, Zebediah would pick him up again in days.

Whatever happened, he had to get word to Mum.

She'd be ill with worry. If he had money he could bribe Ambrose to take a message…but he had nothing. And he couldn't trust Ambrose not to tell. Not yet.

Tobias sighed, leant his head back against the wall, closed his eyes. The sunshine pressed on his eyelids. He rested, his ears full of the familiar street noise of the other boys. The warmth and light bleached his thoughts to stillness, and he felt himself relax for the first time that day.

A cloud passed over the sun, and Tobias shivered. He opened his eyes onto the black expanse of Zebediah Petch's waistcoat. Against his will, his eyes travelled up, past gold watch chain, white collar, black beard, eagle nose, cold, seaweed eyes and bushy black hair. Zebediah stood over him, haloed by the spring sun.

'My office, boy. Now.'

As Tobias got to his feet and walked, slightly unsteadily, towards the house, he glimpsed Ezra gathering up the other boys, shepherding them towards the classroom, looking for all the world like a benevolent parson.

Six locks lay spread out on the desk. A set of lockpicks lay beside them, glinting dull silver in the dusty light. 'Show me,' said Zebediah.

Tobias stared down at the locks. Licked his lips. He needed to think, but his heartbeat kept pounding in his head. If he opened the locks quickly they'd know he'd been messing them around. If he did them slowly…well.

That's why he was here now. But they couldn't prove anything. Couldn't prove he hadn't lost his touch. He risked a beating either way. Best to carry on.

His hands fumbled over the picks. He chose randomly, attacked the first lock quickly, letting Petch see his nervousness, his uncertainty. It took him half an hour to open all six locks. Zebediah sat silently the entire time, not moving. When Tobias finally looked up from the last lock, he took an involuntary step backwards. His uncle's eyes were granite pebbles.

Zebediah reached out a massive hand and snapped the locks shut, one by one. 'Now do it again,' he said. 'Only this time, do it right.'

'I-I did it as quick as I could!' Tobias stammered. 'I'm out of practice, that's all. I ain't done no lockpicking for five years. Honest, Uncle, I can't do it no quicker.'

Zebediah leant back and his chair groaned in protest. 'I thought better of you than this, Toby,' he said, his voice dangerously quiet. 'Oh, I can't blame you for trying it on. No, I'm disappointed that you're stupid enough to take me for a fool. And Ezra too. You should know better by now.' His fist slammed down onto the desk with an almighty crash, sending locks and picks flying. Tobias backed away.

'I didn't!' he cried.

'Off the tools for five years? When Ezra and Perce saw you pick the lock of your own house just the other day? Right sweetly too, Ezra told me. Under fifteen seconds, and Barty put a good lock on that door. Forgot about that, didn't you, Nephew? You're going to have to sharpen your memory if you plan to keep on lying to me. That was downright pitiful.' He lurched up from the desk and Tobias retreated another step. His legs ached to run but there was no point.

Zebediah rounded the desk with a terrifying swiftness in such a large man. He grabbed Tobias by the scruff of his jacket and shook him until his teeth chattered. 'I don't rightly know what to do with you, boy. I'd beat the living daylights out of you right now if I thought it'd do any good. But it wouldn't. Just set your back up further.'

He lifted Tobias so that his feet dangled. He hung limply, too terrified to struggle. Zebediah's face was inches from his. He saw the pores in his nose, smelt the brackish breath, saw the yellowed whites of the pebbly eyes. Then the eyes blinked, the hand let go, and Tobias dropped to the floor, stumbled, nearly fell. He backed away, gasping.

'You just missed a beating by a hair's breadth,' Zebediah said. 'I don't want to beat you. It ain't the way to handle you and I pride myself on handling my men. So I'm gonna do a deal with you.'

'A deal?' Tobias gaped at his uncle. 'What deal?'

'A letter a week,' Zebediah said. 'To your mother. In exchange, you do your work here and you do it right. Any more slacking, and not only will I stop the letters but I'll thrash you good and proper. Have we got a bargain?'

Tobias stared at him. Fear and fury tumbled inside his head, fighting like tomcats. A letter to Mum. Zebediah had known just the bait to dangle under his nose. His stomach writhed, but he couldn't help himself: he took the bait. 'Two letters a week,' he said.

'One,' said Petch.

'Done.' He spat the word out, hating himself, but hating Zebediah more.

'Right.' His uncle's eyes gleamed as he hitched his pocket watch out of his waistcoat and placed it face up on the desk. 'Do them locks again, boy. Do them in under five minutes and you can write to your mum. One second more, and I'll beat the cussedness plum out of you.'

When the last lock snapped open, Tobias dropped the lockpick and stepped back, wiping his sweaty hands on his trousers. His heart pounded inside his head like Ambrose's hammer as he looked up at his uncle.

'Two minutes and seven seconds.' Zebediah leant back in his chair. 'My little brother was right about you.' A cold, satisfied smile spread across his face.

Sixteen

'Charlie?' She felt someone grab her shoulder and shake it. 'Charlie! Wake up. Are you ill?'

'Mmmph,' said Charlie, and rolled over to peer through bleary eyes at Nell, looking far too crisp and neat in a dark blue dress, white lace apron and cap. Charlie groaned. 'Go away.'

'You've missed breakfast. Are you sickening for something?' Nell reached out a hand to feel her forehead but Charlie batted it away. 'No! Let me sleep.'

'Must be something catching. Your mum's still abed and it's gone eleven!'

'What?' Charlie struggled to sit up. 'What's that about my mother?'

'She's usually up and working by daybreak. But this morning when her maid went in to help her dress, your mum was sound asleep. Wouldn't get up. She's sleeping still. Downstairs was agog with it till Mr Moleglass came and set them by the ears. What's going on?'

It couldn't hurt to tell Nell about her suspicions. Charlie took a deep breath: 'I think my mother's duplicating her research.'

Nell looked at her blankly. Then her eyes widened.

'You mean the stuff Windlass was after? The secret weapon? She destroyed all that!'

'Ever since she got back, she's been working in her laboratory. She won't tell me what she's doing. When I asked her if it was her old research, she didn't deny it. Last night I couldn't sleep so I got up to make sure she was all right. Only she wasn't in her bedroom.'

Nell frowned in puzzlement. 'Where'd she gone?'

'I don't know. I waited a long time. When she didn't show up, I came back here. It was nearly dawn. The rooks were just beginning to call.'

'Why didn't you rouse the Castle when you found her missing?'

'She'd taken her candlestick and her pistol. I knew—'

'Pistol!'

'A revolving pistol. She sleeps with it beside her bed.'

'Well, I'll be a...' Nell broke off. 'Why would your mum wander round the Castle all night toting a pistol?'

'She was working in her laboratory, I'm sure of it.'

'In the middle of the night?'

'I guess she couldn't sleep.'

'Maybe. It does sound like she might be working on that weapon again. But why...' Nell broke off.

'What?'

'There's no point in playing guessing games, Charlie. Your mum's in bed asleep. This is our chance to find out what she's up to. Let's make a visit to her laboratory.'

'I've done that! She keeps her papers locked in a filing cabinet.'

'That don't matter,' said Nell, suddenly looking grim.

'Oh,' Charlie said. 'Can you pick locks, too?'

'I'm a Petch, ain't I?'

But when Nell pulled open the door of the Dowager's filing cabinet twenty minutes later, after a slight struggle with the lock, the cabinet was empty.

'I thought,' Nell spoke slowly and carefully, like someone trying to keep their temper, 'you said she locked the papers away in here.'

'She did! I saw her!'

'Well, they ain't here now.'

'I'm aware of that!' Charlie began yanking open desk drawers. Nothing. She collapsed in defeat. 'They have to be somewhere! She's been working nearly every day since she got back. There must be dozens of pages. Wait...' She jumped to her feet. 'Of course! The safe!'

'A safe? Where?'

'There's a great, horrible, greasy safe sitting in my father's office like some sort of metal troll. With knobbly dials for eyes.'

'Sounds like a new-fangled combination lock.' Nell sighed. 'They open when you turn the dial to the right numbers in the right order. Well, that's us sunk. There's precious few can crack a combination lock. But the good thing is, Windlass won't be able to either. Your mum's papers are as safe as houses.'

It was on the tip of her tongue to say: 'You're a Petch. Your family breaks into houses for a living!' Instead she watched Nell relock the cabinet, then the laboratory door.

'I wish I could do that. I keep practising with a buttonhook.'

Nell glared at her. 'Why the devil would you want to learn a dirty trick like this? You're the Queen! Not a housebreaker!' She stomped away down the stairs. Charlie followed. Nell kept disappearing around the next bend.

'But look how useful it is!' she called after her.

A snort floated up the stairwell.

They emerged onto the third floor and Nell stalked away down the thick carpet towards the servants' stairs. Charlie caught up with her and they paced, side by side. 'Are you as good as Tobias?'

'Not even near.' Nell didn't turn her head. 'Mind, I never seen anyone as good as him; he's got a rare gift. Or curse, depends on how you look at it.' She sniffed. 'Most babies are given rattles and dollies to play with. In my family we get lockpicks. Enough of that; it's lunch time and I'm hungry, even if you aren't.'

'I'm starving! But first...' She grabbed Nell's arm and pulled her to a stop. 'I want to talk about Tobias! What did your friends from the Resistance say? Are they going to help look for him?'

'That's sorted. Do you remember Joseph?'

'The one who's sweet on you?'

Nell blushed. 'Don't be silly. Joseph has organised the old network. We have over thirty people out looking. I got a newspaper friend to print out a photograph of Tobias to give to them. It's nearly two years old, but it still looks a bit like him. And of course they have the wanted posters of Windlass. So now we wait.'

Charlie groaned. 'I hate waiting! At least you can get out into the City and help. I'm trapped in here.' And then she had her brilliant idea. 'Do you think your family would help us? To look for Tobias?' she added, when Nell just continued to stare at her as though she were speaking Esceanian.

'The Petches must have connections all through the City – ones the Resistance don't. They must know the sort of people Windlass would use for laundering money, buying weapons or holding someone prisoner.' She trailed off. Nell's brown eyes had gone cold. 'S-so would Zebediah help find him? He is his nephew after all.'

'It isn't a good idea, Charlie.'

'Why not? What harm can it do just to ask your uncle?'

'Zebediah won't pay me no heed. I turned my back on the Family. And he won't give a damn about Toby unless he thought the boy was of use to him.' Nell's voice was bleak. 'You don't want nothing to do with the Petches. Twisted, every one of them. Black as treacle, Petch blood. Black as sin. At least Toby ain't got none of it in his veins.

I have.' She looked at Charlie, her eyes hard. 'Toby's better off dead than having anything to do with that lot. Rose Petch was a simpleton to marry Uncle Barty; worse'n that when she let Windlass out of prison. But the one thing she has done right is to keep that boy away from my family!'

'I don't understand!'

'No,' Nell said. 'I hope you never do.'

Seventeen

Dear Mother,

I am sorry to worry you like this but I have written as soon as I could. I am fine. I have a place to live and am eating well. I will write every week so you will know how I am keeping. I cannot tell you what I am doing or when I will be coming home. But you are not to worry. Take care of yourself and give my regards to Nell. I hope Moleglass and the toffs are not working you too hard.

Your loving son, Tobias

Molly read the letter out in a clear, steady voice, then handed it back to her father.

'It seems Nell Sorrell would rather work as a skivvy than do her duty by the Family,' Zebediah growled. 'Reckon we're well shot of her. You won't be having nothing to do with her in future, Toby. Right, Moll, you can cut along.'

Molly left, and Zebediah folded the letter into quarters and slid it into an envelope. 'Address it,' he said.

Tobias dipped the pen in the inkwell and wrote his mother's name in large letters. Underneath he put: *Care of Mr Ancel Moleglass, Quale Castle.* He watched the shine of the ink dry away. Zebediah took the letter and slid it inside his jacket. 'I'll see it gets delivered,' he said. 'Now off you go to Ezra and keep your end of the bargain.'

Tobias stood still, watching the spot on his uncle's jacket that hid his letter. 'No,' he said, his voice amazingly steady. 'That ain't good enough.'

Silence squeezed the air from the room. Zebediah's eyes rose from the desk, his face flushed strawberry. 'What do you mean?' he growled.

'I want to see it delivered,' Tobias said.

'You calling me a liar, boy?' His uncle's voice climbed to a roar. Zebediah stood, and it was like a mountain hitching itself onto two legs and rising from the ground.

'You can see whether or not I keep my end of the bargain,' Tobias said. His voice was shaking now. 'I want to see your end kept too. Then I'll do my work in good heart. Otherwise, you can beat me till your arm falls off, but I won't never do what you want!'

Zebediah's eyes narrowed and his face darkened further. He said nothing for several moments, then shook his head. 'You're game, boy. I'll give you that. But you better be worth all the bother you're putting me to. Follow me and be sharp!'

Tobias peered through the grimy window of the brougham and watched Ambrose twist his way through the crowd. It was the end of market day. The hundreds of stalls filling

Castle Square were being knocked down and packed up in a riot of bustle and shouting. Soon nothing would be left in the cobbled space except a few rotting cabbage leaves.

Ambrose reached the Castle gates at last: a small, shabby boy in a cloth coat and cap like a dozen others milling about the square. He handed the letter to the guard in the hut and ran off, dodging his way towards the Cathedral. The driver clicked to the horse, the brougham began its stuttering journey across the cobbles, and Tobias leant back on the leather cushions, staring straight ahead, the bitter taste of captivity in his mouth.

Zebediah said nothing and they travelled without speaking all the way to Flearside, pausing at the Cathedral to allow Ambrose to climb up beside the driver. Tobias was aware of a weary gratitude to Zebediah for his silence. He went about the rest of the day in an unthinking haze. Not even the sight of Albert, bruised and sullen, at supper, roused him to worry about the future. He crawled into bed as soon as allowed and welcomed the nothingness of sleep.

'Go it, Tobe!' Ambrose cried, as Tobias went to collect his shilling for the eighth day in a row. A groan rose from the other tables, but his youngest cousin was grinning at him proudly. The cold, sleepy mornings spent listening to Ambrose rattle on about his inventions were paying off.

'Thirteen minutes, Toby. A new record.' Ezra spun the coin through the air at him, and Tobias caught it and put it with the others in his pocket. Eight shillings. Was it enough?

'But the boys are right,' Ezra said. ''Tisn't a fair fight. And it seems there's nothing I can teach you about lockpicking. From now on we'll concentrate on the things you don't do so well: like climbing. You're the worst snakesman in the group, lad. For all you're a skinny fellow, Albert'd swarm in a upstairs window tidier than you. Outside with you. I want you up that wall twice before dinner.'

Tobias groaned. His years of gardening had given him a strong back and arms but these boys could climb walls like flies, and none of them seemed to share his fear of heights. The practice wall, which you were supposed to climb with only the aid of a drainpipe and fingerholds between the bricks, was torture. He reached the ground each time shivering and sweating.

'And this afternoon,' Ezra continued, 'we'll start you on your first safe.'

'Safecracking!' Albert glared up from the table where he was mauling his locks. 'That ain't fair, Ezra. I'm older'n him. I ought to be put on safes first.'

'Age has nothing to do with it, Bert, as you know right well. Everyone has their talents. Toby's is locks. Don't worry, Brother. We'll find yours one of these days.'

The titter that ran around the room did nothing to improve Albert's temper. Tobias caught a glare as he left the room which said as plain as shouting that he'd better be careful to keep out of his cousin's way for a few days.

By dinnertime, Tobias's mood was equally bad. He'd fallen off the wall three times, and although the straw mattresses spread along its base had kept him from serious injury, he was bruised and sore and fed up. He hated climbing, but Ezra didn't seem to accept that he'd never be any good at it.

'Mostly it's confidence with you, Toby,' he had said, calmly picking Tobias up off the ground the third time. You're frightened, and your body knows it. Believe in yourself, boy. You got good strong hands. Trust them. Let them look after you.'

'I can't do it!'

'A good housebreaker knows how to climb. Sometimes you got to climb your way out of trouble. You'll learn.'

Tobias stormed into dinner with such a black look on his face that even Albert steered clear of him. He flung himself into the nearest empty chair and glared at his plate. When food was put on it, he shovelled it in without tasting it. God, he hated this place. He only wished he could climb! Then he'd climb right out of... He froze, his fork halfway to his mouth. What an idiot he was! The answer had been staring him in the face for days.

'Did you fall on your head this morning, Toby?' His eyes jerked up and met Molly's. She was seated across from him, an open book on the table beside her and a look of disdain on her face. 'At least have the good manners to close your mouth,' she said. 'It's hard to concentrate when someone's sitting opposite you looking like their brain has just fallen into their dinner.'

'Uh, sorry.' He put his fork down and forced his mouth shut. It kept trying to open again. He felt Ezra's watchful eyes travel in his direction. He organised his face and looked at Molly's book. 'What's that?' he asked.

'What?' Her eyes snapped up irritably.

'Your book. What're you reading?'

'What do you care?'

'Might've read it, that's all. If not, maybe I could borrow it after you?'

Her eyes narrowed in disbelief. 'You? Read books?'

'I believe that's what they're for.' His own voice grated with dislike. Who was this girl, to talk to him like that? Even Charlie, at her most high and mighty, had never treated him like a peasant.

She raised a scornful eyebrow. 'What's the last book you read, then?'

'*One Thousand and One Arabian Nights.*' Charlie had stolen it from the Castle library for him.

To his satisfaction, Molly's mouth fell open and a dull red flush travelled up her face, clashing with her copper hair. 'Did you really think,' he said scathingly, 'that I'd pretend to like books if I didn't? Why on earth would I, you gurnless girl? Keep your blasted book. I don't want it!'

'You shouldn't be bringing books to the table, Moll,'

159

said Ezra. 'If Dad catches you, it'll go on the fire like the others.'

'Well, he isn't here now, is he?' She turned on her eldest brother furiously. 'And just when am I going to have time to read, otherwise? I'm treated worse than a slave round here...' She began to gasp and Tobias looked up from his food in dismay, recognising the signs. 'And the one thing that gives me a little bit of pleasure...a tiny bit of enjoyment...lets me forget for a moment that I'm trapped in this...this...hellhole!' The last word rose into a shriek and, grabbing up her book, Molly fled in a storm of tears.

Into the careful silence which followed, Tobias inserted a question: 'Don't Uncle Zebediah approve of books?'

'Not story books, no,' Ezra said, spooning up his rice pudding thoughtfully. 'Dad can't read himself, but he allows as how it's got its uses. We was all trained on books. I can read and write pretty well, and Moll and Ambrose are right expert at it. Ambrose is clever with his numbers too. Ain't that so, lad?' Ambrose, busy drawing one of his machines on a scrap of paper, ignored his big brother. 'He can do things with numbers I never even thought of!' Ezra shook his head in fond amazement. 'He's to follow Wilf in the warehouses. But Dad don't hold with wasting time reading story books. Best not let him catch you at it, Toby, if you're that way inclined. It's bad enough with Moll and she's only a girl.'

'Safe locks is a far cry from your ordinary ward lock, Toby. Mostly, we crack safes with brute force: jemmies and wedges. Sometimes we even drill and powder 'em and blow the lock clean off. But that takes a fair bit of time and, as you might imagine, knocking wedges in with a sledgehammer makes a bit of a row, as does gunpowder, and noise ain't always advisable. Also, they're making safes more difficult to wedge open every year. So someone who can crack a safe lock is a fair treasure in our trade.'

Ezra walked over to a three-foot tall iron box sitting in the middle of the floor and patted it. 'This here's called a combination lock. Can't open it with a key. You got to turn the dial to three different numbers, in the right order, mind. There's three tumblers inside this lock that got to fall into the right slots. If your fingers and your ears is good enough, you might just be able to tell when they go. Even with good fingers, it takes a deal of concentration and patience. I reckon you just might be able to pull it off. There's not much I can tell you about how to do it; you got to feel it out for yourself. I'm gonna leave you alone and get back to the boys. You got three hours, Toby. I want the safe opened when I come back, hear?'

Tobias's mouth fell open. 'But...I might be rubbish at this! What if I just can't do it?'

Ezra blinked his goggle eyes and smiled. 'Be positive, Toby. I'm sure if you try hard enough you'll earn yourself a good report to Dad tonight. Now, don't take this the wrong way, but since I can't stay here with you, I'll be locking you in. Just so's you don't get distracted like.' He ducked out of the low door and shut it behind him. Tobias heard the sound of a bolt being drawn.

He stood and stared at the door and swore for a solid three minutes. Then, running out of inspiration, he turned and stumped over to the safe. He would have to do his best. The threat behind Ezra's words was plain: if he didn't get the blasted thing open, he'd get a bad report. And that meant no more letters to his mum. And maybe a thrashing from Zebediah.

He sighed and knelt on the floor in front of the safe. It was one of over a dozen lined up across the room. It was a small room, an unused stable, cold and dark, with a cobbled floor. He heard a rustle of what was probably rats in the loft overhead. It wasn't a nice place to be locked up on your own for three hours, but he didn't have time to worry about that now.

Ezra had said to use his fingers and ears. He leant his head against the door of the safe and began to rotate the dial. He turned it slowly, all the way from zero to fifty. Nothing. He tried again, turning the dial even more slowly. After the fifth attempt, his knees were aching from pressing into the cobbles and sweat was beading on his forehead. Frustration pounded behind his ears; he jumped up and began to pace up and down the room. He wasn't going to be able to do this. It was impossible!

He strode to the stable door and kicked it, then turned and leant against it, hunkering down on his heels and glaring at the safe. He sat like that for a long time, not thinking, not moving, just staring at the safe. Then, with a groan, he rose to his feet and walked to it, squatted, placed his left ear close to the dial, put the fingertips of his right hand on the dial itself, rather than the turning knob, and shut his eyes. He took a deep breath, held it, and nudged the dial one turn to the right. Half an hour later, he felt the first tumbler fall. Nearly an hour after that, something cracked like a gunshot in his left ear, and he jerked his head away as the lock clicked open. Tobias's yell of triumph bounced off the walls and scared the rats in the hay loft.

Ezra's mouth stretched in a wide grin. 'I knew you had it in you, Toby! How long did it take?'

'Must have been two hours,' Tobias said. 'Hour and a half, maybe, after I got the hang of it. It's slow.'

'It'll speed, with practice. Well, you earned a bit of free time, I reckon. Cut along.'

Tobias ducked out of the stable door and stood for a moment, relishing the sunshine and fresh air. The stable was like a prison cell and now he was out of it, he realised how much he had hated being locked in. He thought of Windlass, sitting in a dank cell in the Castle dungeons for weeks. If he didn't get away from the Petches, he'd be risking that himself. At least they didn't hang thieves any more.

He shook himself free of the thought and looked around for something to do. Ezra usually gave them free time at the end of the day: forty minutes or an hour. Some of the boys were roaming the courtyard, playing marbles, rounders, fooling about on the climbing wall. Others were already making their way home. The guard was lounging by the gate, chewing on a pipe, hardly seeming to notice the boys straggling out the courtyard into Flearside. Tobias watched them enviously, knowing full well that if he tried to join them the guard would collar him before he got near enough to the gate to spit through it.

He found a sunny wall and leant against it, fingering the shilling in his pocket. Should he try bribing Ambrose tonight? If the boy peached he'd be in an even worse fix.

He watched the other boys playing, but made no effort to join in. He could hardly remember what it felt like to feel that hitting a ball or winning someone's tolley was something important. Yet only a few weeks ago he would have been running with the boys from his street, full of the heady freedom of that precious hour or two between work and supper.

'Give it back, Bert! That's my best tolley. Give it back!'

A group of smaller boys had been playing ring taw in an area where the cobbles had broken away to expose the dark riverbed soil beneath. A circle was scored in the dirt, and the boys crouched round it every evening with their bags of marbles. Now Albert stood astride the circle, one hand high in the air, Ambrose jumping uselessly for his stolen marble like a short-legged dog after a treat.

As Tobias watched, Albert shoved Ambrose and sent him sprawling onto the cobbles, then pocketed the marble. The other boys had backed off, and even those playing rounders stood silent, watching. Tobias glanced at the guard. The man smoked his pipe, making no move to interfere. Ambrose was sitting where he'd fallen, staring up at his brother, a look of hatred on his face. 'I'll kill you someday, Bert,' he said, and Tobias felt a chill crawl down his spine.

Albert laughed and walked away. He sauntered past the spot where Tobias leant against the wall, stopped and turned. Tobias felt his heart sink as Albert rounded on him, the glint of success shining in his eyes. He was looking for his next victim and Tobias knew who had been chosen.

Albert advanced on him and Tobias straightened, stepped forward from the wall. If it came to fighting, he hadn't a chance, but he wasn't going to back down.

'Ain't you gonna try and get his tolley back for him?' Albert sneered. 'Stick up for your little buddy?'

'It's nothing to do with me.' Tobias stared up at his cousin, keeping his voice and face blank. This close, Albert was terrifyingly large. He would be as big as his dad when he was full grown.

Tobias was tall for his age, and reasonably strong. But he preferred to use his brains to his fists. He didn't much like hitting and he hated being hit. The Castle guards had taught him a bit of boxing, but that would be useless against a mauler like Albert – like trying to stun a bull with a popgun.

'I'll fight you for it,' Albert said.

'I don't want it.'

'You're yellow!' Albert reached out a finger and jabbed Tobias in the shoulder. A circle of boys surrounded them at a safe distance, and Tobias saw Ambrose watching him, wide-eyed and tremulous. He ignored Albert's finger and smiled up at him.

'I just ain't stupid, Albert. No way could I win a fight with you. Why should I give you an excuse to give me a licking? And before you start something, you'd best give a thought to your daddy. The guard over there's watching. You looking for another thrashing?'

Albert's eyes narrowed and his face grew sullen. Tobias felt his muscles relax. He'd talked his way out of a beating.

'So much for your hero, Ambrose.' Albert turned and sneered at his little brother. 'He's as yellow as you are. Right well suited the two of you. Well, I'll just keep this tolley, then.'

Tobias saw Ambrose's eyes dim, the look of hope in them dying. Damn! No way would he be able to bribe Ambrose now with those eight shillings. It had been a near thing when the boy was keen on him. He gritted his teeth.

'Bit big to be playing ring taw, aren't you, Albert?' He kept his voice light – even cheerful – but the taunt in the words was plain, and Albert swung back to him, eyes narrowing. God, but this boy was dim. He could march him about like a lead soldier. But not without risk. He grinned cheekily up at his cousin. 'That tolley can't be of much interest to a big, grown up chap like you. What say we race for it? Three times round the courtyard? Winner gets the tolley.'

'Yeah, race! Go it, Albert! Race him for it!' Excitement burbled through their audience, and the other boys crowded round, their fear of Albert forgotten, pushing him forward as champion against the newcomer. 'Show him what for, Albert!' Ambrose pushed forward too, his eyes locked onto Tobias's, hope back in them, and even more importantly, hero-worship. Tobias blinked and looked away.

Albert seemed almost stunned, then he grinned and began to bask in the unfamiliar glory. *Good*, thought Tobias. He's taken the bait. He could beat Albert easy in a foot race. But a look of cunning crossed his cousin's face.

'Not a foot race, no,' he said, waving aside the groans and jeers of the smaller boys. 'Shut up, you lot! I got a better idea.'

'Oh yeah?' Tobias said. 'What's that?'

'Climbing wall,' Albert said, with a nasty grin. 'First one to the top wins.'

In the uproar of shouts and cheering that followed, Tobias stared at his cousin with a bitter smile on his face.

Albert wasn't as stupid as he seemed. Tobias shrugged. He'd have to do it, even though he had almost no chance of winning. Oh well, at least the climbing wall was better than getting beat up. Just.

Halfway up the wall, he was having second thoughts. He climbed steadily, trying to keep the fear out of his head, refusing to look down, concentrating on Albert's ugly red face and the look it would have on it if he won. But Albert was a head and shoulders higher than him and going well. Tobias glanced up. The top of the wall seemed as far away as ever. He felt a wave of vertigo coming and dodged it. This was his only way out of this place. *I'm going to get out of here!* He began to chant it under his breath. He closed his eyes and climbed blind, pretending that he was climbing out for real – that he was going to climb onto the roof, clamber down the front of the house and run through the streets of Flearside. Run and run until he got home.

He only knew he'd reached the top when a cheer rose from the courtyard and he opened his eyes. He was clinging to the guttering. It was almost impossible to stop himself scrabbling onto the roof and running for it. Instead, he turned his head and looked for Albert, bracing himself to see the grin of triumph on his cousin's face. But Albert was two feet below, snarling up at him in rage. Tobias nearly fell off the wall. He'd won! He'd actually won.

He looked down and saw Ambrose jumping up and

down and waving his arms with delight. Behind him stood Ezra, smiling up at him with a look of pride on his face.

His little cousin ought to be easy to bribe now. And Ezra might figure he'd knuckled down to being in the Family and ease off watching him. He'd moved a step closer to freedom. So why did the look of hero-worship on Ambrose's face make him feel so uncomfortable?

Eighteen

She followed. She was the shepherd. They mustn't look back, mustn't look down, mustn't stop. Her father was first. He strode confidently along the ridge, his shirtsleeves fluttering in the wind. Her mother bunched the skirt of her dress in one hand and slipped along in flimsy court shoes. Mr Moleglass's black coat-tails flapped as he trotted after her. Tobias was the slowest. He kept stopping, swaying. The wind tore his curses to fragments and threw them to the clouds.

A storm was boiling up. 'Hurry!' Charlie shouted. A lightning bolt sliced the sky and the world disappeared in a sheet of white fire. Thunder cracked overhead, beating the rooftops like a thousand drums. It rolled away and Charlie opened her eyes. Her father had gone. The others merged into the fingers of cloud hanging low over the Castle roofs. She lost sight of her mother, then Moleglass. She began to run along the ridge, trying to reach Tobias.

A figure crawled out of the darkness, clinging to the sloping roof below them. 'Tobias!' she shouted. 'Look out!' But he didn't hear her. Watch crawled up the roof that had killed him, snaked out a gory hand of bone and gristle, grabbed Tobias by the ankle, and pulled him over the side.

The nightmare woke her long before morning. She did not sleep again. Outside her window, she heard the dragon hissing with laughter.

Nell came to her at dawn. 'There's news, Charlie. Toby's alive! Mr Moleglass wants us in the library, sharpish!' Her voice quivered with suppressed excitement and her hands trembled as she helped Charlie scramble into her clothes. They clattered down the staircases and arrived puffing for breath.

The library faced west and the morning light could not reach it. The gas was not lit and the half-dozen candles did little to dispel the gloom. Mr Moleglass hurried forward to take her hand and squeeze it between his own gloved ones.

'Something has happened!' He was as carefully dressed as ever, his hair pomaded, his moustache curled. But his brown seal's eyes glowed. 'It may be important. We need to put our heads together.' He led them towards a sofa and Rose Petch, who had been sitting in a nearby chair, stood and dropped a curtsey.

'Have they found him?' Charlie was too nervous to sit, so the others remained standing. They clustered in a circle in front of the sofa. Charlie's heart was thudding fit to burst out of her chest.

Mr Moleglass shook his head. 'No. But someone handed this to one of the Castle guards.' Moleglass was holding a letter in his hands. Now he read it aloud. As

Charlie listened, her excitement died and she felt like she might be sick with disappointment.

'That can't be from Tobias,' she said.

'I agree – it's odd,' said Mr Moleglass. 'But it is most definitely Tobias's writing. I cannot be mistaken about that – I taught him to write myself. And do you see how he mentions Nell especially? It must be a clue. Do you have any ideas, Nell, as to why Tobias would single you out in such a way? I know you are cousins, but…'

Nell had been staring at the floor. Now she raised troubled eyes. 'I reckon I do. And I reckon Rose has an inkling too, haven't you, Rose?'

'It can't be!' Rose cried. 'Not after all this time. I had it out with Zebediah when Barty died.'

'Zebediah Petch? Charlie looked from Rose to Nell, totally confused. 'What's he got to do with this?'

'We were wrong about it being Windlass who'd got Toby,' said Nell. 'I reckon Zebediah's taken the boy into the Family. And if he has, Charlie, it'll be near impossible to get him back.'

Charlie stared at Nell, her mind a jumble as she tried to readjust to the idea that, for once, Windlass was not to blame. Surely this was good news. Whatever else it meant, Tobias wasn't dead! But then why was Nell looking so upset? 'Into the family? I don't understand. Tobias is already a member of your family. And why can't he come home?'

'Nell means the family business.' Rose was twisting her

172

hands together, her voice shaking. 'Thieves – that's what the Petches are. Housebreakers. That's why I never let Toby near them. Barty wanted Toby to follow him into the business, but I said no. I threatened to leave him. When Barty died, Zebediah came to see me. Wanted to take Toby then and there. I told him I'd have the law on him. He just laughed, but he didn't come back no more. I thought that was the end to it.'

'Uncle Zebediah don't give up easy as that,' Nell said, her voice bitter. 'My dad tried for years to keep Perce out of the business, but Zebediah took him in the end, and my little brother Will, too. He's being trained up now.' She shook her head. 'I'd give a deal to get Will away. It's too late for Perce. And he has too much Petch in him anyway. Always did have, my big brother. Zebediah's welcome to him!'

'At least we have an idea of where Tobias is,' Charlie said. 'And if his uncle has him, he won't be able to go looking for Windlass and get himself killed!'

'Alistair would never hurt him,' Rose said.

'He pointed a pistol at his head and threatened to pull the trigger.' Charlie struggled to keep her voice calm. 'I was there! He meant it.'

'A discussion of Alistair Windlass's intentions is a fruitless exercise,' Mr Moleglass said. 'But I regret that I cannot share your view of the situation, Charlie. Tobias is not the sort of boy to knuckle under to coercion easily, and even if he were, housebreaking is not a gentle career.'

'Is it true, Nell?' Charlie cried. 'Is Tobias in danger? What will they make him do?'

'I don't rightly know what to say to you. Look, Charlie, Toby'll be all right. He's Family. The Petches look after their own. He'll be training up with the other boys now – that's not so bad. And Zebediah's got to keep him alive and well to get any work out of him, hasn't he?'

'Tobias won't steal for him. He's too stubborn. What will your uncle do then?'

Nell pressed her lips together. 'You ain't never met Zebediah. Toby won't have no choice.'

A chill crawled down Charlie's spine. She felt slightly sick. 'You mean he'll beat him – like his stepfather used to!' She heard Rose make a small, broken noise. Out of the corner of her eye she saw Moleglass put his arm around Tobias's mother and lead her to the sofa.

'Toby told you about that?' Nell's face was amazed.

'No. He never talks about his stepfather. Only once…he said he was a thief. But never a word since. Someone else told me about the beatings.' She shuddered. 'Is it true?'

'It's true all right. Poor Rose took the worst of it, but Toby got his fair share. And no, he never talks about it. The Family know, of course. My parents used to row over Uncle Barty. Ma wouldn't hear no bad of him. But Zebediah ain't a drunk. He won't hurt Toby that bad. He'll want him in one piece.'

'If your uncle beats Tobias, I'll make sure he rots in

prison for the rest of his life!' Charlie whirled to face the butler. 'Send a message to Blundell. Search Flearside, starting with Petch's house!'

'That'll do no good,' said Nell. 'Zebediah's got half the police force in his pocket. He'd be tipped off before you got anywhere near the place. And there's no way of knowing where he's keeping the boy. He's got warehouses all over Flearside. You start searching for Tobias and Zebediah will hide him away so deep and twisty you'll never find him!'

'But your brothers would know,' Moleglass said.

'They won't tell me,' Nell said. 'They have no truck with me at all. I'm the first in the Family to ever break free, and it's only 'cause I'm a girl that I managed it. Zebediah don't consider I'm worth worrying about.'

'Would they tell your father?'

She considered. 'Perce wouldn't. But Will might say something. If Dad were to put it casual-like. But I don't know if Dad would be willing. It don't pay to cross Zebediah. Them as does is usually found washed up along the river.'

Charlie stared at Nell in horror. How could this sort of thing happen in her City? And why hadn't she known about it? 'How does Petch get away with it? Why haven't the police arrested him?'

'Arrests need evidence,' Nell said. 'Uncle Zebediah makes sure there ain't none. He's clever and ruthless, and the whole of Flearside belongs to him. Folks call him the King of Thieves.'

Charlie began to pace. She frowned into space, thinking. 'What if we paid for him?' she asked. 'Would your uncle give Tobias up for money?'

Nell shook her head. 'It ain't just money with Zebediah. It's family. It won't matter to him what Rose wants: she's just a woman. Ever since Barty died, Zebediah will consider that it's not just his right to take charge of Toby, it's his duty. You'd be asking him to sell his brother's son.'

'Perhaps, but it is worth a try,' Moleglass said, leaving the sofa to join them. 'A large enough sum might tempt even your uncle. And I think we should let Mr Petch know that Tobias is not so alone in the world as he supposes. I have an idea which should make the gentleman think twice before employing our young friend as a common thief!'

Charlie turned to look at him and was amazed to see that his eyes were twinkling.

'But first,' he continued, 'I have to ask Your Majesty about your views on the subject of fostering.'

'Fostering?' Charlie stared at the butler. Had the strain of worrying about Tobias affected his mind?

'No, I haven't gone mad.' He smiled at her. 'But I believe that even an outlaw such as Mr Petch might think again before employing the official ward of the Queen of Quale as a thief and housebreaker.'

It took her a moment to understand. 'You want me to *adopt* Tobias?'

Nell spluttered and began to laugh.

Charlie stared at them, appalled. 'Do I have to?' She really didn't see what Mr Moleglass and Nell found so funny. 'He'll be absolutely furious with me when he finds out.'

Nineteen

Ezra was pleased with Tobias's new determination as he attacked the climbing wall. Tobias wasn't stupid enough to stop complaining of his hatred of climbing, and his progress was painfully slow, but he clung to the wall with all the strength his desire to get out of Flearside could give him. Things went more quickly with the safes. On his thirty-seventh evening as a member of the Petch household, Zebediah called him to his office.

'In a moment you can take up the pen and paper, boy, and write your mother. Ezra's give me a good report, so you've earned your letter this week. But first I got some news.' A smile cracked Zebediah's beard. 'Ezra says he's done all he can with you. You've trained up faster than I dared hope. You're going with Perce tomorrow. Congratulations, Toby. You're a proper housebreaker now.'

Tobias stiffened in dismay. He'd never thought Ezra would finish with him so quickly. If he didn't get out of here soon, he'd end up a thief like his stepfather. Zebediah would push him in so deep he'd never be able to climb out. Doubtless that was what his uncle had in mind. He looked into the face of the man who was wrecking his life and smiled. Practice was making it easier. 'Thanks, Uncle.'

'Someday you'll mean that. You hate me now. Oh, don't pretend, boy. You're a good liar, but you're not that good.' He grinned. 'I got plans for you, Nephew. I hoped Barty was right about you, and he was.

'Not one of my sons is like me. Oh, Ezra's a good man, but he's no leader. And Albert? Well, I never had hopes of Albert. The spit of my uncle Archie and just as thick. Ambrose, now, he's the clever one. A bit too clever, and odd with it, drawing those ruddy machines all the time. And he's timid. He'll never amount to much.'

Zebediah paused and looked at him, his eyes burning with such intensity that reddish sparks seemed to jump from them. 'Do you understand what I'm saying to you, boy?'

Tobias stared at him, open-mouthed. Someone rapped on the door and he turned to see who it was, thankful for a moment's reprieve.

'Come in!' Irritation turned Zebediah's voice into a growl. His scowl deepened as Perce walked into the room, a paper rolled in his fist. 'What is it, Perce? It had better be important!'

'Oh, I think you'll find it is.' Perce threw a dark look at Tobias. 'I'd want to think twice before I invited our dear Queen's Royal Ward along for a spot of housebreaking, wouldn't you?'

The air flew out of Tobias's lungs. He stared from

Perce to Zebediah. His uncle's face was ludicrous with surprise, but Tobias had never felt less like laughing. He edged towards the door.

'What the devil are you talking about, Perce?' The words ground out black and slow.

'This,' said Perce, and slapped the paper face up onto Zebediah's desk. Tobias saw what it was at once. A wanted poster. His own face stared back at him.

He sprinted for the door but had only gone two steps when an arm grabbed him round the neck and choked off most of his air. Perce dragged him back to the desk, spluttering and kicking.

'Hold him good, but let go of his neck.' Zebediah's voice was soft and cold. 'I got a job that requires his windpipe.' Perce twisted Tobias's right arm up behind his back. He yelled and doubled over, his nose inches from the poster. 'Good,' Zebediah said. 'Now, Toby. Read it out nice and loud.'

Gasping and gritting his teeth against the pain, Tobias stammered out:

£500 Reward Offered
For information leading to the safe return of
the Queen's Royal Ward,
Tobias Petch, aged thirteen.

Believed to have been abducted and held
against his will by person or persons unknown

within the City. All informants given complete
confidentiality. Reply to Superintendent Blundell
of Her Majesty's Constabulary.

'Let him go, Perce.' Tobias fell against the desk. He
staggered up, clutching his arm, then backed away from
the sight of Zebediah's face. It was the colour of lead.

'And just when were you planning on telling us this
little secret, Nephew?'

'I-I didn't—'

'I'll bet you didn't! *Royal Ward?* No wonder you
weren't keen on coming into the Family! You've made a
fool of me, Toby. I'm gonna need time to figure this out.
It may be that I can turn it to our advantage but no matter
about that, you've earned your beating this time.'

He lay face down. Ezra had helped him to the attic room,
eased him into bed, pulled the blanket up to his hips,
leaving his back uncovered. 'I'll send Mum up with some
salve, Toby,' he said. 'I'm sorry, boy, but you've only
yourself to blame. And you got off lightly, considering.
Dad spared his arm.'

Tobias, remembering the leather strap lamming into his
flesh, shuddered. His back was a mass of welts. But he
knew what Ezra meant. Despite his fury, Zebediah had
judged each blow of the strap precisely. He had given
Tobias twelve fierce, well-placed strokes and stopped.
Ezra and Perce had held him up, one on either side, Ezra

181

with his head turned away, Perce with a grim smile on his lips.

He'd had much worse from Barty. Barty had never hit him except in a drunken rage, but he'd knocked him silly half a dozen times. Next day, he'd beg forgiveness, tears flowing into his beard, sobbing and holding onto Tobias like a drowning man.

Zebediah had beaten him cold-bloodedly, like a man training a dog. Somehow that made it worse. Tobias bit his lip and squeezed his eyes shut against the tears stinging behind them. He clenched his fists and longed to hit out at something. He had promised himself, when Barty died, that no man would ever have the power to beat him again. He'd sworn it.

The door opened and someone came into the room. Tobias buried his face in his bolster and glared furiously at grey blankness. 'You all right, Tobe?' It was Ambrose. 'I gotta go to bed but I won't be able to sleep till I know you're not dying.'

'I'm fine,' Tobias growled into his pillow. 'Go to bed and leave me alone!'

'Your back looks like it been dragged through a nettle patch *and* an ant hill. Sure must hurt.'

'And do you think that sort of talk is like to make your cousin feel better?' It was Elsie. 'Get on into bed now, Ambrose Petch, and not another word out of you. Toby will be right as rain in the morning.' His aunt's footsteps approached his bed, and Tobias gritted his teeth and scowled harder. 'I've brought salve for your back, Toby,' she said in her dry, quiet voice. 'I'm going to rub it on now, and it will hurt, I'm afraid.'

'I don't want it. Go away!'

'It's comfrey, child. Knitbone. It'll heal you quicker than anything and take the sting out of those welts. You're having it. Just hold on tight to something. I'll try not to hurt you more'n I have to.' She sat on the edge of his bed, and fire raked his back.

'Ow!' he yelled, rearing up. Her hand cupped the back of his neck and pushed him flat as easily as if he'd been Ambrose. Ezra had obviously inherited his phenomenal strength from both parents. 'Be still, boy!' she ordered. 'I told you it would sting. Don't act the baby! Ezra said you never hollered once when Dad was whopping you. Where's your pride, Toby Petch?'

'That hurts!' he shouted into his pillow.

'Then hold still so's we can get it over quick.' He gave up, gasping and groaning as she rubbed the salve into his welts. 'Well done, Toby,' she said at last. 'I hope Dad won't have cause to hit you again. I never do like it, but Dad don't do it without he has reason. Try and make sure he don't have reason again, son.' She sighed and stood up. 'Sleep if you can and don't rush up in the morning. I'll be in to check on you first thing. You won't be going out with Perce, so there's no hurry.'

She walked over to Ambrose's bed and bent her long neck to give him a kiss. 'Look after your cousin, sweetheart, and fetch him a chamber pot if he needs it in the night, to save the journey.' She blew out the candle and left them.

Tobias was just falling into an uneasy sleep when Ambrose's voice floated out of the darkness. 'Mum's soft on you. She never let me piss in a pot when Dad belted me.'

Tobias groaned. 'Go to sleep, Ambrose!' He tried escaping into sleep again, but it was no use. Five minutes later he was still wide awake, his back throbbing in time to his heartbeat. 'Zebediah beat you as bad as this?' he asked.

'He took a switch to my legs. But it hurt real bad and he said, next time, he'd take the strap to me.'

'And has he?'

'No. I hate getting hit. So I ain't done it again.'

'What?'

'Run away.'

Tobias lurched onto his elbows, peering through the moonlight at the dark shape in the other bed. 'You ran away? How?'

'Shinnied up the climbing wall at night, cut across the roofs and down the front of the house. Easy as pie. Only they wouldn't let me in, even when I showed them my drawings. So I had to come back again. Mum cried for a week 'cause I'm the youngest and she likes me best. After Ezra.'

'Wait a minute!' Tobias's head was swimming. He lowered himself back onto the bed. 'Who wouldn't let you in? What are you talking about?'

'The Academy, of course. The Royal Academy of Engineering. I'm going to be the greatest engineer that was ever born. I'm going to invent machines that fly and boats that travel under water, and wire bridges and iron ships and propulsion engines and bicycles with gears and...'

Tobias fell asleep and dreamt that Ambrose flew down out of the sky in a sapphire blue flying machine and carried him off on a journey to the sea.

'Well,' he said. 'Will you do it?'

'I don't rightly know.' Ambrose frowned at the eight shillings laid out on his work table. 'Dad wouldn't like it.'

'He won't never know. Look, Ambrose. It can't hurt anything. It's only a letter to me mum. You've taken 'em before. And how else are you going to get hold of eight bob? You could buy an engineering book with that!'

Ambrose licked his lips. He blinked long bronze lashes and frowned up at Tobias. 'You ain't fixing to run off, are you? 'Cause I don't want you to. I like you better'n anyone, even Molly. You talk to me like I got sense, and you like my drawings, don't you, Tobe?'

'I think your drawings are great,' Tobias said gently. 'And no,' he lied, 'I'm not fixing to run off. How can I, locked in this room day and night?'

Ambrose stared at him with a twisted, wizened face, then darted at Tobias and wrapped his arms around his middle, squeezing him with all his considerable strength. 'Ow!' Tobias gasped. 'Give over! Mind me back!' Ambrose loosened his grip slightly, but clung on, his face buried in Tobias's shirt.

Tobias gazed down at the top of his cousin's head. What was he supposed to do? What was wrong with the boy? He felt a dry ache in the back of his throat. 'Hey, kid,' he said. 'It's all right.' He tried to say: 'I'm not going anywhere,' but the words refused to come out.

'I'll do it,' Ambrose muttered into his shirtfront. 'But only if you promise to take me with you.'

'What?!'

As suddenly as he had attached himself, Ambrose let go. He spun round to the table and picked up the shillings, one by one, until they were a silvery pile in his hand. He frowned at Tobias and shoved the fistful of coins into his trouser pocket. 'I said, I'll do it. But only if you swear to take me with you, Tobe.'

'I told you, I'm not going anywhere!'

'This letter's supposed to bust you out, isn't it? Come on. I'm cleverer than you, you know. I'm cleverer than anyone I ever met. It's obvious. And if you're going, so am I. When your friends come to bust you out, you got to promise you'll take me along with you.'

'Why, Ambrose? Even if I was leaving – and I'm not – why would you want to come? You don't really want to leave your family: your mum, Ezra, Molly. They love you.'

Ambrose shrugged. His face was wearing the stubborn

look Tobias had come to recognise. 'Maybe. But if I stay here, Dad won't let me be an engineer. He'll make me work in the warehouses when Wilf dies, just 'cause I'm good with numbers, and I never forget nothing. I'm going to be an engineer and nobody is going to stop me! So promise, or I won't help.'

'Ambrose, I…I can't promise something like that. I can't take you away from your mum!'

'Promise!' Ambrose's face turned carrot-red and he glared up at Tobias. 'Promise, or I'll go right now and tell Dad what you asked me to do!'

Tobias's mouth fell open. 'You little pismire!'

Ambrose shrugged. 'Promise.' His eyes were as hard as Zebediah's.

'All right!' Tobias shook his head. 'You Petches! You're all alike. Right! I promise. If I ever get out of here, I'll do my best to take you with me.'

'And come back for me if you can't!'

Tobias groaned. 'All right, Ambrose. All right.'

The boy's face broke into a glorious grin, and he pushed Tobias towards the table. 'I got paper and pen here. Write your letter, Tobe. Write it now!'

Tobias gave up and closed the book. He stretched out on the lumpy mattress and stared at the ceiling. Five days he had been locked in the attic bedroom, with only Ambrose's engineering books for company, and they were as dry as dust. He was let out for meals and to visit he privy, but otherwise he was as close kept as any prisoner in Charlie's dungeons. Zebediah ignored him at mealtimes, which suited Tobias fine. The sight of his uncle made his throat squeeze up with hatred.

He watched a spider inching careful-footed across the cratered surface of a ceiling beam, and wondered if Ambrose had managed to slip out of the house yet to deliver his letter. He'd told him to take no chances. He just hoped the boy was fly enough to make sure he wasn't seen. Perhaps he shouldn't have involved him, but he had to get out of here. He'd go back to the Castle. He'd forget about finding Windlass. He'd even go to that poxy school. He didn't care what he did as long as he never had to see Zebediah Petch again!

A sound whispered across the room. It made the hairs on the back of his neck stand up, and he rolled off the bed. Someone was picking the lock. But who? Moleglass would arrive with police klaxons clanging and whistles tooting: it couldn't be him. And if it wasn't a friend...He darted across the room, snatched one of Ambrose's heavier wrenches out of the tool box and turned around in time to see Molly open the door and slip inside.

'You going to hit me with that?' she asked. 'In that case, I'll take the books back again.'

He lowered the wrench and felt his face turn bright red. 'Sorry,' he said. 'I didn't know who—'

'Hoping it was Dad, were you?'

'*I* don't beat people up!' He closed his eyes and turned

188

away. 'Sorry. Look, you shouldn't be here. You'll get in trouble.'

'So you don't want the books? I'd be going spare by now if it was me, locked up in here with only Ambrose's engineering books. I tried to bring these days ago, but there always seems to be someone hanging about.'

'Books?' The word sank in at last and he whirled around.

'Yeah. You know. Those things with words in them?' Moving to his bed, she dumped the blanket she was carrying on top of it and half a dozen books came tumbling out. Tobias pounced on them: *Gulliver's Travels, Robinson Crusoe, Tales of the Brothers Grimm, The History of Tom Jones, A Foundling.* He sat on the bed, turning the pages in wonder.

'Where did you get these?'

'Stolen, of course.' She grinned at him. 'Working in the warehouse has to have some compensations. Mind you keep them hid, underneath some of Ambrose's junk would do, and I want them back.'

'Sure.' He frowned up at her. 'Why are you being nice to me?'

She looked uncomfortable. 'It's to say sorry, really. For being so nasty at dinner the other day. I thought you were like all the other boys. Most of them would sooner have a bath than read a book.'

'That's bad,' Tobias said gravely.

She laughed. 'See? You are different.' Her smile faded. 'You're in trouble, you know.'

'Tell me something I don't know.'

'I've never seen Dad so flummoxed. He don't know what to do with you. Perce don't want to take you housebreaking in case someone recognises you from the posters. They're all over the City, by the way. Most of the men want to hand you over to the Queen and collect the reward.'

'Really?'

'Don't get excited; Dad won't have it.'

'Why not? Five hundred's a blinking fortune!' Tobias thumped the bed in frustration.

'Maybe, but Dad's got plenty of money. You haven't figured him out yet, have you?' She sat cross-legged on the floor and gazed up at him, her copper hair and sapphire eyes glinting in a shaft of sunlight.

She's pretty, he thought. He hadn't noticed before. He felt himself begin to blush and picked up a book and thumbed through it to hide his embarrassment.

'Dad's what they call an entrepreneur,' Molly announced grandly. 'Do you know what that means?'

'Of course.' He allowed himself to peek up at her. 'It's someone who starts their own business.'

'Yes. But a bit more than that. They invent a new way of doing things. Dad is probably a genius. It runs in the family, you know. Ambrose is one. And I may be – I'm not certain yet. But Dad invented a new way of being a thief. He looked at the trade and saw where the profits were being made.' She paused. 'Put that book down,' she ordered. 'This is important.'

He sighed, closed the book, and sat with his head on his hands, watching the sunbeam outline her nose in a halo of fuzzy brightness. It was a pretty nose, he decided.

When she saw she had his attention, Molly smiled, then began again with great seriousness: 'The profits in thieving come when the stuff's sold on by the receivers: pawnbrokers, second-hand shops, jewellers. Receivers never give the thief a fraction of the true value. So Dad decided to do it differently. He figured out that his main asset was the family, and we're a huge family, if you count all the children his sisters had – the Sorrells, the Tofts, the Quilters, the Ketleys. And Dad's head of them all.'

'So,' Tobias said slowly, paying attention at last. 'The warehouses—'

'That's right. We steal it, transport it to the other warehouses in the City till it cools off; then it comes here, where it's sorted and logged; then we ship it off to our second and third cousins, who run the shops: the pawnbrokers, the market stalls, the jewellers. Very respectable they are! And all the profit comes to the Family, see, for Dad to divvy up.' She grinned in admiration.

'Everyone's better off, 'cause we're getting full value for our goods. You have to admit, it's clever. And the boys are trained up, and those that like a bit of excitement go on the tools, and those that like a quiet life go into the shops. Suits everyone, you see. As long as you're male, and as long as you do everything Dad says. And it suits Dad most of all, 'cause he's in charge. He controls everything and everybody.'

'I had noticed.' He didn't try to keep the bitterness out of his voice.

'You haven't noticed half of it. You still don't get it, do you? Why do you think you're here? Why do you think Dad won't give you up for the reward?'

Tobias stared at her. 'I don't know! You've got it all figured out, do you? Go on then, tell me.'

'Because you're a *boy*. Because you're a boy whose last name is Petch. I hated you when you first came. If I'd been a boy it would have been me. I've got the brains.'

He shook his head, completely lost. 'What are you talking about?'

'The Business, of course. The Family. Dad's creation. It's his whole life. He loves it more than he loves Mum or any of us. Oh, he loves us, but only because we belong to him. What he really loves is this…this Machine he's invented. And he can't bear the idea that when he's dead it'll die with him.'

Tobias's mouth fell open in dismay as he finally understood what Molly was telling him. 'But…Ezra… Albert, Ambrose. They can carry on. And Perce. What about him, or your other cousins? You said yourself the Family is huge!'

'It has to be a Petch. Not a Sorrell or a Tofts. Certainly

not a Quilter! There's only four Petch boys: Ezra, Albert, Ambrose and you. And my brothers are useless.' She shook her head. 'Oh, Ezra's a sweetie, but he's a born second-in-command. Albert's just thick. And violent. He'd never learn to manage people. Because that's what it's about: management. And Ambrose? He'll run away and be an engineer some day, even if he has to kill Dad to do it. You think I'm joking? I'm not. I love Ambrose, but he's utterly ruthless. Like Dad. Like me, a bit. So you see, it's got to be you.'

'That's crazy!' Tobias lurched off the bed and began to march around the room. He wanted to kick something. 'I'm not even a real Petch! I'm adopted! I haven't got a drop of your blood in my veins. Doesn't he care about that?'

Her bright blue eyes gazed up at him, and she shook her head. Her face was sombre. 'He cares about the name and that you're clever and brave and stubborn and have the makings of a brilliant thief. He's ready to love you better than a son, Toby, if only you give in to him. Besides,' she paused, blushed, 'he's figured out how the blood can carry on.'

'Oh yeah? And how's that going to work?'

She brightened to scarlet and stared at her hands. 'He's planning to marry us off.'

'W-what?' He stared at her in utter horror.

'Not till we're older. And you don't have to look so disgusted.' She glared at him. 'I'm not that bad, am I?'

'I-it's not that.' He felt his own face burn red.

'You're...real pretty...and clever...but... Sweet Betty, I'm thirteen! And you're what?'

'Fourteen.'

'He's mad! He can't tell us who we're likely to want to marry in five or ten years. I may never marry at all. I haven't had much luck with families so far.'

'I'm never marrying,' she said.

'Girls always marry.' As soon as they left his mouth he wished he could catch the words and put them back. She clenched her fists and her face scrunched into a mask of fury. It was scary. He didn't know what to do if a girl hit him. He'd always hit Charlie back but that was different. Charlie was Charlie, but Molly – Molly was a girl!

'Don't make that sort of stupid generalisation ever again, Toby Petch! It's not even true. And I have no intention of wasting my life slaving after menfolk. I've had enough of that already. If I were a boy, I'd be taking over the business, and I'd be good at it – as good as Dad. But since he's too stupid to see past my long hair and dresses, I'm leaving. Just like Ambrose.'

Tobias gulped. 'What're you gonna do?'

'I'm going to university.'

'But—'

'Don't you dare say that girls can't go to university. They can! The Queen's mother is a famous scientist.'

'Yeah, but she's rich. How're you gonna pay for it?'

'I don't know. Maybe I'll steal. I can pick locks and

climb walls as good as any of the boys! But I'm going.'

'Good,' said Tobias.

'Do you believe me?' Her eyes flashed blue lightning.

'I absolutely believe you.'

Twenty

'What about your spies, Nell?' Charlie asked. 'Are they still looking for Tobias?'

'We've sent some into Flearside.' They were sitting in front of the fire in Charlie's bedroom, waiting until the household was safely in bed. 'Now them posters are out, Zebediah will keep the boy well hid. I've told 'em to concentrate on Windlass. He's the man we've got to find. Toby'll keep.'

'I want him back!'

'So do we all, Charlie. But whatever happens, Uncle Zebediah won't kill him. Windlass is our target.'

'Once he's dead, will your people help find Tobias?'

'If they can.' Nell stared into the fire.

'You don't think Mr Moleglass's plan will work, do you?'

The older girl shrugged. 'It's worth a try.' She glanced at the mantel clock. 'It's gone eleven. Mr Moleglass and the rest'll be asleep. Let's go.'

They crept down the attic stairs and along the fourth floor until they reached the north wing, where they climbed an identical twisting stairwell to find the laboratory door locked. Everything was dark and silent.

They took up stations in the furthest corner of the corridor and waited. Midnight came and went. Charlie slumped with her back against the wall, dozing. One o'clock. She was too cold and stiff to sleep properly. When the Cathedral bell chimed two, Nell jumped to her feet with a swear word Tobias would have been proud of.

'She ain't coming, Charlie! Are you sure you didn't dream all this up about your mum going missing at night?'

'Maybe it was just the once,' groaned Charlie, staggering to her feet.

'We'll check on the way back.' Nell strode off, rubbing her arms against the cold.

But when they got there, they found the Dowager's bedroom unlocked and empty. Charlie ran to the bedside table. The candlestick and pistol were gone. The bed had not been slept in. Where was her mother? If she wasn't working, what was she doing? 'I'm searching the Castle!' Anger and fear were fighting for control. Charlie chose anger. 'Will you help?'

'Yes,' said Nell. 'I'm beginning to think it's important to find out what your mum's up to.'

They spent the next hour searching the Castle from top to bottom, carefully avoiding the footman who slept in Mr Moleglass's pantry, guarding the silver. When they were in the kitchen, with the chill of the flagstones soaking through the soles of her boots, Charlie thought she heard a noise. 'What was that?'

'What?'

'Listen!' But the noise didn't come again.

'What was it?' Nell hissed.

'A thud. Sort of faint and echoey.'

'I didn't hear anything.'

Charlie said nothing. She was too busy fighting fear. There was no sign of the Dowager. Charlie's panic grew with each room that did not contain her mother. Perhaps the gun and candle weren't important. Perhaps Windlass had broken into the Castle after all. He could be here now.

'We need to rouse the Guard!'

'Calm down! Let's search her bedroom again. There might be a clue.' Nell grabbed Charlie's hand and pulled her up the servants' stairs to the second floor. She opened the door onto the landing, stiffened, and quickly blew out their candle. 'Shhhh! There's someone there!' Nell pushed open the door, slowly, until Charlie could see a yellow circle of light trailing away from them. It paused outside her mother's door, then disappeared inside.

'Well, Charlie,' Nell's whisper hissed in her ear. 'She's back.'

Charlie yawned over her porridge, bacon and toast, then went to find Nell. The older girl was bent over an ironing board, pressing one of Charlie's black dresses. The knobbly bun of curly brown hair threatened to collapse from beneath her lopsided maid's cap, and her face was so white Charlie could have counted her freckles. 'You look dreadful,' she said.

Nell glared at her, then slapped the heavy black iron on the stove's hotplate. 'I've been up since six this morning, Your Majesty! I work for my living!'

'My mother's still asleep.'

'Hrumph.'

'And I order you to stop ironing and help me search her study.'

Nell shot her a dangerous look from beneath her cap, then smiled. 'Good. I hate ironing.'

The study door was open, and when Charlie clattered in, the first thing she saw was her mother's secretary, sitting at the desk, pushing shut one of the drawers. She was a prettily dressed, plump young woman of about twenty-three, her light-brown hair hanging in loops over her ears according to the latest fashion. When she saw who it was, she jumped up and curtsied. 'Oh, Your Majesty! I'm sorry, your mother isn't here. I believe she's—'

'Still asleep. Yes, I know. I-I've run out of writing paper. If I could—'

'Oh, let me! I've just been tidying your mother's desk, so I know where it is.' She twisted around and took a sheaf of writing paper from one of the drawers. She held it out to Charlie with a smile. 'Will this be enough, ma'am?' She glanced over Charlie's shoulder at Nell, curiosity plain on her face.

199

'Thank you,' Charlie said. There was nothing to do but take the paper and retreat.

'Drat!' she said, as soon as they were out of earshot. 'I wanted to look for the combination to my mother's safe.'

'I wondered if that's what you were after. What would you do with the papers if we got that safe open?

'Burn them,' said Charlie.

Nell looked at her consideringly. 'Perhaps I'd best come with you and look at it now. At least I can tell you what sort it is.'

'Yup. That's a combination safe all right.' Nell stood with her hands on her hips, surveying the large metal box squatting against one wall. They had slipped into the ministerial wing unspotted and, after fifteen minutes of bad temper and equally bad language, Nell had managed to pick the lock of the door to Charlie's office.

The safe was nearly four feet tall and wide and made of greasy grey metal which gave off a sharp, metallic stink. She bent to twirl one of the knobs on its door. 'But it's a double lock, see? Two dials. Must have cost a ruddy fortune! Even Zebediah himself couldn't break into that thing. And it's too blessed heavy to nick.' Nell straightened and smiled at Charlie. 'You can stop worrying. If the papers are in there, they're safe.'

'But I want them destroyed!' Charlie said. 'I'm going to try and find the combination.'

Nell shook her head. 'I'm after Windlass, Charlie.

I don't care about the papers as long as he can't get at them. I'll be staying in town to help the others look for him. And I'll try to get news of Toby.'

Charlie stared at her. 'You don't want me to burn the papers, do you? Why?'

'Because Quale may need them.' Nell's face was determined. Charlie knew she wouldn't change her mind.

'If you're going, go! Go now! I don't need your help.'

'Sorry, Charlie.' Nell's voice was soft. 'Still friends?'

Charlie turned away. She stared at the safe, hating it, and listened to Nell walk from the room. Then she looked up at the portrait of her father, gazing down at her from the opposite wall. He'd been barely older than her when it had been painted.

'Don't worry, Father,' she said. 'I'm not giving up.'

Twenty-one

He was deep in the shipwrecked woes of *Robinson Crusoe* when footsteps approached his door. They clumped nearer with the implacable heaviness of trouble, and Tobias slipped the book under his pillow and stood up, his heart thudding. What now? But he knew, even before Ezra unlocked the door and opened it.

'Don't you never learn, Toby?' His long face was sorrowful. 'And now you got Ambrose into it. I begin to wish you'd never come, the trouble and strife you cause.'

'As I recollect,' Tobias spat, fear sending his temper soaring. 'I didn't exactly ask to be here!'

'Downstairs, boy. And don't try nothing, 'cause I'm that upset, I might just thump you.'

Wearing his fury like armour, Tobias marched down the stairs in front of Ezra. When they reached Zebediah's office, he flung open the door with a crash and looked for Ambrose.

His cousin was hunched on the floor, hugging his knees to his chest, tears running down his face. One side of his mouth was bruised and swollen. Albert lounged against the wall beside him, and Tobias was aware of

Zebediah and Perce standing in front of the desk. But he only had eyes for Ambrose.

'Who hit him?' His voice cracked on the words, but he didn't care. He turned eyes cold as polar ice on his uncle. 'Did you hit Ambrose?' His voice was as arctic as his eyes, and he saw Zebediah blink in surprise.

'*I* hit him, you louse. I knew the two of you were up to something so I been following him. He had it coming, sneaking on the Family.'

Albert. Of course. Tobias stepped forward. He had never felt so cold and calm. He hit Albert in the mouth so hard his fist felt like it had exploded. His cousin crumpled without a sound. Tobias felt an almost overwhelming desire to kick him, but he smothered it. Hands grabbed and hauled him backwards. He didn't struggle.

He looked Zebediah in the eyes and was amazed that he wasn't scared. It had gone too far for that. It was a relief, in a way. 'Leave the boy alone,' he said to his uncle. 'He didn't know what he was doing. He never knew what was in the letter. He just thought he was doing me a favour, that's all. If you hit him, I swear to God, I'll kill you.'

Ambrose was sobbing loudly now. It was like a rasp grating in Tobias's head. It hurt. This was his fault.

'Ambrose,' said Zebediah. 'Go on up to your room now. No one's gonna beat you. Go on.'

Tobias heard Ambrose sob and sniff and stand up with a groan. He didn't turn his head to look. Ezra and Perce were holding his arms so tightly he was losing feeling in them. 'I won't go till you promise not to hurt Toby!' The boy's voice was shrill, like the trill of a terrified robin, and Tobias felt tears pushing behind his eyes. He clenched his jaw, holding onto his anger with the desperation of a man hanging from a cliff. If he let go, he was lost.

'Don't back-talk me, boy!' Zebediah roared.

'Go on, Ambrose.' Tobias kept his voice steady. 'I'm going to be fine. I promise. Go to our room. I'll see you later. Go on!' He heard the boy sniff, then run out of the door and clatter away into the distance. He closed his eyes for a moment. When he opened them, Zebediah was still there.

'Let go of him, Perce, Ezra, and take Albert to his mum. Yes, both of you. Tobias and me got things to discuss, ain't we, Nephew?'

'Yes.' He stared his hatred at Zebediah, and Zebediah looked back. His seaweed eyes flickered green and brown and red, and Tobias saw the enormity of his will and knew it would rather crush him than let him go.

Ezra released his arm but Tobias didn't move. He heard Ezra lead a groaning Albert out of the room. 'And you, Perce,' said Zebediah. 'Go with your cousins. He's past wanting to run. Aren't you, Toby Petch?'

'Don't call me that!' He ground the words out. He didn't notice Perce letting go of him or the door closing. 'I'm not a Petch. I've none of your blood in me, thank God! It's just my bad luck that your drunken sot of a brother persuaded my mother to marry him. That man beat us every time he got drunk. Did you know that, Uncle? Do you even care?'

'He loved you. And your mum.'

'I don't need that kind of love! And I'm done pretending. You brought me here by force, and you're keeping me against my will, and I hate you for it!'

'I can see that.'

'I'm not your heir! I'm not going to run your thieving kingdom for you. If you're clever, you'll send me back to the Castle and collect the reward.'

'And leave you to rat on us? You know too much, boy.'

'Do you think I'd do that to Molly or Ambrose? Or even Elsie? They never hurt me. It's you I hate. Just like I hated your brother Barty!'

'That's enough—'

Tobias was shaking. His face felt frozen; his heart turned to ice. 'I'll tell you, dear Uncle, what I never told nobody. I did love Barty. He was the only dad I'd ever known and I loved him something fierce. But I hated him too. I hated him most of all for what he did to my mother. If someone hadn't knifed him and thrown him in the canal, I would have ended by killing him. They beat me to it is all.'

Zebediah stared at him for a moment in silence. His face was impassive. 'I'd give a deal to know who your real daddy is, boy,' he said. 'He give you more than just them light eyes.'

The thought of Alistair Windlass was a bucket of cold water poured over his head. He shivered.

'Thought so,' said Zebediah. 'You know him. He's alive then?'

'No!' Tobias shook his head in denial.

'One of the Castle guards? Or maybe that Moleglass fellow of yours?'

'It's none of your damn business! And Mr Moleglass ain't my dad, though I wish he were. His eyes are brown.'

'I know.' Zebediah smiled grimly. 'I went and had a look at him. Natty little gent. Downright comical. But you're fond of him, aren't you? Shame if something were to happen to him.'

Tobias stared into seaweed eyes and felt the blood drain from his face. 'You...You're bluffing!'

Satisfaction shone from Zebediah's eyes; his voice rumbled, treacle-rich. 'Accidents happen so quick these days. Blokes get knocked down by carriages, fall into the river, go down the wrong alley and end up with a shiv stuck in their gullets. It's a dangerous city. A gent like your Mr Moleglass can hardly walk the streets in safety no more.'

'You low, filthy...' Blood thudded in Tobias's head. It boiled behind his eyes, and the icy fury that had been sustaining him melted. He lunged at Zebediah, hitting out with all his strength, blind to everything except an overwhelming need to cause damage.

It was like punching an oak tree. Zebediah shrugged

him off, raised an arm and smashed the back of his hand into Tobias's face. Tobias crashed to the floor. Pain bloomed in his mouth and blackness swarmed over him. A hand grabbed the back of his shirt and yanked him to his feet, slung him in a chair. His head throbbed and the metallic taste of blood made him feel sick. It oozed from his mouth, began to dribble down his chin. He groaned and tried to focus his eyes.

'Listen good.' His uncle's voice snarled in his ears; sour breath clogged his nose and made him retch. A hand slapped across his face, knocking the nausea out of him. He gasped and stared up at Zebediah's eyes, inches from his own. 'I said *listen*! You can faint when I've done with you, but you'll listen now!' His uncle's teeth glinted in a fearsome grin. His eyes glittered. 'I'll never let you go. I'll see you dead first. Understand this: what's mine is mine, and no man takes it from me!

'But I don't want you dead. I got uses for you. So I'm gonna break you. There's two ways of doing that. I could beat you till I hammered the rebellion out of you. But you're as stubborn as me. I might kill you, and if I didn't I'd kill your spirit, and you're gonna need that to do the work I got in mind for you. So I've got to do it the other way.

'You give yourself away today, boy. You're soft. You're as soft as your mother. You're the sort of fool who'll sacrifice himself for someone he cares about. Like you just done for Ambrose. Used proper, that sort of thing can be a strength. Ambrose'd follow you to the grave now, I reckon. But it's your weak flank. It can be took advantage of. And that's what I aim to do.

'You're going out on a job with Perce tomorrow. You're gonna break into a house and you're gonna steal. Tomorrow and the next day and every day that I tell you. And if you don't – if you run away, or step one foot out of line – that funny little Moleglass fellow is dead. Do I make myself clear?'

Drizzle dripped from the sky, smudging the sickly glow of the streetlights. Tobias trudged behind a second cousin called Quilter. Another, a Tofts, walked on his left. Perce kept pace with him on his right. Perce was waiting for him to make a break for it. He hadn't believed Zebediah. The more fool him. Zebediah didn't make that sort of mistake. He was beginning to wonder if Zebediah ever made a mistake. Ever got it wrong. Ever left an opening, a crack, a mouse hole, that one of his victims could squeeze through.

It was the second time he had been out of the Petch fortress since his kidnapping. The brougham had brought them into one of the wealthy quarters, but they were walking the last bit. People noticed a carriage at this time of night. Idly, Tobias wondered about the duty constable, making his rounds. But Zebediah would have sorted it. Planned it. Dealt with it. Zebediah dealt with everything.

As he walked, he opened his mouth to the cooling

drizzle. His lower lip was split. Two of his teeth wobbled. Ambrose had cried at the sight of him. Cried and cried, until Tobias crawled out of bed and went to his cousin, holding the child until he slept at last. After that, he himself slept as though drugged and had to be shaken awake by a tight-lipped Elsie at midday, whose own eyes were red and swollen.

She cleaned the blood from his face, gave him fresh clothes, fed him, and spent the rest of the afternoon cutting his hair short and dying it black. When Tobias caught a glimpse of himself in the mirror he saw a stranger: a Flearside tough. The pale blue eyes were all that was left of Tobias Petch.

Perce came to collect him at midnight. Zebediah saw them off. He issued instructions to Perce; said nothing to Tobias. But his eyes said everything. They told Tobias of the enormity of his satisfaction, his knowledge that Tobias was done, broken.

'Here.' Perce grabbed his arm, pulled him sideways. Down an alley. Behind the great row of stone houses smeared by damp and dark. No streetlights here, but Perce seemed to find his way blind. He pulled Tobias through the gravel, the smell of cat's piss, past high walls black in the darkness. He pushed him against a wooden gate, thrust a cold lockpick in his hand.

'Your moment, Toby,' he said, biting the words off short and soft and deadly. 'Mess up and I'll loosen the rest of your teeth.'

Tobias picked the lock. It was a nothing lock, a ward lock. It took ten seconds, even with his hand quivering like a rabbit in a snare.

'That's the first,' said Perce. 'Your housebreaking career has begun, little cousin. Watch your step, 'cause I'm just waiting for you to mess up. You follow me and keep quiet.'

He followed. Time stretched five times its normal length. He heard every breath of the three men, every footstep, the crunch of each pebble beneath their feet. He leant against the back door of the house, his forehead pressed to its cold wooden surface to keep himself from falling over, and picked the lock. Twenty seconds. Climbed the creaky kitchen stairs to the hall. Waited in darkness smelling of beeswax and linoleum. Listened to his own hoarse breathing outrun the tick of the grandfather clock. Perce and Cousin Tofts and Cousin Quilter lit their dark lanterns and whipped through the house like ferrets: snakelike, silent, efficient. He imagined the family asleep upstairs waking to the early morning howls of the parlour maid come to light the fire; felt his mouth go dry as he saw himself being run down and collared by a copper, thrown into a police cell. Again, the image of his father, lying on the bunk in the Castle dungeon, flashed into his brain, and he shivered.

The men were back. Perce ushered him into a room and presented him with a small metal safe. This was more difficult. He had to concentrate. Listen. Feel with his

Evelyn Gregory
Toronto Public Library
Evelyn Gregory
416-394-1006

User ID: 27131027051251

Payment date: 04 May 2013 14:
52
Bill reason: OVERDUE
Item ID: 37131109251348
Title: TPL CHILDREN'S
PAPERBACK
Amount billed: $8.00

OVERDUE $8.00
Total Paid: $8.00

Telephone Renewal 416-395-
5505
www.torontopubliclibrary.ca

fingers. His mouth was throbbing, and a profound tiredness seemed to be welling up from some deep spring far inside his very depths, but he knelt and cracked the safe's lock in just over twenty-five minutes. Not brilliant, but fair.

They hauled him to one side, emptied the safe; then collected him and retreated from the house as efficiently as they had come. The brougham was waiting for them two streets away. He fell asleep in the carriage. He didn't wake when they returned to Flearside, nor when Zebediah carried him upstairs and put him to bed as though he were a small child let to stay up too late.

Twenty-two

'No response at all?'

Superintendent Blundell puffed his cheeks out and shook his head. 'Time-wasters. Oh, we've had a fair helping of those! If Your Majesty had seen fit to consult with me before taking this step—'

'So people have come forward!'

'If you will forgive my presumption in saying so, ma'am, the amount of money offered as a reward is ludicrously high. For a mere gardener's boy—'

Charlie rose to her feet. She said nothing, but Blundell's words dried in mid-stream. His ruddy face turned several shades paler and he jumped from his chair. Grumbling and muttering under his breath, Lord Topplesham began to rise from his own chair, collapsing back into it with a groan of relief as Charlie waved him away. 'If you must be such a fool, Blundell,' he snapped, 'kindly keep it to yourself.'

But Blundell hung onto his sense of ill-usage with a terrier's tenacity. 'I merely meant that the amount of the reward has ensured that we've had a queue of unsavoury individuals blocking the Constabulary's doors for the past fortnight. Every layabout in the City has scrounged up some scruffy lad and brought him along. Those that haven't boys bring maps and ridiculous stories of kidnapping. I've wasted hundreds of police hours already on this enterprise. And yes, I do consider it ill-conceived. I should have been consulted!'

'You are checking these people's stories, aren't you?' Charlie asked. 'They might be genuine!'

'Rest assured, ma'am,' Blundell said through gritted teeth, 'we investigate any lead which falls anywhere near the realms of possibility. Most, however, do not! As I said, police hours are being wasted on this which would be better spent elsewhere. For instance, searching for the boy's father.'

'Aye. Well that's the next point of business.' Topplesham mopped at his perspiring face. 'My people and the Resistance have drawn a blank. A few possible sightings, but all in different parts of the City and not one description matching another. If I didn't know better, I'd almost believe the scoundrel's fled the City.'

'He wouldn't do that!' Charlie cried. 'You have to keep looking for him.'

'I agree, ma'am. But I have to tell you that with each week that passes, our chances of catching him get worse. He'll have had time to set himself up nicely. Made his plans and arranged his escape route.'

'And what are my mother and I supposed to do?' Charlie glared at her Prime Minister. 'Hide away in the Castle for the rest of our lives, because you can't catch one man?'

First Nell, now Topplesham. They were giving up. Leaving her to fight Windlass on her own. 'You have your orders,' she told her Prime Minister. 'Find him.'

Her mother had disappeared again. Only this time, it was broad daylight. Nell was gone, so Charlie went to find Mr Moleglass. He was in his pantry, polishing the silver.

'I can't find Mother. Do you know where she is? She keeps disappearing.'

'A moment,' he said, putting down the polishing cloth and peeling off the stained leather gloves. 'I'll put the kettle on.'

'Mr Moleglass, I don't want a cup of tea! I want to find out where my mother keeps going. What do you know about it?'

He bustled about, putting the kettle on the hob, clearing the end of the table and putting out cups and saucers. 'Your mother is taking a turn in the rose garden, I believe.' It was a poor lie. He did not look at her. 'Try not to be so anxious about her, child. You are following her about like a spy. It is not good for either of you. Now, tea.' He poured the boiling water into the teapot and Charlie watched without a word.

She was not sure she could have spoken. For as long as she could remember, Mr Moleglass had been her best friend, her comfort and support. Nell had gone, Topplesham was weakening, but she had thought she could always count on Mr Moleglass.

214

He looked up and saw her face. 'Charlie…' he said. His seal's eyes brimmed with worry and guilt, and she saw the struggle he was making. It was unfair of her mother to trap him like this. Charlie stood up and smiled.

'It's all right, Mr Moleglass. I'm not thirsty and I have something I need to do.' She turned and left.

Charlie searched the Castle systematically. Anger gave her strength and she raced up the grand staircase to check her mother's bedroom, bathroom, morning room, study. All the places her mother should be. When she didn't find her, she started to look in the places the Dowager shouldn't be. Including Rose's workroom.

Rose looked up from her sewing, a look of hope in her eyes.

'Have you seen my mother?' Charlie asked, and Rose's eyes dimmed.

'No, Your Majesty.' She bent her head over her work, and Charlie turned to go. Something made her stop, look back at the small, brown woman sitting on a hard chair in a shaft of sunlight.

'Rose,' she said.

The woman looked up at her. Her eyes looked huge in her pale face. Charlie noticed that she was thin. Rose had always used to be plump, she remembered. And pretty, with her oval face, fawn and pink skin and thick hair the colour of conkers. Charlie stared at her and realised she was searching for a glimpse of Tobias in his mother's face.

Rose threw her a puzzled look. 'Yes, ma'am?'

Charlie blushed. She had been standing like a goose, staring, not saying a word. 'I-I just wanted to say…we *will* find him. We will get him back.'

Rose stared down at her sewing. Her fingers shook as she pushed the needle through the fabric. 'It's my fault,' she said in a voice like the whisper of autumn leaves. 'Zebediah's got him now. And it's my fault.'

Charlie bit her lip. Words did not come. She could not even think them. She closed the door behind her and the click of the latch echoed like a thunderclap. Then she ran even faster to find her mother.

The kitchen last, then the gardens. She was racing past the housekeeper's office on her way to the kitchen stairs when a noise reached out and yanked her to a halt. The clank and grind of the service lift.

Unbidden, a vision of Mrs O'Dair, the dead housekeeper, lurched into her head, and Charlie backed away from the lift doors. She retreated as far as the corner which led on towards the kitchen stairs. It would only be Maria, or Moleglass, or one of the footmen, on some sort of errand. Fetching something from one of the cellars. A bottle of wine, perhaps.

The lift doors groaned and shuddered open, and Charlie's mother stepped out of the lift, turned towards the state apartments, and walked around the far corner and out of sight.

Charlie stared after her. The cellars? What on earth

could her mother want down there? Charlie shuddered. She intended to follow her mother tonight, no matter where she went. But she had hoped never to have to descend into the Castle cellars again.

Twenty-three

Tobias lost track of the nights. They melted in his memory into slush: long journeys in the brougham; houses rearing black beneath indigo skies; cobblestones glinting in the moonlight; the insides of strange houses glimpsed by the scant light of dark lanterns; the knowledge of servants asleep in the attics, gentry on the first or second floors, dogs drugged, snoring in their kennels. And always: the locks, the picks, Perce at his elbow, the sound of tumblers teasing him to find the pattern, release their secret.

By the third night, numbness left him and fear took its place. But it stayed only briefly. They were never caught – never came close to it. He recognised Zebediah's hand. A drunken housekeeper or deaf, elderly manservant. A family out of town. A police constable short of money.

The routine inside the houses was always the same. Most did not possess a safe and his job ended once they were inside. With practice, his clever fingers grew more clever, and in a strange way he began to take pleasure in his skill. No one could match him, he knew. Not Perce or Ezra, not Zebediah himself. He was a creature of the night now, waking in the afternoon to stare up at the grey rafters keeping the weight of the roof from

smashing down on him. They were, he noticed, riddled
with deathwatch.

'Big job tonight, Toby.'

He looked up from the office fire and frowned at
Zebediah. Why was he being told this? It was none of his
business. He saw Perce shoot the same look at his uncle.
But Zebediah was looking at him, not Perce. 'New
type of safe. Double tumbler mechanism. Think you're
up for it?'

He shrugged. 'It'll take a lot longer. Are they interlocked
or separate?'

'That I don't know. But the crib's empty. Not even staff
sleeping in, so you'll have all the time you need. Do your
best with it, boy, but we don't expect miracles. If you can't
crack it, no one can.' Zebediah's eyes surveyed him with
pleasure before turning to his older nephew. 'Perce can
take along some wedges in case.'

Tobias slumped back against the wall and watched
Perce pouring over the map spread across the desk,
repeating Zebediah's instructions according to the nightly
ritual. This part of a job was restful. No thinking. No
worrying. Just do as he was told. He considered his
uncle's news and felt a stirring of interest. Ezra had told
him about these safes, but hadn't yet managed to get hold
of one to practise on. It would be chuffing if he could
crack it tonight, never having touched one before.

As the brougham clattered over invisible cobbles,

Tobias stared out at the moon floating above the City. It shone full and bright in the clear, crisp night. Only a few chimneys stretched fat ropes of smoke into the violet sky, and the normal city fug had vanished along with the smell of coal.

He felt the kick of adrenaline as it began to trickle through his blood. Edginess, making his heart beat faster, his breathing quicken, his stomach tense. He was used to it now, was beginning to enjoy it: the awareness of risk, of danger. It numbed his misery like a dose of laudanum.

The house was a solitary giant, silent and dark behind high brick walls. It had been built before the City came and now stood isolate in a sea of smaller, poorer houses. A smell of abandonment greeted Tobias as he pushed open the front door: damp, mould, dust, mice. He cast a puzzled glance at Perce, but his cousin pushed him inside with an irritated hiss. The door shut behind them; the men lit their dark lanterns.

'Perce! This house ain't been lived in.'

'Someone's just let it. Some rich cove. Moved the safe in already. Don't pester me with stupid questions, boy. Just do your job!' Perce didn't bother to whisper. The house was empty. The men darted off. Returned almost at once. 'Safe's in here. Come on!'

He followed Perce into a small, gloomy room to the side of the house. He saw it at once: humped against a wall, large and squat, gleaming slightly in the dim light. He could smell the metallic, oily newness of it.

'Get on, boy,' growled Perce.

Tobias knelt before the safe. The men put down their lanterns. Waited. He nestled his ear against the metal door, touched both dials with questing finger tips, rotated them slowly, evenly, listening to the tumblers rolling in their hidden pathways. Interlocking. He was sure of it. His heart accelerated; his mouth was dry, but sweat prickled the palms of his hands, dampened the hair beneath his cap and itched his shirt collar. He tore the cap off, wiped his forehead on the sleeve of his jacket and began again. Sweet Betty, this was difficult.

The men were silent. They respected his fingers. Even Perce trusted him now to do his best.

He lost himself inside the mechanisms of the lock. His eyes were closed; he knew nothing beyond his fingertips and his left ear. A picture built in his brain, a picture of the tumblers as he found each one and sent it safely home. He didn't know how long it took, but he felt the lock give beneath his fingers with a shudder like an earthquake. There was hiss of metallic air as the safe sighed and opened its mouth.

'Got it!' Tobias slumped as the tension left him, grinned to himself in the darkness. He'd done it! He'd beaten the best they could throw at him.

'Well done, Toby.' Perce's voice was full of respect, of awe. Hearing it gave him a bitter satisfaction. 'Just under thirty minutes. You're a bloody marvel!'

'Yes. Congratulations, Tobias. An impressive performance.'

The voice seared through him.

He sensed Perce and the others freeze. Saw Perce reach for the pistol he carried inside his jacket. Light punched across the room, blinding him. Someone had unhooded a lantern.

'Don't try it, Mr Sorrell! Hands up. Unless you want a bullet in your head.'

Tobias crouched on the floor beside the safe, blinking up at the figure standing in the doorway, pointing a revolving pistol at Perce. He stared, unable to believe, even as his body began to shiver with shock.

Slowly, Perce raised his hands above his head. So did Cousin Tofts and Quilter. The three men looked as shaken as Tobias felt.

'What is this?' growled Perce, his voice vibrating with anger and fear. 'Who are you? What d'you want?'

'You have something of mine. I want it back.'

'Yeah? And what's that?'

'My son.'

'Bloody hell!' said Cousin Quilter.

Perce just stared. Stared at Alistair Windlass, standing tall and smiling in the doorway, a neat moustache and beard hiding the lower part of his face. He was meticulous in a black coat and pearl-coloured waistcoat, grey trousers; his shoes and beaver hat gleaming in the lantern light nearly as brightly as the barrel of his pistol. Except for that item, he might have been a bank manager, a barrister, a Member of Parliament.

'The eyes,' said Perce. 'Look at his eyes. By God, it *is* his dad. You filthy little brat! You set us up!'

'Don't be absurd,' snapped Windlass. 'The boy is more shocked than you are. And even less pleased to see me, I fear. Your hands too, Tobias. Above your head. Past experience tells me I cannot trust you to be sensible.'

Mechanically, Tobias raised his hands. He couldn't take his eyes off the man in the doorway. His mind seemed frozen inside a vast desert of numbness.

'Who are you?' roared Perce.

'That is not your concern. Using your left hand, Mr Sorrell, ease your gun out of its holster and toss it behind you. Don't do anything stupid, or it will be your last action on this earth. I chose this house because it's out of the way. No one will hear a gunshot, and if they do, they won't investigate. If you three gentlemen want to carry on living, I suggest you do exactly as I say.'

Perce put a shaking hand in his jacket, pulled out a small pistol and dropped it on the floor behind him.

'Well done,' said Windlass. 'My informant tells me that you are the only one who habitually carries a firearm, Mr Sorrell, but it would be as well to check. Gentleman, one by one, walk slowly to the opposite wall. Stop three feet away from it and lean forward onto your outstretched hands. You first, Mr Sorrell. Then you, Mr Quilter. Mr Tofts, now. And yes, you too, Tobias. I need you where I can see you.'

Tobias rose from his crouch, walked on unsteady legs and leant against the wall next to Cousin Tofts. His cousin was breathing heavily, and the smell of sweat and fear was thick in the room. He turned his head and watched Windlass pat down each man for weapons, then back away, still holding the pistol.

'Tobias, I have a job for you,' he said. Tobias stared at the wall and shook his head. 'Come here, son.' Tobias didn't move. Windlass sighed. 'Your stubbornness can be extremely irritating. If you don't do as I tell you, I will put a bullet through Mr Sorrell's left leg. I'll try not to hit a major blood vessel, but I can't promise. Now, come here.'

'Do it!' rasped Perce.

Tobias pushed away from the wall. He was shaking worse than ever.

'Take these.' Windlass pulled a tangle of handcuffs from his coat pocket. 'Cuff them. Start with Sorrell.'

Tobias attached a cuff to Perce's right hand, pulled it down behind his back, then cuffed the left. He did the same with Quilter and Tofts. None of them spoke.

'Thank you, Tobias.' Windlass lowered the pistol. 'Now, stand over here in the middle of the room, where I can see you. Gentlemen, you may turn round.'

The men shuffled around. Their faces were red. Anger was getting the better of fear, and Perce snarled as he spoke: 'Zebediah Petch will kill you.'

'I'm not easy to kill,' Windlass said. 'Ask Tobias. I have

a message for Mr Petch. Don't look for us. He's had the lend of my son for three months now, but enough is enough. Tobias, we're leaving.'

'No.' He shook his head. Took a step backwards. 'I won't go with you.'

'You'd rather stay with this filth?' His father's voice was icy with contempt.

'No!' He glared at Windlass, aware that his own voice was uneven, that he was shivering with fear and hatred. 'But I'm not going anywhere with you.'

'I'm rescuing you, boy! Or haven't you grasped that simple fact?'

'*No!*' He shouted the word. Gritted his teeth. 'I don't know why you're here, but it's not to help me. I won't have anything to do with you! You can shoot me, but I won't go with you. Never. You murdering—'

The click of the pistol being cocked cut off his words. It was still pointed at the floor. Windlass's eyes never left Tobias's face. His voice was cold. 'You'd rather stay with Zebediah Petch?'

Tobias found his breath was coming in ragged gasps. He stared at the pistol in his father's hand, then up into Windlass's frozen eyes. 'Petch is a villain! I hate him! He's a demon! But you – you're the Devil himself!'

'This is what will happen, Tobias.' The words were calm, matter of fact. 'If you don't come with me, I'll put a bullet through Mr Sorrell's head. If you still refuse, I'll do the same to Mr Quilter. Then Mr Tofts. The decision

225

is yours.' Windlass lifted his arm, took careful aim at Perce's head.

'For God's sake, Toby!' The words stuttered out of Perce's mouth in short gasps. 'Go, boy! Please! Just go with the man!'

Despair cut through him as he looked at his cousin's face. He had no choice. He didn't like Perce, but he couldn't stand by and see him shot dead. 'All right,' he said. 'I'll come. Leave them be.'

'Certainly.' Windlass pulled a key from his waistcoat pocket and flung it onto the floor. 'For the handcuffs,' he said. 'I wish I could stay and watch you try to use it, but, alas, my son and I must be going now. My regards to Zebediah Petch. And tell him, if he comes after us, I'll kill him. Good evening, gentlemen.' He uncocked his pistol, slipped it into his coat pocket and turned his pale eyes on Tobias. 'A step in front of me the entire time, son. And no bravado, please, or I shall take measures you won't enjoy.'

Tobias left the room without a backward glance. Windlass stood back to let him pass, and he was relieved that the man didn't try to touch him. It was bad enough to hear him following close behind. The hairs on the back of Tobias's neck prickled at his father's nearness.

Every muscle in his body was singing with adrenaline, his heart pounding in anticipation. The fog of shock had cleared from his brain at last, and now it seemed to be working at twice the normal speed: images, super-sharp, raced through his mind. He retraced the movements of the evening, every step they had taken during the break-in – saw the overgrown garden, the high walls, the wrought-iron gate, tall and spiked, vicious with rust and malice. The people who had built this house had not wanted unwelcome visitors.

Windlass would have a carriage waiting outside that gate. Once inside it, he had no chance of escape. Just get him far enough away from the men. Far enough – so that Windlass couldn't shoot them. He himself was safe enough. Windlass surely wouldn't kill him. Not having gone to this trouble. The man wanted him alive. But why? *Why?!*

They reached the hall. The foot of the stairs. The door stood opposite.

'Open it, Tobias.'

He pulled the door open, breathed in the air of the garden, rank with weed and cat, rich with the scent of wisteria blooming invisibly overhead. He stumbled on the threshold, nearly fell. Windlass reached out a hand. Tobias twisted away, grabbed the door and slammed it with all his might, catching his father's arm below the elbow. The roar of pain found him already running. He flung himself against the gate and was stunned to find it locked. The picks were in Perce's pocket. In any case, there was no time. He turned, saw his father stumble down the front steps of the house, clutching his arm; begin to run towards him.

Tobias raced for the nearest wall. Ivy covered it. He

swarmed up like a monkey, like Ambrose, like a Petch. But it was a high wall. The ivy ran out. He paused ten feet above the ground. Ten more to the top.

'Tobias! Get down from there! Come down at once! You'll fall, you fool!'

He looked down. Windlass's face glimmered up at him in the moonlight. His cold eyes glittered. The ground seemed to veer at Tobias. Then sway and dance away. He clutched the ivy and rested his sweating forehead against the grit and dust of the bricks. He heard Ezra's voice in his head: 'It's all confidence with you, boy. You got good strong hands. Trust them.'

He began to climb. He climbed slowly, his fingers searching the bricks for crevices. The mortar was old and crumbling. Full of handholds. It was easier than the climbing wall at Flearside. The top of the wall lowered itself towards him.

'*Tobias!*' There was a note of urgency in Windlass's voice he had not heard before. It broke his concentration for a second, but he batted it out of his mind, strained his left hand up…'*Tobias! Stop! It's not safe!*'…found the coping stone that capped the wall. He had made it! He heaved himself up with all his strength, and the stone moved. It walked towards him. He flung his right hand up, grabbed another stone, hung by his two hands for a fragment of a second, and felt the top of the wall bend. The mortar had long since turned to dust. The coping stones slid from their sockets like rotten teeth. There was a long, timeless moment as he leant back from the wall, grasping nothing but air – a long, timeless moment as he thought of his mother and Mr Moleglass and Charlie, and felt a sharp, bitter sense of loss. And then he fell.

Twenty-four

Charlie woke with a gasp. She couldn't remember the dream, just the sensation of falling. She must have been dreaming about the ridge again.

The rooks whirled over the Castle, scraping the grey light of early dawn with their voices. It was mid-April, and the sun folded the darkness away earlier each morning. Her favourite time of year: a time of promise and new beginnings. Charlie shivered, curled on her side and tried to go back to sleep.

But sleep had finished with her and at last she gave up. She rolled out of bed and went to her wardrobe. She pulled out a box and carried it to the table. It held one of her most precious possessions: the suit of Tobias's old clothes she had worn when she had escaped from the Castle with him to find her mother. She began to dress, pulling on the trousers and shirt, fastening her boots, sliding her arms into the warm sleeves of the jacket before sliding her body out the window and onto the roof. She was going back to face the dragon. No more running from nightmares. She had been wrong to hope that others would defeat Windlass for her. Queens fought alone.

The sky was pearl-coloured and cold. Dew lay on the

leads, shimmering between water and frost. The rooks screamed, hoarse with excitement at the freshness of the day. Charlie filled her lungs with silvery air.

She took her time climbing to the ridge, pausing to watch the rooks wheel overhead and to look, when she was high enough, for the distant glimmer that was the sea. When she reached her enemy and stood staring at its long metal backbone, she couldn't tell whether she was shivering from fear, excitement or cold.

She knew what she was going to do. She had thought it out during the climb. She did not want to die. She needed to do this, but she no longer trusted in the magic of her balance, the magic of her feet and head to keep her safe. She knew now, as she had not before, that she *could* die. She knew it with her body and not just her mind. The knowledge brought sadness. She had lost something, and it wouldn't come back.

Charlie knelt down and sat astride the ridge. She lay forward, stretched her hands out and inched onto it. She crawled across on her belly, legs hugging the sides of the roof for balance. It was slow, awkward, ungraceful. But she crossed. The dragon was dead.

It had been months since she had climbed into the dumbwaiter and given herself up to darkness and fear in order to travel to the cellars. Charlie pulled the dumbwaiter door shut and waited for sickness to flood her stomach, for her heart to pound in her ribcage. But all she felt was a slight tightness in her chest and a dry mouth. Amazed, she reached for the rope that lowered the lift and began to pull. The dumbwaiter lurched and groaned downwards.

She must have grown stronger, now she was twelve. It was easier to haul herself down. She must also have grown larger. The inside of the dumbwaiter seemed too small ever to have held her *and* Tobias.

It stopped at the lower-ground floor, and she scrabbled out quickly into the dust and the dim light falling from narrow windows high in the walls. The Dowager would be stepping into the service lift at any moment, and Charlie needed to watch and see where she went. The lift might stop here, or it might continue on. If it did, she would have to watch which floor it stopped on, take a risk on calling it when she judged it safe, and follow her mother down. The dumbwaiter went no further.

She crouched behind a dusty corner and watched the lift door and the semicircle above it where a long pointed arrow like the hand of a clock showed the lift's position. The arrow quivered and began to move. Down it dropped, past F2, F1, GF, LGF. Charlie held her breath, but the needle barely paused on B1 before sweeping on past B2, B3, and finally coming to rest at B4. Her heart sank. Basement Four.

Clutching her lantern, Charlie forced herself to walk to the lift. She pushed the call button and hoped her mother was far enough away not to notice. She stepped into the lift and pulled the inner doors shut. The outer doors swung together, the gears clanked, the lift lurched, and she was on her way down. She watched the needle begin its quivering journey: B2, B3, B4. The lift shuddered to a halt, and she clashed the inner grille open and waited the terrifying mini-seconds until the outer doors slowly opened.

She lit her lantern and stepped out into the smell of damp stone and the taste of air that was never dry. The lantern light made a bright circle on the stone floor, and her spiky shadow danced within it. Charlie shivered, took a deep breath, and marched into the dark to find her mother, taking her circle of light with her.

Twenty-five

Pain scraped away the darkness. Pain like dull knives sawing his flesh. Not cutting cleanly, but tearing, ripping. He fled, seeking the dark, but there was light now. Stabbing light. And someone pushing something into his mouth, forcing him to swallow bitterness. He tried to vomit, but even that was denied. He was held down as he struggled to escape the pain, forced to lie still and listen to his own screams. And then the darkness returned, dissolving him and the pain together.

Periods of light came again, but the pain was never so bad. Visions spiralled past like shards of coloured glass in a kaleidoscope: men's faces, bending over him. Sometimes it was a stranger's face, sometimes Zebediah or Barty or Perce. Sometimes his father's face slid into view, and he would shudder with fear. Men's hands lifted him from the darkness and placed him back inside it: hurting, holding, feeding, soothing, cleaning. Never his mother. He called and called, but she didn't come.

The kaleidoscope faded, and he opened his eyes on a grey world. He was lying in a strange room on a high brass bed. The curtains at the window were pulled, but light glowed through them. The curtains were dark blue, and the light was cold and dim. His right leg throbbed with a fierce, deep ache. He could wiggle his toes, slowly and painfully, but the leg would not move. It lay like a dead thing beneath the eiderdown.

Something awful had happened to him. He knew it. He knew he ought to do something about it. But he was so tired. He closed his eyes and slept.

A shaft of sunlight slanted from the window. Its warmth sliced through the room and fell across the face of Alistair Windlass, asleep in an armchair. He shouted at the sight of his father's face – a bark of pure fear. Windlass's eyes opened and gazed into his. Tobias lay, trapped by his dead leg, and remembered. After a long time, he swallowed and said: 'My leg.'

'Is broken.' His father shifted in the chair, leant forward. His face was haggard: pale above the beard, the eyes red-rimmed. His left arm was in a sling. 'To be more precise, the tibia of your right leg is fractured. Rather unpleasantly. But the doctor says you will walk again, although there may be a slight limp.'

'Doctor?'

'The best surgeon in the City. He operated on you here.'

'Operated?….*He cut me open?!*'

'Your bone had done that already. But yes, he made an incision in your leg and repaired the damage. It took a long time and you lost a lot of blood. But it was that, or amputate.'

Tobias stared at his father in blank horror. 'You let one

of them crazy sawbones cut me open? I might have died!'

'It was a risk, yes. But the leg would not have healed. It would have become gangrenous. Amputation might have killed you anyway. I took the decision in your best interests. Chose the best man, a surgeon well versed in the latest research on the use of carbolic acid as a disinfectant. And you have survived.'

Tobias stared at his father in disbelief. 'You! It was your fault!'

Windlass nodded. His eyes didn't flicker. 'Yes. If you had died, I would have been responsible. I'm fully aware of that fact. It would have been the cause of lasting regret.'

'You sod!'

'Enough, Tobias! If you stoop to vulgar abuse I shall leave the room. Now, do you feel well enough to take some broth?'

Tobias ignored him. The desire to close his eyes and sleep was becoming overwhelming, but there was so much he needed to know. 'Where is this place?'

'Nowhere in particular. A house I have rented. Under an assumed name, of course.'

'Why?' He fought the exhaustion away. He wanted, needed to know.

Windlass understood him. 'You're my son, Tobias. Do you really think I would leave you enslaved to a man like Zebediah Petch? Go to sleep now. We'll talk later.'

'I don't believe you,' Tobias said. And slept.

In the beginning, he slept away great chunks of time, waking only for an hour or so, intervals where Windlass gave him bowls of broth or gruel, helped him to use the bedpan, washed him, administered the laudanum that eased him back into a twilight world of strange dreams and fancies. Despite his father's promise, they did not talk. Tobias found the situation too embarrassing to speak in more than monosyllables, and Windlass tended him in silent efficiency.

Soon he was sleeping less, lying awake for hours of the day and night, gritting his teeth against the needle-sharp pains of his bone knitting itself back together. He fumed at being trapped in a bed again, at the weakness of his body and – most of all – at the fear he felt every time Windlass came near him. He watched his father with a kind of horrified fascination: every movement, gesture, facial expression. What did the man want with him?

'Books.' His father placed a parcel on his bedside table. 'You need something to occupy your mind.'

'My leg hurts.'

'You'll have to put up with it,' Windlass said. 'I'm reducing your doses of laudanum. I don't intend to have a son addicted to opiates, as frequently happens after injuries of this kind.'

Tobias made no move to open the parcel. He was torn between a desire to see what books Windlass had brought him and the strong urge to throw the lot in his face. He shifted, trying to ease the pain. 'When can I get up?'

'Soon.' Windlass had been drawing back the curtains. He turned and was outlined in the glow of morning light. He had obviously been out of the house already and wore morning dress, his collar and tie impeccable. His fair hair was fashionably cut, his beard and moustache neatly trimmed. His pale eyes were tired, but the sling was gone from his left arm, though Tobias had noticed a slight stiffness in his movements as he opened the curtains.

'When are you gonna let me go?' The question had been burning unspoken in his mouth for days.

Windlass watched him cooly for a moment. 'I'm not,' he said. 'At least, not yet.'

He had been expecting the answer, but still had to fight to stay calm. 'What do you mean? You can't want me. I'm nothing to you. Why not get shut of me? I'll live now, if that's what was on your conscience.'

'I didn't think you believed me to possess such a thing.'

'I don't!'

Windlass smiled and walked to the door.

'Wait!' Tobias propped himself on his elbows, saw his father turn and raise an enquiring eyebrow. 'You owe me an explanation.'

Windlass shook his head. His mouth slanted in a contemptuous smile. 'Three months with Zebediah Petch and you still believe that life is a game played to a set of childish rules? I don't owe you anything, Tobias, and if I don't choose to share the innermost workings of my mind, I'm afraid there is nothing you can do about it. Now please excuse me; I must go and see to some food.'

'Surely,' he spat the words out, 'a fancy gent like you don't soil his hands with cooking! Ain't you got no servants?'

'Cleverly done, Tobias. No. I cannot afford servants – they see too much, ask too many questions. A woman comes in for two hours a day to clean downstairs and cook the evening meal. I'm always in the house when she's here. She's elderly and deaf, and I have told her I have a poor, deranged son locked upstairs. She'll be no help to you. And it's "*Haven't* you got *any* servants?". Your grammar is appalling.'

He looked up from his book and saw Windlass standing in the door, holding a wooden crutch. Despite himself, a grin spread across his face. 'I can get up?'

'Yes.' An answering smile flitted across his father's face. 'The leg must stay splinted for another week or so, and you must not put weight on it yet, but yes, you may get up for brief periods. You'll find it tiring. You've been bedridden nearly three weeks. Your strength will take time to return.'

Tobias manoeuvred his leg over the side of the bed and reached out for the crutch. 'No!' he said, when Windlass made to help him. 'I'll do it myself.'

His father stood near the door and watched as he failed three times to lever himself out of bed. On the fourth attempt he stood, swaying, his head swimming, his heart pounding with effort. He began a slow circuit of the room, balance and hop, balance and hop. He was shaking by the time he got back to the bed. He sank down onto it and the crutch slipped from his fingers. He flopped back, exhausted, and waited for his breathing to slow.

Through half-closed eyelids, he saw the dark shape of Windlass approach, pick up the crutch, prop it beside the bed, then stand, silently, looking down at him. He saw the glint of a watch chain as it rose and fell in time to his father's breathing. An image flashed into his mind: the shining open mouth of a pistol promising death; his father's hand, as steady as though carved from stone, aiming the gun at his head. Fear flared his eyes open. 'Get away from me!' he yelled, scrabbling backwards on the bed.

Something moved behind his father's eyes and he stepped away. Tobias shivered as the fear subsided, edged himself onto his pillows.

'You hate me that much?' Windlass's voice lacked all expression.

'What do you expect?' His own voice was shaking. 'You threatened to put a bullet in my head. Or have you forgotten? You murdered the King. Charlie's dad! You should have hung. I went that morning. Did you know? I went and waited for them to bring you out. I waited to watch you climb the gibbet and see them put the rope round your neck, like you did to him. *I wanted to see you hang!*'

240

'I'm sorry to disappoint you.' Windlass turned and left the room.

The door was locked. And not a lockpick or buttonhook to be had. Tobias cursed. Each night he checked, and each night the disappointment cut deeper. He stumped over to the window and stood, looking out over the Georgian houses gathered round a minute square garden. It was the middle of night, and the moon was waxing nearly full. It glowed like a mellow Durch cheese, smiling down benevolently. When he was little, he had believed that the man in the moon granted wishes. Tobias gazed up at the moon with something like hatred.

He turned to go back to bed and glimpsed a movement in the garden square. Beneath the trees. He shrank back behind the curtain. Had it been...? Again the shadow shifted, adjusted itself with the unconscious weariness of the night watchman. He backed away from the window. He was certain. It was not the moonlight playing tricks. There was a Petch in the square. Watching. Zebediah had found them.

'Windlass!' He tapped the crutch on the wall again. Blast the man! Why didn't he wake? At last, bedsprings creaked. 'No light! Don't light a candle!' He didn't dare shout too loudly. Had he been heard? Yes. Footsteps.

'What is it?' His father's voice floated beneath the door.

'There's a Petch in the square, watching the house.'

Silence. Then: 'I'm going to unlock the door and open it two inches only. Hand me your crutch and retreat to your bed. I will not come in until you have done so.'

'I'm not lying!'

'Perhaps. I'm opening the door now.' There was the sound of the key in the lock; the door cracked open. Tobias pushed his crutch through the opening, felt it taken, hopped back to his bed. In the moonlight he saw his father, wrapped in a dressing gown, hair tousled with sleep. Windlass studied him for a second, said: 'Stay on your bed,' and moved to the window. He stood to one side, peering out into the square. Then he backed away from the window as carefully as he had approached it.

'A shame,' he said, turning towards Tobias. 'My informant has missed a trick. But it was only a matter of time. I've made arrangements. I had just hoped not to have to use them until you were steadier on your feet.

'You'll find clothing in the wardrobe. Put it on. There are slippers; they'll have to do. Be ready in twenty minutes.' He turned to go, still holding the crutch.

'Wait! What's happening? Where are you going?'

'To deal with our unwanted visitor.' Windlass's voice was placid.

'Deal with…you're not going to kill him? No! I won't stand by and let you murder—'

'Unless the man's head is unnaturally fragile, he'll have nothing but a headache as a result of his night's work.

Sorry to disappoint you, but I'm not quite as bloodthirsty as you imagine.' Windlass's voice was cutting, and Tobias stared after him as he strode from the room. The door thudded with slightly more force than was necessary. The lock clicked. In a moment, Tobias heard the subdued noises next door of his father dressing.

He hopped to the wardrobe, pulled the clothing out and scrambled into it as quickly as he could: trousers, shirt, waistcoat, a woollen coat. Quality clothes: he could tell from the cloth. Tailor-made. Gent's togs. He gave a grunt of contempt at Windlass's finicking ways before hopping to the window. His father's footsteps had travelled downstairs a few minutes before. Tobias intended to see what happened. He had a ringside seat, and he certainly didn't trust a murderer like Alistair Windlass to keep his word.

The moon shone down on the small square of greenery, with its orderly shrubberies, its miniature grove of ornamental trees. Once, he thought he saw a movement on the far side of the square, but he could not be sure. The smaller branches swayed in an occasional breeze, but otherwise, the scene could have been painted on canvas in silver, indigo and mossy green. Nothing happened for a long time. Then a gig rattled into the square and stopped before the house. A man climbed down. The moon smiled, and Tobias heard footsteps climbing the stairs: the light, confident tread of his father. He dodged away from the window, and his eyes sought his father's face as the door opened, but it remained in shadow.

'I can't trust you not to try to crack my head open with your crutch, so you'll have to do the best you can with this.' Windlass held up a gentleman's slender cane. 'My apologies: there is no sword inside it.' He tossed the cane to Tobias. 'Keep the weight off your foot as much as possible. Now, come on. And do be sensible. I will give you your freedom, eventually. Petch will not.'

He stood back, and Tobias limped out of the room and pegged slowly down the stairs. The front door stood ajar.

'There is a gig outside. Get in.' Windlass closed the door behind them and leapt into the driver's seat. He took up the reins and clicked to the horse. Tobias shivered in the cool night air and watched the garden square disappear behind them, wondering what sort of thing now lay in its heart.

Twenty-six

Basement Four was a long, twisting passageway, with smaller tunnels sprouting at every turn and burrowing into the earth beneath the Castle like the roots of an enormous tree. Dust did not drift across the floor here, as it did in the higher basements. Instead, the damp seeping through the stone floor mixed with grit filtering from the walls to form a riverbed of slurry.

Her mother had worn a wide path through the slurry. Charlie forced herself not to run as she followed it. The track branched from the main passage almost at once and led far back, curving gently to the left the whole time, until Charlie was sure she was no longer beneath the Castle itself, but somewhere under the garden.

The passage grew narrower and the ceiling lowered itself until it was only a foot above Charlie's head. Her old fear of being shut in quivered at the edges of her mind, but she made herself walk on. She rounded a corner and the tunnel ended. A thick, curved wooden door, strapped and hinged with rusty iron, stood in front of her. It was shut. She put out her hand and took hold of the corroded door handle, turned it slowly, and pushed the door open.

For a moment, she stood in the doorway, blinking at the glare of light, and saw her mother turn from the table where she was standing and stare at her with shock and guilt. More guilt than shock, and Charlie knew that she had been right not to trust her mother. Because she was doing it again. She was making the thing that Windlass wanted. The thing he had wanted so much that he had murdered her father in an attempt to get it. She was making the crystals.

'So,' said her mother. 'You've tracked me down again. I was hoping for a bit more time.'

'Why?' Charlie asked.

The room had been hacked out of the rock upon which the Castle stood. It was more a cave than a room, with curved walls and a rough ceiling of lumpy stone. But it was large, well lit by kerosene lanterns, and obviously a sort of laboratory. Tables held scales, magnifying lenses on stands, racks of glass tubes full of powder, burners for heating chemicals. And one long table in the middle of the room carried what looked like a miniature railway track with a truncated ramp at one end, like a viaduct cut in half. The wall facing it was black with scorch marks and pockmarked with holes.

'Why didn't I want you to find me?' her mother asked. 'Or why am I recreating my research?'

'Why couldn't you tell me? Moleglass knows.'

'Yes. Ancel knows everything. And Topplesham.'

'But not me? Didn't you think I have a right to know about this? I lost you for five years because of your science. My father died for it!'

Her mother bowed her head, then raised it defiantly. 'No, Charlie. Your father died because he no longer wanted to be a weak king and a poor father. My science didn't kill him.'

'It did! It's at the root of everything. Windlass wanted it enough to enslave Father and an entire kingdom. What did you discover that Windlass wanted so much?'

Her mother looked at her, her face grave. 'Do you know how gunpowder is made?'

Charlie shook her head.

'Come,' said her mother, pulling out two chairs from a nearby table. 'Sit down. You're right. It is time you understood about the crystals. I've tried to protect you for too long.'

Charlie sat next to her mother and found she was trembling. She was about to find out why her life had changed forever when she was six years old.

'Gunpowder,' her mother began, 'is more correctly known as "black powder". It is a mixture of three substances: saltpetre, carbon, in the form of charcoal, and sulphur. Of these three, saltpetre is the most important and the most difficult to obtain. In much of the world it is derived from urine.'

'Ugh!' Charlie said.

'Yes.' Her mother smiled. 'It is a long, tedious, and

extremely smelly process. There are a few mineral deposits of saltpetre in the world, but they are nearly depleted.'

'Why is saltpetre so important?'

'It is a crystal, Charlie. That makes it interesting to me, but its importance as the main ingredient of black powder is as an oxidising agent.'

'Oxidising agent?'

'Put simply, it helps the fuel, carbon, combine with oxygen in order to create energy – an explosion. Left to itself, once lit, the carbon would simply burn like a lump coal, which is what it is. In order to create an explosion, the carbon must be made to combine rapidly with a large quantity of oxygen. The more oxygen, the bigger the explosion. Do you understand?'

'What does sulphur do?'

'It acts to control the process. The fuel, the carbon, is finely ground and thoroughly mixed with saltpetre. A small quantity of sulphur is added to keep the mixture from exploding randomly. Given the correct proportions, you have gunpowder. And you know what that does.'

'It kills people,' Charlie said, her voice icy.

'Precisely,' said her mother. 'Now I want to tell you a story. Do you remember the last time? It was the night I disappeared all those years ago. That story had a happy ending. This one almost certainly will not, although I am doing all I can to try to change that.' She put her arm around Charlie's shoulders and drew her close.

'Eighty years ago there was a war between the

countries of the Eastern and Western hemispheres. The West had large mineral deposits of saltpetre. The rulers of those countries grew rich trading saltpetre to Eastern countries such as ours. Alas, the Western rulers were greedy rather than wise. Their people were largely uneducated and poor, and their countries suffered from periods of drought, when many of their people starved.

'Instead of using the wealth from the saltpetre to educate their people, invest in irrigation systems or stockpile grain reserves in case of famine, the rulers of the West amassed huge personal fortunes. But greed is never satisfied. So they formed a coalition between themselves and began to blackmail the Eastern countries. The price of saltpetre soared. It became more costly than gold or diamonds. Quale could not afford to buy it. Not even the growing imperial power of Esceania could meet the price the Western coalition was demanding. So the inevitable happened.'

'War?'

'War. And the only blessing was that because of the shortage of saltpetre, the countries of the East sent their soldiers armed with sabres, swords and pikes, with long bows and crossbows. It was a medieval war fought on a modern scale: great sailing ships crossed the Western Ocean and spewed out a medieval army.'

'But the Western countries had saltpetre. So they must have had gunpowder.'

'Oh, they did. But relatively few muskets or cannon.

And the East had refined enough saltpetre from urine to fuel an equal number of firearms. The war was brutal, but relatively short. Fewer women, children and old people died in the Saltpetre War than in any other war of that century, purely because of technology. It is much harder to kill quantities of human beings when armed only with bows and arrows or blades.'

Charlie shuddered. She had not lived through a war, and although the threat of Esceania always hovered at the edges of her mind, she had never really thought about war like this before: about the tools and machines human beings created to kill one another.

Her mother continued: 'The East triumphed. Quale and Esceania had formed an uneasy alliance, and the smaller Eastern nations looked to us for leadership. We colonised the Western countries, absorbed them into our empires, and used the saltpetre mines to fuel our colonial expansion into the Northern and Southern hemispheres. But everything runs out in time, and the saltpetre reserves in the Western hemisphere are nearly depleted. Explorers have been sent throughout the word, searching for other reserves, but none have yet been found.'

Charlie frowned up at her mother. She thought she could see where this was leading.

'Your father and I,' her mother said with a sigh, 'were naive and foolish. We were glad that saltpetre was running out. We hoped that a world where the technology of death is limited might be a more peaceful one. But then Alistair

Windlass came to us with disturbing news. Our spies had learnt of vast stockpiles of saltpetre stolen secretly over the years from the Western deposits and brought by shiploads to Esceania. We had been double-crossed by our ally. Esceania was playing a long game: they would wait until the other Eastern countries had run out of gunpowder, and then expand their empire until they ruled the entire world. And that time was nearly upon us.'

Her mother blinked, seemed to come to herself and looked down at Charlie. 'So you see,' she said. 'When Alistair asked me to try and synthesise saltpetre, I felt I had no choice but to try my best.'

'And you succeeded.' Charlie shivered. This was why her mother had run away. This was why her father was dead.

'No. I never managed to synthesise saltpetre.'

Charlie stared at her in amazement.

'I created something new.' Her mother sighed. 'Something worse, Charlie. Far, far worse.'

Twenty-seven

'Petch will turn the City upside down till he finds us. He don't give up.'

'Neither do I,' said Windlass. 'It's a big city, and Petch's lair is in the heart of it. Even his resources are finite. He'll find the new suburbs more difficult to negotiate.'

The horse clopped forward steadily, its iron shoes striking an occasional spark from the cobbles. When the clattering changed to the crunch of macadam, Tobias's head jerked up. He had dozed off. They were heading north, towards the miles of terraces of new brick houses devouring the countryside.

'This is daft,' he said, as though the conversation had never stopped. 'You're just putting off the inevitable. Petch'll find us. Why don't you get out of the country? Just go! Either Petch'll slit your gullet, or someone'll recognise you and you'll end with a rope round your neck.'

'I thought that's what you wanted.' His father's voice was light and smooth. He had no reply, so he stayed silent, struggling to sort the confusion in his mind. What did he want?

'I want things to be like they used to,' he said at last, above the rumble of the iron-rimmed wheels.

'Except that you aren't the same person. And which part of your past do you want to return to? The time when your stepfather was alive, beating you and your mother? Or the time when you slaved in the Castle gardens and your mother worked herself to exhaustion for Mrs O'Dair?'

'Them was both your fault!' Hatred raged afresh and spat itself out of his mouth.

'Yes.'

And that was all. No apology. No regret. Merely an acknowledgement of fact. 'Why are you doing this?'

Silence.

'When are you going to tell me what you're after? Why did you take me off Petch? Why not just leave me back there?'

The clopping of the horse's hooves was the only answer he got. He turned his head and stared at the profile of the man seated next to him. It was an attractive, intelligent face. The face of a man of no background who had raised himself to become Prime Minister. It should have belonged to a good man, even a great one. Instead, it might as well belong to the man in the moon. It was smooth and smiling and stuffed full of false promises and lies. Unlike Zebediah, whom he understood only too well, he couldn't fathom Alistair Windlass. The man was a monster. Best leave it at that, and be done with him.

'One thing puzzles me,' his father said. 'Having come

to know you slightly over the past weeks and become even more familiar with the extent of your sheer pigheadedness—'

Tobias snorted.

'—I wonder how Petch convinced you to steal for him. Your mother no doubt did her best to instill her somewhat primitive moral code in you. I'm convinced you would not willingly embark on a career as a thief.'

'No.' The word was a grunt.

'Did he beat you?'

'No.' His mind had built a wall around the whipping Zebediah had given him. He wouldn't speak of that to anyone, least of all this man.

'Then what, Tobias? What was his hold over you?'

The sound of the wheels spun a hypnotic peacefulness out of the night, and Tobias found himself answering. 'He threatened to kill someone.'

'Your mother?' The words were sharp.

'Mr Moleglass.'

'Ah. So that's why…'

'What?'

'You haven't mentioned the Castle or your friends. You have no intention of returning and endangering Moleglass, do you? What a noble little idiot you are! If I were to let you go, what would you propose to do after that, alone in Petch's City without friends or protection? How do you imagine you would survive? He's a shark and you're a tiddler. He would swallow you whole.'

'What do you care?' He couldn't keep the bitterness out of his voice. It had seeped deep into his soul in the years he had watched his father from afar. The grand Alistair Windlass, who had cast him off before he was born.

'I didn't steal you out from under Petch's nose, setting him on my trail and dislocating my shoulder in the process, just to hand you back to him.'

'Dislocating your...' Tobias turned his head and frowned at his father. 'What do you mean?'

'It doesn't matter.'

'Was that why you was wearing a sling? I thought it was because I slammed the door on your arm.'

'Singularly unobservant. That was my right arm, which you bruised most effectively.'

'Then how did you—'

'You must weigh over six stone. Six stone falling nearly twenty feet is enough to dislocate anyone's shoulder.'

'I *fell* on you?'

'I caught you. Or tried to.'

The journey continued in silence as Tobias struggled to digest the notion that Alistair Windlass had almost certainly saved his life.

The eastern sky was bleaching pale when Windlass turned the gig into a newly built mews. He stopped in front of one of the stables, jumped down, pulled wide the stable door, lit a lantern, guided the horse and gig inside, and began to unfasten the traces. Tobias remained in the gig, slumped in a half-doze, listening to the clink of the harness, the horse blowing and stamping; smelling the rich reek of horse and watching his father in the golden glow of the lantern.

Windlass worked quickly and efficiently; soon the horse was unharnessed, curried, blanketed, and shut in its stall with a manger of hay. He turned to the gig and saw Tobias watching him. 'Well?' he said.

'I'm just surprised you know your way round a horse, that's all. You got muck all over them fancy boots.'

Windlass grinned up at him, looking, for a moment, almost human. 'They'll clean,' he said. 'That would be your job, I think, as you can't make yourself useful in any other way.'

'If you think I'm cleaning your—' The sight of his father's grin stretching wider shut his mouth.

Windlass pulled a carpet bag out of the back of the gig and reached a hand up to help him down. 'I started work as a stable hand when I was fourteen,' he said. 'My father took me out of grammar school on my birthday and put me to work. I never forgave him.' The grin had gone.

'My grandad,' Tobias said. 'Who was he?'

'A farrier in Reavedale. Up north.'

'Mum comes from there. Is that where you met?' But Windlass ignored the question. He stood, holding the stable door open.

'Hurry, please. I want a few hours' sleep.' He led the

way through the mews to the row of houses fronting onto the road. They were newly built, the bricks raw, the front gardens rectangles of mud. Windlass strode up the short path and unlocked the door. Tobias stepped into a dark, narrow hall smelling of wallpaper paste and varnish.

He heard the chink of a key in a lock, and then Windlass took his arm and pushed him up the stairs and into a small room at the back. 'In here. The bed is made up; there's a chamber pot should you need it. And water in the jug. Get some sleep if you can. I'll wake you mid-morning. And, Tobias, the window is barred and the door will be locked, so you needn't waste energy exploring. You'll find a nightshirt beneath the pillow. Goodnight.'

'Wait!'

'What?'

Tobias stared through the stripes of dawn light filtering through the barred window, searching without luck for his father's eyes. 'Who was it? Back in the square?'

'I didn't recognise him.'

'And…did you…What happened?'

Windlass turned and left the room without another word. Tobias heard the key turn swiftly, ruthlessly, in the lock.

He woke in a panic. Where was he? He lunged up in the bed, heart pounding, and saw sunshine streaming through a barred window, remembered the lock clicking. He was somewhere, nowhere, lost in a maze of red-brick houses and mud. He sat on the edge of the bed and listened. Silence. Not a sound of Windlass. Was the house empty? What time was it?

He grabbed the cane off the floor where he'd dropped it the night before, peg-legged to the window. It looked out over a scrap of back garden, the privy pushed against a raw wooden fence at the back. Beyond a narrow access road were identical gardens in reverse. Brick walls divided up the weed and rubble into squares on a games board. There was no sign of a living human being.

The top sash of his window was pulled down a few inches to let in air. He squeezed his hand through the bars and tried to push open the lower sash. It wouldn't move, and he saw that it had been nailed shut. He limped to the door. Locked. He retreated to the bed and flopped onto it, staring at the ceiling. Not even books, now, to get him through the waiting. Unless... He swivelled his head and spotted a small bookcase beside the wardrobe. He sat up slowly, shaking his head in a weariness of admiration. The man thought of everything.

Except food. Tobias snapped the book shut and sat up with an irritated hiss of hunger and pain. His stomach was empty and his leg was complaining. He rubbed the long jagged scar on his shin. The splints and bandages had come off two weeks ago, but the leg still felt hollow and spindly. And ached at odd moments, like now.

It was evening. Shadows slanted longways. Windlass

had been gone all day. The worry had been growing on him for hours. Had Zebediah got him? Windlass might be dead, and no one would know to come here and unlock the door. Panic washed over him and he fought it off with difficulty. He'd get out. Find some way to break the window. The houses either side seemed to be empty, but he could shout. Shout for hours till someone heard. If they did.

He grabbed his stick and jumped off the bed. For a moment he stared at the window, racked with uncertainty. Then he gripped the stick tightly and rammed its ebony head between the bars. The pane of glass shattered and half of it fell onto the invisible pavement below with a brittle crunch. He turned the cane around and used the small end to punch at the jagged shards sticking out from the frame, sending them spiralling out of sight. He was about to smash the second pane when he heard the front door open and close. Footsteps climbed the stairs.

Relief was washed aside by a wave of fear. The window! He turned to face the door, clutching the stick so tightly his knuckles turned white. It wasn't much defence, but no way would Windlass hit him and not get something back. He was done taking beatings.

The door opened and Windlass stopped on the threshold, taking in Tobias and the stick. His eyes flicked to the window, widened slightly, then returned to Tobias's face.

'My fault for being so late,' he said. 'I'm sorry, but it

was unavoidable. Come downstairs now and let's find something to eat. You must be starving. I certainly am.' Without another word, he turned and left the room, and Tobias heard his footsteps patter down the stairs and disappear into the room below. He stood, frozen in amazement, until hunger drove him after his father.

Windlass was in the kitchen, his jacket hung on the back of a chair, his shirtsleeves rolled up. He was slicing bread. 'Shall we eat in here?' he said. 'As it's easier. Set the table, will you? Plates are on the dresser.'

Tobias hobbled between dresser and table, setting out plates, cutlery and glasses. Windlass brought ham, cheese, a jar of mustard and a large earthenware jug from the larder and set everything in the middle of the table. He slumped into a chair with a groan and closed his eyes for a moment before leaning forward and attacking the food. He piled bread, ham and cheese onto Tobias's plate, and then his own. They ate in unison, silently, intently, until the first pangs subsided.

Windlass leant back, rubbed his eyes, sighed, and reached for the earthenware jug. He uncorked it, poured out two glasses of small beer and handed one to Tobias, who watched his father down his beer in one go, refill it, and cut a new slice from the ham. Windlass's face was pale, his eyes red-rimmed. He looked as though he hadn't slept. Except for the time in the dungeons, Tobias had never seen Alistair Windlass looking so dishevelled. His hair flopped across his forehead, his boots bore traces of mud, his shirt was rumpled and Tobias smelt the acrid tang of dried sweat.

'You're in a state,' he said, through a mouthful of bread and ham. 'What have you been doing? Something's up, isn't it?'

'I need a wash and a change of clothes,' said his father. 'And we need to talk. But first, I fear, I must get some sleep. I'm sorry, Tobias, but I have to lock you in again. I can't trust you not to run off and Petch would have you in fifteen minutes if you showed your face in the City. His men are everywhere.'

'You had a run-in with the Petches? I knew it! I told you to get out of the City. What happened?'

'Not now, Tobias. I'm too tired. Bring the plate with you, but I want you upstairs, please.'

Windlass paused before locking his door. 'Don't knock out any more glass, son. The only result will be a draughty bedroom. Most of this estate is empty. You could shout for days and no one would hear. I shall sleep for three hours, then we'll talk.'

Three and a half hours later, the door opened. Windlass's face floated above a candle flame. 'I've lit a fire in the sitting room. Come. We might as well be comfortable.'

It was a small, square room with a bay window and a narrow cast-iron fireplace. The curtains were drawn, a coal fire burned in the grate, and a gate-legged table held a teapot, cups, plates and a large fruit cake. 'I don't know about you,' said Windlass, 'but I'm hungry again. Sit down and I'll pour the tea.'

He was wearing grey flannel trousers and a dark blue smoking jacket, a silk cravat loosely tied at his throat. His hair was smooth and gleaming. Tobias sat in one of the two armchairs, feeling a hysterical desire to laugh pushing up his throat. He took his teacup in shaking fingers and watched his father relax into the other chair, cross one long, elegant leg over the other, and sit eating cake and sipping tea.

'You're the strangest man I've ever met,' he blurted. 'Sitting there as though you hadn't a care in the world. Togged out in your fancy clothes, smelling sweet as a daisy. I'll never understand you.'

Windlass looked up at him. His eyes shone silver over his teacup. 'Would you rather I stank?' he asked with a smile. 'You could use a bath yourself, you know.'

Tobias blushed, then scowled at his father. 'I've other things on me mind just now. Like what happened earlier. Did the Petches catch up with you?'

'Let's just say they got closer than was comfortable.' Windlass put his teacup down on the table with a sigh. 'Very well, the time has come for a serious discussion.'

'So what happened?' Tobias persisted.

'I had business in town. But it soon became obvious that this beard is no longer a sufficient disguise. Your stepcousins had a good, long look at me that night. I rather fear they have recognised me from the wanted posters, which complicates things somewhat.'

Tea sloshed out of Tobias's cup and splashed onto his lap. 'Ow! Blasted—' he jumped out of his chair, spilling more tea. 'What do you mean?' he shouted, thumping his cup onto the table with a clatter. 'And stop laughing, it's not bloody funny!'

Windlass put back his head and roared.

'Shut up, will you?' Tobias was near hysterics himself. The damp patch on his trousers was no longer scalding and he sat back down, all too aware of looking as though he'd wet himself. 'It wasn't that funny.'

'Oh, it was.' Windlass sighed, sniffed. 'Thanks, Tobias. I haven't laughed so much in…' The laughter died from his eyes. 'Well. A long time.'

Shock jolted Tobias: punched him in the stomach. He had forgotten. He had actually forgotten. He was starting to forget, for minutes, sometimes hours, what this man had done. Charlie's face floated before his eyes and he blinked, stared at the floor. What was wrong with him? He was sitting having tea with Alistair Windlass, traitor and murderer! Laughing with him! His father, who, only a few months ago, had killed the King and threatened to kill him, his own son. Tobias groaned and put his face in his hands.

He hadn't cried when Zebediah strapped him or belted him in the mouth. He hadn't cried since he was eight years old and Barty Petch had been found floating face down in the canal. He cried now. Now, in front of the man he hated most in the world. Tears flooded out of his eyes, sobs choked his throat, and his shoulders shook as weeping mastered him.

'Tobias...Tobias, please stop.'

'Damn you!' His voice broke between the sobs, deep and husky one moment, squeaking the next. 'Just go away! Leave me alone, can't you? Have the decency for once in your life to do something for someone besides yourself and go away and never come back!'

'I'll go, Tobias,' Windlass said. 'I'll go on one condition. Here.' Something dropped in his lap. He shuddered, made a tremendous effort and stopped crying. He took the handkerchief, wiped his face and looked at his father. One pair of pale blue eyes stared into the other.

'What?' he said. 'What condition?'

'That you go with me.' Windlass's face was without expression, but his eyes glowed with such intensity that Tobias couldn't look away.

'You're mad,' he gasped, certain that he'd found the truth of it, made sense, at last, of his life. 'You must be. Mad! Why would I go with you?'

'Because you're my son, and I love you.'

Tobias felt the blood drain from his face. 'Liar,' he said. 'You never loved anyone but yourself.'

'That isn't true.' Windlass shut his eyes and rested his head on the back of the chair. Then opened them and stared at the ceiling for a long moment before looking at Tobias once more. 'But I understand why you should think so. I have loved four people in my life.

'I loved my mother. She died a few days before my fourteenth birthday. I loved your mother. I met Rose when we were hardly out of childhood, and I loved her because she loved me. I didn't think anyone could, you see. And over the past weeks, to my amazement, and – if I'm honest – against my better judgement, I have found that I love my son. You, Tobias. More, perhaps, than all the others.'

Twenty-eight

'What?' cried Charlie. 'What did you make?'

'I'll show you,' her mother said. She rose from her chair and went to the work table with the railway track. Working with quick, graceful movements, she took a small metal tube from a box under the table, went to another table and filled the tube with a fine black powder. Then she fitted a pointed metal hat to the open end and returned to the long table. She placed the tube in a metal carriage with four wheels, which sat at the lower end of the track. Then she turned to Charlie. She held out a packet of safety matches. 'Would you like to light the fuse?' she asked.

Charlie looked at the twist of string protruding from the bottom of the tube and took a step backwards. She shook her head. Her mother seemed another person: cold, efficient, clinical. It scared her. And whatever was inside that metal tube scared her even more.

The Dowager's smile was brief and bitter. 'I think you're right, darling. I'll do it.' She struck a match, and the reek of sulphur stung Charlie's nostrils as her mother turned and lit the end of the fuse. A spark hissed, glowed, then darted up the string and into the small black tube.

There was a bang like a firework exploding. Charlie jumped and backed away as the tube shook like a beast trying to free itself from its bonds. Fire belched from its end and the tube shot forward, propelling the carriage along the track. The carriage stopped at the end of the track, but the tube did not. It leapt into the air and flew fierce and straight as an arrow, whining like a mad hornet, and smashed into the stone wall. A sheet of fire engulfed the wall and an explosion shook the floor beneath Charlie's feet. She screamed and dropped to her knees, but the explosion was over. Drifts of bitter-tasting smoke wafted through the air, and she heard the sound of pebbles dropping onto stone.

Charlie climbed to her feet and walked on shaking legs towards the blackened wall. A new hole had been dug out of it, large enough to hold both her fists. It glowed and smoked as though it lay at the heart of a volcano. Charlie turned a horrified face towards her mother.

The Dowager stood, tall and beautiful, her hair curling like a golden thicket around her face. 'It's a new form of explosive,' she said. 'I synthesised a crystal which contains within it both the carbon fuel and the oxidising agent. Its ability to oxidise its carbon element is so efficient that the energy released is beyond anything previously known. And the gases the chemical reaction release act, as you have seen, as the perfect propellant. It is a rocket bomb. A high-explosive rocket, which can be launched from a distance at a target or dropped from airships.'

'What I have done, my child, is invent a new technology for killing people. For killing people by the dozens, by the hundreds, perhaps thousands. I have done nothing less than invent a new way of waging war, where those who die will not be soldiers on a battlefield, but entire cities – and the children, women and men who live in them.'

Charlie thought she would remember the journey back from the cellars, holding her mother's chilly hand, for the rest of her life. She stayed in the Dowager's bedroom that night. She did not want to leave her mother alone and Caroline seemed pleased to have her near, although she was silent and withdrawn. Neither of them slept. At dawn, Charlie sent for the Prime Minister. The audience chamber was cold and draughty. They drew their chairs close to the hastily lit fire, and Charlie watched the flames flicker across her mother's face. Caroline seemed near to emotional collapse, but the questions had to be asked.

'I understand the technology, Mother. Enough of it, at any rate. What I don't understand is where Alistair Windlass stands in all this. Why did you tell him about this crystal you'd made? Why didn't you just destroy any evidence of your experiment and forget you'd ever done it?' Charlie couldn't keep the edge out of her voice, although she tried.

'It was the greatest mistake of my life, Charlie. I will

die regretting it, but I can't change the past. Science does not allow that. Yet.' Her mother gave a wan smile.

'And you must remember that Alistair was Prime Minister,' Caroline continued. 'He was also a close friend. He had expressed an interest in my scientific research for years. As Prime Minister, he had asked me to attempt to synthesise saltpetre; it was inevitable that he should enquire about my progress. Hardly a day went by that he did not visit my laboratory. It would have been difficult, if not impossible, to hide the results of my experiments. But I didn't try. I synthesised this new crystal and saw the implications at once. I had no illusions about the use that would be made of it. I told Alistair the latest attempt was a failure. Then I made the mistake of telling him why.

'I'll never forget...' Her mother's voice faltered. 'I'll never forget the look in his eyes. It was as though I'd never truly seen the man before.'

Charlie saw with a shock that her mother was crying. Tears welled on her bottom eyelids and rolled slowly down her cheeks. The Dowager sighed. 'When I realised what Alistair wanted to do with my research, I knew I would have to disappear. I couldn't take all my papers with me, so I destroyed the most dangerous.'

'And just what did Windlass want to do with your research?' Charlie asked. 'Did he tell you?'

'Yes.' Her mother's voice was full of pain. 'Enough, anyway. But he's quick, Alistair. Adept at reading people. And I wasn't good at disguising my reaction. I was horrified.

I couldn't believe that a man I trusted…someone I thought I knew as well as I knew myself…'

'What did he want it for?' Charlie's voice was sharp.

'Power, darling. What else?' The Dowager shook her head. 'Oh, he wrapped it up in pretty colours: talked about seeing off the Esceanian threat once and for all; about a weapon which would put an end to war forever. I expect he even mean some of it. But it was power he was after. He's a politician, my child. A clever, clever man who rose from nowhere to the greatest position of power in Quale. And it wasn't enough. Nothing is ever enough for him. He's a born adventurer, Charlie. He would use my crystals to conquer the world. With as little bloodshed as possible, to give him credit. He does value human life. But not enough to let it stand in the way of what he wants. That, my love, is Alistair Windlass.'

'And that,' said Topplesham suddenly, from the depths of his armchair, 'is why the man has got to die. Once he's dead, the crystals can die too. Your mother can destroy her papers, destroy every last speck of crystal, and the world will carry on much as it's always done: bumbling and tottering, but getting through it somehow. But as long as Windlass is alive, he'll carry the knowledge of this power with him and he won't give up. Even if he has to find another scientist and get them to duplicate your mother's results.'

'That is unlikely,' said the Dowager. 'But not impossible, I suppose. Alistair studied what I was doing at the time. But he would have to be very lucky.'

'The man has the devil's own luck!' Topplesham muttered. 'I've had every spy in my employ after him with a shoot-on-sight policy. Nothing. Nothing! It's as though he's disappeared off the face of the Earth.'

'But surely,' Charlie cried, 'Windlass is the very reason we must destroy the papers and the crystals now! Why have you been making more crystals? And recreating your papers? You have! Don't deny it!'

'Don't get all huffy with your mother, Charlie.' Topplesham said. 'I asked her to. Well, ordered, really.'

'What?!' Charlie sat up straight, stared at Topplesham in disbelief. 'Why would you do such a thing?'

'We are on the brink of war. The only thing stopping the Esceanians is the fear that we have the crystals ready to use. The situation is even more desperate now that Windlass is on the loose. If he gets to Esceania, he'll sell the lot of us. He'll promise them the crystals in exchange for Quale. The only way to prevent a full-scale invasion is to have the weapon made and ready to use.'

'I can't believe what I'm hearing!' Charlie jumped to her feet. 'You want to use it?'

'No!' Topplesham puffed and patted his red face with his handkerchief. His little puffy eyes stared at her miserably. 'That's the last thing I ever want to do! But if it comes down to using your mother's crystals or letting Esceania and Windlass have Quale for dinner and the rest of the world for desert, well...yes, Charlie. I'll use 'em.'

271

Twenty-nine

'I won't go with you!'

'Then I must remain here, Tobias. I can't abandon you to Petch.'

'You abandoned me for thirteen years. Why stop now?'

'I've told you why.'

'And I don't believe you!'

The conversation continued at the breakfast table as though it had never stopped. 'You want me to think you're some sort of reformed character,' Tobias said. 'Well, forget it. A snake can shed his skin, but he's still the same viper underneath.'

Windlass gave an exasperated sigh and continued buttering toast. 'You are incredibly pigheaded!' He raised frowning eyes. 'I could compel you,' he said. 'But I would rather you came willingly. Think logically, Tobias. You have no other alternative.

'You refuse to return to the Castle because of the threat to Moleglass. I don't know if Petch was bluffing or not, but the truth is that as long as he's at large, neither you nor Moleglass would be safe. If you decided to go back to the Castle and give evidence against your uncle you would put your own life at risk. The Petch family is spread like a disease through the City. The police could not possibly take them all. Any informer against Zebediah Petch would have, I think, a short life expectancy. And you certainly can't survive on your own in the City. Petch would snap you up within a day.'

'It's none of your damn business what happens to me,' Tobias growled. 'I...I'll get out of the City. Go north. I can get a job gardening somewheres.'

'You hate gardening.'

'So what?'

'Petch would find you within the week.'

'You don't know that! You think you know everything! You think you're so clever. If you're so clever, why are there wanted posters all over the City with your face on them? If you're so clever, why aren't you still Prime Minister, instead of a convicted felon with a price on your head?'

Windlass's eyes turned from pale gentian to silver. 'We both know why,' he said, his voice as cold as his eyes. 'Because you decided to play hero. You and Charlie, between you. You've had your revenge, Tobias, for my abandonment. I have sat in the condemned cell, knowing I was about to die. In a way, I did die. That life is over, for both of us. We need to start again.'

'I can't forget what you did. And I can't forgive it. Not ever.' Tobias spoke in a kind of despair.

His father nodded, unsmiling. 'I understand that. I don't ask you to forgive me. I ask you to come with me out of the country to a place of safety where we can both recover from the events of the past months. I ask for your company for the period of one year, Tobias. One year only. After that, you may go wherever you wish, do whatever you wish. With my assistance, both practical and financial.'

'I don't want your money!' Tobias closed his eyes against the tears that threatened to break out again. Windlass's logic was beating him down. He searched frantically for a weapon. 'It's dirty.'

'You can't survive on your own, Tobias. Just at the moment, you need me.'

'I'd rather take my chances.'

'And go back to being Zebediah's pet monkey?' The contempt in his father's voice was intolerable.

'Better than being yours!' he spat.

Windlass put down his cup, raised furious eyes that froze Tobias to his chair. He realised that – for the first time – he was seeing Alistair Windlass without his icy control. 'You little idiot!' His father's voice was low and deadly. 'Petch will drag you so deep into the mire you'll never climb out. He'll tie you to him with theft and murder. He wants you body and soul, and he won't stop until you're as corrupt as he is.

'I'm offering you a way out. I want your companionship – not your soul! One year and you're free. No strings, Tobias. No conditions. Or do you feel that you have to prove your hatred of me by destroying yourself?!'

He couldn't move, couldn't speak. He stared into the sky of his father's eyes, and what he saw shocked him to his very core.

'You'll come with me?'

'One year,' he whispered.

'One year,' said his father.

Snippets of black hair floated from his head to encircle him.

'I don't know who hacked off your hair, but it's been butchered,' Windlass grumbled. 'It'll take months for this to grow out properly, but at least we'll get rid of the black. Piebald hair would attract more attention than is agreeable.' He worked round him with comb and scissors, round and round, till Tobias was ready to scream.

'Leave off,' he said. 'It don't have to be posh, just all one colour.'

'When I get you to Esceania, my son, you'll learn what a haircut is. And a tailor. And you'll certainly become more acquainted with soap and water than hitherto.'

'I washed this morning.'

'That was a wasted effort then. You'll have a bath when I'm finished.'

'I won't!'

'You will, if I have to put you in it. You're as ripe as a Gorgonzola cheese, and I will not travel in a confined space with someone smelling as you do.'

'Plenty of breeze on board ship,' Tobias grumbled.

'We share a cabin. Twenty portholes would not provide sufficient ventilation. We shall have one.'

'Very funny.' He glared sourly up at his father, who was spruce and odour-free as usual. 'Humans is supposed to smell. We're animals, like horses and dogs. They smell. It ain't natural to wash as much as you do.'

'Isn't. It isn't natural. And according to your logic, we should live in caves and eat our meat raw. No thank you, son. The main advantage we humans have over the other animals is that we can choose not to live as they do. There, finished. Come into the kitchen for your bath, please. The copper should be boiling by now. And then, we have an appointment.'

'An appointment? At this time of night? Where?'

'With my informant. In the City.'

Tobias opened the door of the sitting room to see his father break apart a revolver and spin the chamber, inserting bullets. Windless snapped the chamber closed and raised his eyes to Tobias's face. 'Are you ready?'

The sight of a pistol in his father hands sent a sickening judder through his stomach. 'Who are you planning to shoot?' he said, controlling his voice with difficulty.

'The price on my head,' Windlass said, 'is paid whether I'm dead or alive. Dead is not only easier for Petch, it's safer. He can collect the reward and not have to worry about news of his own activities reaching the ears of the authorities.'

'Then why go into the City? Let's just find that boat of yours and get on it! Do you want to end up dead?'

'No,' said his father. He slid the revolver into a shoulder holster. 'This trip is unavoidable. Believe me, I would not risk it otherwise. Now, a change of clothing, please.'

For the first time, Tobias noticed Windlass's clothes. His normally elegant father was wearing filthy brown trousers, a moleskin waistcoat and a coarse striped shirt. Now he shrugged into a short, shabby black coat, concealing the pistol, and nodded his head to a jacket and trousers flung across an armchair. 'On with them, please.'

The clothes were dirty and torn. Tobias hesitated, wanting to refuse, to argue again about the madness of this trip. He looked up at his father, and felt his courage slide away. With a sick feeling in the pit of his stomach, he realised he was more afraid of this man than he'd ever been of Zebediah Petch and an army of stepcousins. It made no sense. Windlass didn't hit him, wouldn't kill him. He knew that now. So why was he afraid? What was he scared of? Tobias looked away, busied himself dressing. When he couldn't put it off any longer, he glanced up, and his mouth dropped open.

Windlass's eyes were hidden behind spectacles with round, smoked lenses. He gripped a white-tipped cane. 'A blind man and his boy,' he said, pulling a battered hat low on his forehead. 'Like a thousand other beggars in the City. Pathetic. Unimportant. Seen and forgotten in a moment. Pull your cap low, Tobias. Shade your eyes and keep them fastened on the ground. Remember, you are guiding me over uneven pavements. Cap down, face down, and we shall pass unnoticed.'

It was a mile's trudge through the rutted mud of the suburban streets before they found a cab. Tobias's leg began to ache before they had gone halfway. He had not walked without the cane before, and each step sent a ripple of pain from ankle to knee. Windlass reached out and gripped him under the arm. 'Let me take your weight,' he said. 'Keep off that leg as much as possible.' The pain eased, but it was all Tobias could do not to tear his arm from his father's grip.

A hansom cab crouched in front of an inn on the main road to town, the driver dozing in his seat, the horse dozing in its traces.

'Gi'us a ride into town,' said Windlass, his voice blurred in a northern drawl.

'You?' scoffed the cabbie, yawning hugely. 'Show us your brass, blind man. If you've got any.'

'How much?' Windlass rifled in his coat pocket and pulled out a handful of coins.

'Half-crown for the two of you.'

'Highway robbery! I'll gi'ye two bob.'

'The fare's half-crown. If you ain't got it, shove off.'

'Bleedin' cheek,' muttered Windlass. 'Here, boy. Find us a half-crown in this lot and show the man.' He held out the coins, and Tobias dug out a large, silvery half-crown and held it up.

'You get it when we gets there,' Windlass said. 'Now help me into the cab, boy.'

'Where d'you wanna go?' called the cabbie as they climbed in.

'Flearside!' Windlass replied. Tobias stiffened and shot his father an amazed stare.

'You would,' grumbled the cabbie, snapping the reins to wake his horse. 'Low-lifes and beggars in me cab now. What's the world comin' to?'

The horse clattered along the macadam of the main road, and Windlass groped in a pocket and pulled out a clay pipe. He thumbed tobacco into the bowl and lit the pipe. Soon drifts of smoke wafted up into the sky. It was a bright, moonlit night. Tobias glanced at his father and saw that the pipe was the final piece of the disguise: gripping it in his teeth changed the shape of Windlass's jaw. Clothes, spectacles and pipe combined to make him almost unrecognisable.

'I trust the smoke doesn't bother you?' his father murmured.

'No,' said Tobias. 'I have a pipe myself sometimes.'

'Not any more you don't. I agree with Charlie. Smoking isn't good for children. She has quite an aversion to tobacco smoke, as I recollect.'

'Don't talk about her!' hissed Tobias through gritted teeth.

'Sorry.' Windlass's voice was cool.

'And why the blazes are you taking us to Flearside? Are you mad?'

'I sincerely trust not. It's the last place Petch will be looking for us. Right under his nose. I'm not a fool. Even you must admit that. And I have every intention of surviving. Hate me if you must, Tobias, but don't underestimate me. That would be a mistake.' He smiled around his pipe and blew a great puff of smoke into the air.

Tobias stared at him in amazement. 'You're enjoying this!'

His father's spectacles reflected the shine of the moon. He grinned. 'Aren't you? Don't you feel even the slightest thrill at the adventure? The risk? Admit it; you do. I heard it in your voice the night you cracked that safe of mine. You loved it. You're my son, Tobias. You can't deny your inheritance forever.'

'I'm nothing like you!' Tobias clenched his fists and stared at the road in front of them, at the horse's bobbing neck and uninterested ears. Windlass settled back into the cracked, leather seat and the rest of the journey passed in silence.

The cabbie dropped them off in a dingy street in the heart of Flearside. Tobias recognised it: the street with the pub. His heart began to pound, and he shot Windlass a quick glance. What was he up to?

His father held the cane in front of him. 'Your arm, boy,' he growled. 'Keep your eye on these blasted pavements. I've no mind to be tumbled into a ditch. An' it happens, you'll smart from my cane!'

Windlass glinted a sharp eye at him over the top of his spectacles and reached out his arm. Tobias took it and began the sham of guiding a blind man. He kept his face down, his cap pulled low. His heart was thudding in his ears, and his stomach felt full of sour apples. Enjoy himself? The man was mad. And yet…like a maggot in his brain, the thought kept wriggling: there was an aliveness. It had been the same when he'd gone housebreaking with Perce: the tingle in his blood, the buzzing quickness in his brain. He shot a glance at Windlass and saw the hint of a smile stretching the man's lips as he chewed on his pipe stem.

The street was empty, the pub lantern dark. It must be two in the morning. Where was Windlass taking him? And who were they meeting at this time of night, in Flearside? Down several alleys, stepping over rotting muck, overflowing sewers. The smell of Flearside dug into Tobias's nostrils, rank and unforgettable. And the thought sneaked into his head with sullen satisfaction: *I bet he's not enjoying this.*

Windlass guided him while appearing to be led. Tobias was soon lost in a maze of winding, narrow lanes. The houses either side were sinking into rottenness. The ground sank with them, and he smelt a new rottenness: the unmistakable stench of the river. Sewage and seaweed, salt, muck and decay. He heard it lapping its brown wet tongue against the wharves and warehouses. Windlass led him in a twisting path down steps, along the wharf front, beside warehouses with blackened windows for eyes.

'What are we doing here?' Tobias hissed.

'Shhh!' His father gripped his arm in painful warning, led him alongside the river. Tobias felt a sudden fear of that brown water licking at his feet. He couldn't swim. One push, one slip and…Windlass stopped, looked at him, his eyes invisible behind dark lenses. His fingers still digging in Tobias's arm, he turned to the warehouse behind them and knocked on a small, wooden door: three times, gently. Pause. Five times. Pause. Twice.

Tobias's heart was clattering in his chest as he watched the door swing slowly inward almost at once. Before he could see who had opened the door, Windlass grabbed his shoulders and pushed him inside. Tobias tripped, sprawled forward on hands and knees onto a rough stone floor. The smell of the place rang alarm bells in his head. It couldn't be!

He scrabbled to his feet and whirled round. The warehouse was lit with a single dark lantern. By its light, he saw two figures: Windlass – and someone smaller. Much smaller.

The smaller figure launched forward and embedded itself in his middle, squeezing with thin, monkey arms. 'Tobe! Oh, I'm so happy to see you. Gosh, I missed you! We're

282

gonna be together now. Isn't it great?'

Horrified, Tobias stared at his father. Windlass was watching him. He had taken off his spectacles. His eyes were narrowed, calculating, and the look in them made Tobias's blood freeze to its very marrow.

'Ambrose!' Tobias hissed. He grabbed the boy's shoulders and gave him a shake. 'What are you doing here? You shouldn't be here! Get out, now! Go back to bed!'

The boy stared up at him, his face blank with dismay. 'But...I'm comin' with you, Tobe. Your dad said I could. He's gonna pay to send me to engineering school.'

Tobias raised his eyes to his father's face. Cold horror battled rage. Windlass watched him, his eyes glinting, the hint of a smile lurking on his lips. 'So,' Tobias said, 'this is your informant. You rotten—'

'Careful, Tobias!' Windlass's voice cut the darkness like a knife. 'This isn't the time or place. Take Ambrose out—'

'No!' He looked down at his cousin. 'Ambrose, you can't come. You gotta go back to the house. I'm sorry, but it's too dangerous.'

'You promised!' cried the boy. 'You promised to take me with you. You swore it, Tobe.'

'Yes. I'll come back for you. I will – I swear, Ambrose. But not now. Not with him. You don't know—'

'Course I do,' said Ambrose. 'He's the traitor. The one they're all after. He killed the King.'

Tobias stared at the boy in disbelief.

'Ambrose and I have a bargain,' Windlass said. Amusement rinsed through the words and set Tobias's teeth on edge. 'You underestimate your cousin, Tobias, and you delude yourself. You see him as you want him to be, rather than as he is. Ambrose may only be ten years old but he knows what he wants out of life, and he knows that I can help him achieve it. He's coming with us of his own free will and there is nothing you can do to prevent it. Now take your cousin outside and wait for me. I shall be five minutes.'

'I'm coming too.' A figure stepped out of the shadows. Windlass whirled round, pulling the pistol out of its holster and pointing it at the speaker.

'Don't shoot! Please, Dad!' It was the first time he had called Windlass by that name. 'It's Molly!'

'Step forward slowly, so I can see you,' Windlass said. He kept the pistol pointed at the intruder. The figure moved forward into the lantern light. Molly wore trousers and a jacket; a cap hid her hair. Her face was white and she was trembling.

'I'm Molly Petch,' she said to Windlass. 'Ambrose is my little brother. If he's going with you, so am I. He needs me to look after him. I won't be any trouble.'

'Moll!' Ambrose cried. 'You're ruining everything! Go away! Send her away, Mr Windlass!'

'Quiet!' Windlass's voice was soft, but the effect was immediate. Ambrose stood still and put his fist against his mouth.

284

'Send them both back. Please.' Tobias's voice was a soft as his father's.

Windlass lifted his head as he listened, but did not answer. He stared at Molly, his eyes narrowed in thought, the pistol pointing at her head. Slowly, he raised the pistol, eased the hammer down, slid it back under his coat. 'I think not, Tobias,' he said. 'Molly may come with us, on the understanding that she does exactly as I tell her.'

'I will,' Molly said.

'No!' hissed Tobias. 'Molly! Don't be a fool! Take Ambrose and get out of here while you still can.'

'You're overruled, Tobias,' Windlass said. 'Take the young lady and her brother out and wait as I directed. I will follow in five minutes. Do it, son. Every moment we delay increases the chance of discovery.'

Tobias looked at his father, frozen with despair and mistrust. Molly walked swiftly to him and took his arm, pulled him to the door. 'Come on. Outside! Like he said.' She tugged him through the door. Ambrose followed.

Moonlight glinted down on them and in its light he stared at his cousins in blank dismay, his mind racing. He had no choice now. 'Five minutes,' he said. 'Come on, Molly! We only got one chance! I'll take you and Ambrose to the Castle. My friends there'll look after you and see you get home all right. Come on! Now! If we run, we can get clean away before he comes out!' He grabbed her arm.

'Get off!' Molly said, and gave him a shove that sent

him sprawling into the slime of the path. 'We're staying here, like he said, aren't we, Ambrose?'

'Yup.' Ambrose stared down at him. 'You all right, Tobe?'

He ignored the hand Ambrose put out for him and scrambled up. 'You two! What d'you think you're playing at? You can't trust him! He's using you. I don't know what for yet, but he's not bloody Father Christmas!'

'Shut up, Toby,' said Molly. 'Don't tell us what to do. It's all right for you. You've got away. I doubt you gave us another thought. Well, we're getting away from Dad now, and you can't stop us!'

He stared at them in despair. There was nothing he could do but stay with them. Ambrose sidled over to him and took his hand. Molly stared back at him, her face white in the moonlight. It was silent, except for the noise of the river lapping against the slippery stones.

The door opened without warning, and Windlass came out. His eyes glinted at them. 'Quickly and quietly,' he said. 'Follow.'

There was no pretence of blind man and guide. Windlass set a pace which was only just not running. Molly and Ambrose trailed him like hounds on a scent. Tobias struggled in the rear, limping, hopping and half-running to keep up. Before ten minutes had gone, he was gasping with pain and exhaustion.

He had no energy left to notice where they were headed until Windlass halted at last, in the shadow of an old church. Tobias paused a few feet away from his father, leant forward with his hands on his thighs and struggled to catch his breath. Finally, he looked up. His father was in shadow, but he could feel his eyes on him, watching, gauging his recovery. Ambrose had run to him, was standing beside him anxiously. Molly stood back, watching him as silently as Windlass.

Tobias drew a shuddering breath and straightened, took his cap off and wiped his forehead. And then he saw. He heard himself gasp with shock as he realised where Windlass had brought them. 'Why? Why have you brought us here?'

He knew this street, this tiny church, had passed it hundreds, thousands of times. At the end of the street was an obscure alley, stinking of sewers. One side of the alley was formed by the ancient wall that marked the end of the gardens of a row of unimaginably old stone houses. The other side was the even taller, even older wall that surrounded the gardens and grounds of Quale Castle.

Thirty

'The papers are secure, Charlie,' said Topplesham. 'No one can break into the Castle; the Guard has been doubled and the dogs are out day and night. Even if they did, the papers are locked inside the finest safe in the country. It is said to be impregnable. Alistair Windlass may have many talents, but I don't believe safe-cracking to be one of them.'

'He can hire someone.'

'True. But no thief could possibly get past the dogs, the Guard and the safe. The papers are secure.'

'No!' she said. 'Not while there is even the smallest risk. Not with that man still out there.' She turned to her mother. 'How much have you written? Could Windlass make the crystals if he got hold of the papers?'

'Yes,' said her mother. 'It's all there. Any decent chemist could—'

'That's it!' Charlie whirled on the Prime Minister. 'I want the papers destroyed.'

'No!' Topplesham struggled to his feet. 'You're wrong, Your Majesty. I'm sorry, but the Privy Council wants this weapon. We need it, in case—'

'Politicians!' Charlie shouted. 'You're all alike. Power. That's what it's about!'

'It's about protecting this country!' Topplesham was redder that she'd ever seen him. She wondered if he was about to have an apoplectic fit, but she was so angry she didn't care.

'I am Queen,' she said, 'and I order—'

'I'm Prime Minister, ma'am,' Topplesham roared, 'and in matters of State Security I take precedence! This is a constitutional monarchy, ma'am. You have no say in the matter!'

Charlie stared at him. 'That can't be true.'

'I'm afraid it is.' Her mother looked up at her, her eyes weary. 'In times of war or threat of war, the Privy Council, in the person of the Prime Minister, can override the decisions of the Monarch, should it be decided they endanger the Kingdom.'

Charlie shook her head. She couldn't believe it. She was furious. And she was right. She knew she was. But she was beaten. She sought for a solution, any solution.

'Lord Topplesham.' Charlie turned to the Prime Minister. 'At least, promise me. Take the safe away to prison. Lock it in your most secure cell and mount a full-time guard over it. Please.'

'And what about me?' her mother asked. 'Would you like Topplesham to lock me in prison, too? Don't forget, the knowledge is all here, in my head. It will never be sufficient to destroy the papers without destroying their source. You will have to have me killed.'

'Mother!' Charlie stared at her in horror.

'I'm sorry. I'm just pointing out that there isn't any safety any more. The knowledge exists. I wish it didn't. But short of killing me and destroying all evidence of my work, I don't see how you can safeguard against the Alistair Windlasses of the world. Even if you did kill me and destroy my work, some other scientist might eventually stumble across this discovery. Should we ban science? Where do we stop?'

Topplesham stared at the floor, his face still beet-red. 'I'm trying to act for the best, Charlie. I hope you believe me.' He looked up at her and she nodded, her heart heavy.

'It's just,' she said, 'that "best" doesn't seem to exist any more.' And then she went to her mother and allowed herself to not be Queen. For a few moments, she wanted to be a twelve-year-old girl. Her mother gathered her in her arms and held her tight.

Charlie clung to the top of the airship, crawling towards the ropes that supported the undercarriage with its belly full of death. She pulled her knife from its sheath.

She looked down and saw the Kingdom of Quale spinning below her. It was dawn. Lights flickered in farmhouse windows. Cock crows spiked upwards, thin and shrill. And there – there were the roofs and cathedral spires of Quale City. She reached the ropes and began to saw at them. They seemed made of iron; her arm began to tire. Quale City floated ever nearer. Soon the bombs would fall.

A movement tickled the corner of her eye. She turned

her head and saw Tobias creeping across the body of the airship towards her. He clawed his way, fast and furious.

'Tobias!' she cried, relief sweeping through her. 'Help me!' She held out the knife to him, then watched in horror as he snatched it and threw it over the side. Charlie watched it glint and spiral out of sight.

'What have you done?'

He didn't answer. Instead, he grabbed her hands, dragged her to the side of the dirigible and pushed her off. He held her by the wrists as they floated over the City walls. She heard people scream as they looked up and saw the airship floating overhead. And then she heard the first explosion. The shockwave hit her, and then the backwash of heat. She looked into Tobias's pale eyes as he let go.

Charlie shot up in bed. She was drenched in sweat and gasping. It felt early. The small hours – two or three in the morning. She shivered and waited for her breathing to slow, her heart to stop hammering. That had been bad. The worst for weeks. She shuddered at the memory of Tobias's face, the coldness in his eyes.

She wouldn't sleep now. She got out of bed and groped for her jacket. She shrugged it on, found her trousers and pulled them on too, stuffing the tail of her nightdress inside. She was going on the roofs.

It was a warm night. Summer was here at last and she had barely noticed. Charlie leant over the parapet. It must be later than she thought. Nearly dawn. There was a red glow over the eastern part of the City.

She shivered and wished her body would make up its mind. Was she cold or hot? Perhaps she was sickening for something. She felt uneasy. Deeply uneasy. Something was wrong. What was it? And then she saw. It wasn't the sun rising in the east. Spreading above the red glow was a plume of smoke, darker than the night sky, blotting out the stars. The City was on fire.

Thirty-one

Windlass stepped out of the shadows towards him, and Tobias stared into his eyes. They were empty, and that emptiness answered his question. He had been right to fear his father.

'Oh my God,' he whispered. 'You've never stopped, have you? That's why you're still in the City. You must have been laughing at me for weeks. Wondering when I'd finally catch on! All those lies. That you cared for me! That you were a changed man who just wanted his son! Oh, you wanted me all right: to steal for you!' Tobias backed away, shaking his head.

As he turned to run, strong arms wrapped round him, bore him backwards. Windlass's hand clamped over his mouth. His father hugged him close, squeezing him so tightly he could barely breathe. He was pulled into the shadows. 'Tobias!' The voice hissed in his ear. 'Stop struggling, you little fool!' His father's breath was warm on his neck. Tobias fought frantically, nearly insane with fear and rage, trying to wrench his mouth clear and bite the hand crushing his lips against his teeth.

'Yes!' Windlass said. 'I have a spy in the Castle. I know that Caroline has obligingly recreated the papers she destroyed six years ago.' His arms seemed made of iron; Tobias wore himself out fighting them, until he hung, exhausted, inside their prison. 'I've lost everything for the sake of those papers. They're mine – I've paid for them, and I mean to have them. Ironically, they're kept in a safe in my old office. A safe identical to the one I supplied for you and your cousins' entertainment. That safe is supposed to be impossible to crack, and yet you did it in less than thirty minutes. It will take your cousin rather longer, but I can afford to be patient.'

Tobias stopped breathing.

'Have I got your attention at last?' his father said. 'Good. That's right. It isn't you who's breaking into the Castle tonight, it's Ambrose. He's been training on interlocking combination safes with his brother, Ezra, and he assures me he can crack one in under two hours. Now, if I let go of your mouth, do you promise not to yell?'

Beneath his father's hand, Tobias nodded his head fractionally up and down. Everything slowed except his brain, which was whirring faster than the wheels on a train carriage. Windlass lifted his hand and he had time to remember every event of the past weeks before he loosened his numb lips enough to whisper: 'I won't run off. Let go.'

The arms unlocked, and he slid from them onto the ground. His brain was racing, but his body seemed to have stopped working properly. Great shivers tore through him, and he sat hunched forward, arms around his legs and head on his knees, until they subsided. He was aware of Ambrose crouched beside him, stroking his arm and crying softly. Tobias waited. Gradually, the sickness faded, his muscles stopped shaking, and he lifted his head. His mind was frighteningly clear.

'You win.' He spoke without turning around, his voice barely above a whisper. 'You had it all figured, didn't you? I was right when I said you were the Devil. You see into people's souls, and then you use whatever you find to get what you want.'

'It's all right, Tobe,' Ambrose said. 'I'm gonna do it, not you. If I do, he'll pay to send me to engineering school, see. That's our deal. I can do it, you know. I cracked Ezra's safe five times now.'

'No!' Molly stepped forward, yanked Ambrose up. 'You're not breaking into the Castle, Ambrose Petch. The guards have guns, you stupid boy. If they catch you, they'll shoot you. I won't let you. You horrid man!' She turned, her face a blur of white fury, on Windlass. 'You can't make him.'

'Shut up, Moll! He'll give me money to go to school, you silly girl. You can't stop me.'

'That's enough!' The bitterness in Tobias's voice shocked his cousins into silence. They stared, open-mouthed. 'I told you both, but you wouldn't listen. He *uses* people. I told you he was using you, I just couldn't figure what for. Now I know. You're not gonna break in, Ambrose. He never intended you should. It's been me all along.'

He climbed unsteadily to his feet, turned to his father. 'That's right, isn't it? You been planning this for weeks. From the very beginning. It's why you tracked me down and stole me off Zebediah, isn't it? *Isn't it?*'

Windlass looked back at him. His eyes glittered, and his mouth was compressed into a thin line. He shook his head. 'Things are not quite so simple. I rescued you from Petch for several reasons. I owed it to your mother. I hated the idea of my son as Petch's slave. And yes, I thought you might possibly be of use. But I wasn't lying the other night when I told you what you mean to me. That was true.'

'No.' Tobias shook his head. 'You don't use the people you love.'

'Nonsense! Them most of all.' Windlass turned to Ambrose. 'Are you ready?'

'*Stop playing games!*' Icy rage swept away the last of the shock. 'You know perfectly well I can't let Ambrose go in there. That's why you brought me tonight. If you meant him to steal the papers you would have left me back at the house. Stop treating me like a fool! Have you got picks?'

'Ambrose has them.'

'Give me the picks, Ambrose,' Tobias said.

'No! I've got to do it, or he won't give me the money.' Ambrose backed away, tears streaming down his face.

'Yes, he will. I promise. Tell him!' he snapped at Windlass.

'You'll have your money. Give him the lockpicks.'

Windlass's eyes never left Tobias's face.

'Do it, Ambrose,' said Molly, her voice shaking.

Ambrose turned a tearstained face to Tobias. 'Is it OK, Tobe?'

'It's OK.'

Ambrose shuffled forward, dug his hand into his trouser pocket and pulled out a set of gleaming lockpicks. He handed them to Tobias. The picks were warm. Tobias clutched them with frozen fingers and turned to his father. 'It'll take me an hour, maybe more. Are the dogs out?'

'Yes.'

Tobias's face twisted with contempt as he gazed into his father's eyes. 'He wouldn't have made it through the grounds.' He turned to go.

'Wait.' Windlass reached out, grabbed his arm and whirled him round.

'Let go!' hissed Tobias.

'In a minute.' His father gripped him by the shoulders and stared into his face. 'I want the papers, Tobias, but I want you too. Be careful.'

Tobias wrenched away, breathing heavily. 'I'll bring you the papers. But then you and I are done, Windlass. You made your choice.' He turned and ran into the night.

The alley swallowed him. He ran between dark walls, listening to his feet slap the cobbles. The smell of sewers settled at the back of his throat. He ran as if in a dream, his old life hanging in front of his eyes like a magic lantern show: the times he had used this alley and his secret door in the Castle wall; the years when it had been his way of getting away from Foss and the garden for an hour or two; and then that terrifying night when he had helped Charlie escape from the Castle. Another life; another boy. He wasn't that Tobias any more. He didn't know who he was, and he had one hour of life left. After that, everything was blank.

Too soon, he reached the wooden door set deep in the Castle wall: small, ancient, almost invisible. It looked as though it had not been used for decades, but he had kept it well oiled. The pick slid into the lock and it clicked open almost at once. He slipped through the door, shut it behind him, not locking it in case he needed to leave more quickly than he had come.

He pushed through the vines that hung across the door and stood for a moment as though in a trance, staring at the garden and the Castle that loomed above it. He felt like a ghost revisiting his old life. He looked up at the Castle walls, and his eyes found the window of the room where his mother slept. He bit his lip, dug his fingernails into his palms, fighting pain with pain. That had been a mistake. He couldn't afford to think of them: Mum, Moleglass, Charlie, Maria.

He moved forward into the garden, noticing signs that the wilderness was being tamed. Foss must have his army of undergardeners and boys by now. He'd be in heaven, the old gnome, leaning on his spade and ordering them all around. Tobias smiled a grim smile at the thought and began to trot from shadow to shadow, his nerves singing with adrenaline.

Halfway to the Castle, the dogs spotted him. One long, baying howl cut through the air, and then he heard the rush of large bodies. Three animals, the size of half-grown calves, barrelled out of the bushes on the other side of the rhododendron walk and raced across the open ground towards him, their bodies long and low in the moonlight. He'd been expecting the dogs, but the sight of them made his heart lurch. He'd forgotten how big they were.

When they were twenty feet away, he gave a low, soft whistle and the lead dog stumbled to a halt. Tobias whistled again and all three dogs stood uncertainly for a moment, then advanced on him, stiff-legged and growling. When they were close enough to catch his scent, the growling changed to excited whining, and the dogs flung themselves at him. Tobias had raised them from pups; even in the darkness, he recognised them. 'Down, Belle!' he whispered as the female reared up and put her paws on his shoulders. But she had him down instead, and he was rolling on the ground, trampled by eager paws and the smell of wet dog, soaked by long, dripping tongues.

The dogs were a whining tumble of excitement and Tobias was terrified in case they forgot their training and began to bark like puppies. 'No! Down!' His voice lashed out at them in a harsh whisper and, hearing his displeasure, the dogs backed away. 'Sit, Belle. Sit! Tully, Caesar, sit!' The dogs hunkered onto their haunches and Tobias rolled up off the ground, groaning and cursing.

'Kennels!' he said. 'Go on! Clear off!' The dogs looked at him, whined, and then bounded up and raced off. He began to walk, then eased into a lope, wincing at the pain in his leg, keeping to the shadows. As he neared the Castle, he slowed. The Guard would be on duty, two men stationed at the main entrance, two men on patrol. He approached the Castle from the east, counting the ground-floor windows until he spotted the one he needed. Then he found a low growing bush, squatted behind it and waited.

After about ten minutes, he saw them. His heart speeded up: this was it. The patrol passed in front of him, the men moving with the weary precision of the practised soldier pacing away the night. They never glanced in his direction. The moment they turned the corner, he sprang up and flew to the window. He'd opened the Castle's casement windows a dozen times, using only a bent piece of metal. With the picks, it was even quicker. It was a simple latch, not even a proper lock. He shook his head. He'd have to have a word with Moleglass...Tobias jerked his thoughts back, blinked the hotness from his eyes, and opened the window.

He stood in the throne room, shivering slightly. His feet seemed glued to the floor. He took a deep breath and made himself move through the room and out of the tall panelled door towards the ministerial wing. Moonlight flooded in at the windows, but he could have found his way in the dark.

His feet were heavy, his leg stiff, and Perce would have cuffed him for the noise he made as he scuffed through the marble hall. Cuffed him for the scratch of his shoes on the floors, the harshness of his breathing. He dodged past the huge entrance door, heart pounding, aware of the men stationed in the guards' hut only a few feet away on the other side. He found the door to Windlass's old office – Charlie's office now – and stood staring blankly at it.

It was wrong to steal these papers. He knew it. Evil would come of it and it would be his fault. He could stop now. Go and find Moleglass and tell him everything. And then? Windlass would be caught and hung. Or more probably shot dead, because he would never give up.

How many people would die with him? Ambrose and Molly? They were the hostages. That's why they were there. Windlass hadn't said: 'Tell Moleglass and these children die!' but Tobias knew. He stood and stared at the door, his eyes wide, his hands shaking so much the lockpicks clinked together like wind chimes. He had to choose. It wasn't fair, but he had to choose. Ambrose and Molly – or the papers. That was the deal. Windlass wouldn't spare them: he hadn't spared his own son.

Tobias groaned and made his choice. He slid a pick into the lock, and his fingers took over. The door was open in five seconds. He stepped into the room and saw the safe at once. It was the same: identical to the one he'd cracked when Windlass had ambushed them. He walked towards it, stumbling over rugs, bumping into tables, and knelt before the safe. He emptied his mind and put his fingertips and ears to work. Just another job. Like all those he'd done with Perce. Gradually, his heart stopped pounding in his head and he was able to listen. He wasn't going to think any more. He didn't exist. Tobias lost himself in the sound of the tumblers.

Minutes later, he didn't know how many, the lock gave. He turned the handle and the safe sighed open. *Please,* whispered part of his mind, *please let it not be here*. But it was: a fat leather portfolio lay on the single shelf. Tobias picked it up, surprised at how heavy it was. He turned and ran.

He knew he was running from himself. If he stopped to think, he'd be lost. He flung himself into the throne room, tore open the window and, without even checking to see if the patrol was in sight, jumped down and raced for the door in the wall. Only once before in his life had he been this frightened.

Voices screamed in his head: Mum, Moleglass, Zebediah, Ambrose, Windlass. And as he crossed a patch of open ground, he heard Charlie call his name: 'Tobias! Tobias!'

Her voice echoed through the night like a silver bell and dragged him to a halt. He stood, shivering with terror, then turned slowly around. His eyes flew up the Castle walls to the rooftops where he had so nearly died all those months ago.

She was there. He saw her plainly in the moonlight, leaning forward over the parapet, staring down at him. Her face was as clear as if she were standing in front of him. He saw the disbelief, the horror in her eyes. They looked at each other for long, painful heartbeats, and Tobias felt the breeze blow cold on his wet face. He shook his head, turned, and ran into the dark.

Later, he couldn't remember getting out of the Castle grounds or running down the alley. His memories began as he held the portfolio out to Alistair Windlass and felt his father gather him and the papers together in a brief, terrifying hug, crushing him against the sour-smelling coat so that he felt the pistol hard against his cheek.

Windlass pushed him away and peered into his face. 'Problems?'

'I was seen. At the end. They'll be raising the alarm now.'

Windlass's face turned grim. 'Follow me, all of you. It's not far. Can you keep up, Tobias?'

He took a deep breath. 'I'm not going. I told you. We're done.'

His father stared down at him, and his eyes narrowed with amusement – or was it contempt? Tobias saw that Windlass had been expecting just this; that he found his son as predictable as ever. His throat tightened with humiliation, and he held the portfolio out again, wanting it finished. His father shook his head with a wry smile. 'You bloody fool,' he said. Then he pulled his fist back and punched Tobias in the stomach.

Pain and shock slammed into him, and air rushed from his lungs as the punch winded him. He dropped the portfolio and slumped to his knees, gasping for breath. His arms were grabbed from behind, twisted up. Cold metal encircled his wrists and he heard the snap of handcuffs. The next moment a handkerchief was shoved in his mouth and he was dragged up and whirled round to face his father.

'I'm sorry,' Windlass said. He knelt, clutched Tobias around the knees, and hoisted him onto his shoulder. Tobias found himself dangling upside down, barely able to breathe. 'Bring the papers, Ambrose, and don't drop them!' Windlass set off at a steady trot, and Tobias heard the others running behind.

He struggled to get the breath back in his lungs, and then he struggled not to vomit as he jounced upside down with his head banging into his father's back at every stride. His mouth was dry as cotton wool and he couldn't spit the handkerchief out, so he tried to kick, but even though Windlass was gasping with the effort of carrying him, he held his legs in an iron grip.

The misery lasted just over five minutes, and then Windlass halted. 'Open the door, Molly,' he said. The next moment, Tobias was sliding onto his feet, which refused to hold him up. Windlass grasped him under the arms and pushed him inside a cab, where he fell face down across one of the seats.

'Here!' he heard a strange voice cry out. 'What's all this about? I don't want nothing to do with no kidnappings!' It must be the cabbie. Was this a rescue? Tobias tried to get up, but someone climbed onto his back and sat on him.

'Keep quiet, Toby!' It was Molly. Why were she and Ambrose helping Windlass? He heard the boy scramble into the cab and onto the other seat.

'Be good now, Tobe,' Ambrose called softly. 'I'm sorry he hit you, but you were being really stupid. He said you might. You don't really want to go to jail, do you?'

So that was it. Damn Windlass and his lies. But was it a lie? Surely there would be jail for this night's work. Moleglass couldn't save him now – wouldn't want to know him. He was nothing but a thief, after all. He closed his eyes and lay still, working at pushing the gag out of his mouth with his tongue.

The cab rocked as someone entered and sat down next to Ambrose. Then it lurched and moved forward to the quickening clop of horse's hooves.

'Did you square him?' asked Molly.

'Obviously,' Windlass said. 'Money works wonders.'

At last Tobias spat the handkerchief out of his mouth and lay gasping for a second. 'Get off,' he wheezed.

Molly slid onto the floor, and Tobias slowly and stiffly rolled himself upright and fell back into a corner of the seat, where he sat, stony-faced, surveying his three kidnappers. Molly sat beside him and, when he looked at her, had the grace to blush. 'We couldn't just leave you, Toby. You wasn't thinking straight.'

'It's none of your damn business!'

'Enough, Tobias,' Windlass said. 'She's right. You choose an idiotic time to exhibit your scruples.' He sat, calm and composed as ever, the portfolio resting on the seat beside him.

'Go to—' Tobias broke off and stared out of the cab window. He didn't want to look at this man, or talk to him. Misery was trickling into him like water through a hole in a dike, seeping into every inch of him. The moment he had taken the papers from the safe, he had sealed his fate. He was cut off forever from his home and the people he loved. Nothing mattered now. Dry-eyed, he stared out of the window and watched the City streets twist away.

Thirty-two

Tobias stared up at her. He had grown again. He looked older, and he limped, and his hair was shorter than she had ever seen it, but it was him. He hugged the leather portfolio to his chest, the portfolio that contained her mother's papers, and tears streamed down his face. His pale eyes weren't cold. They were full of misery. Then he turned from her and ran into the darkness.

She needed to scream for the Guard. But she couldn't do it. They would shoot him. But the papers! She was Queen. Her first duty was to her people. She opened her mouth and screamed. A rusty noise plopped out, like the screech of a baby rook. Shaking and ill, Charlie cast one last look at the fire raging over her City, one last look at the spot where Tobias had disappeared, and scrambled back to her bedroom.

'Windlass has the papers!'

'Charlie, you don't know that.'

'It was Tobias, Mother.'

'You thought it was. You can't be certain. From that distance.'

'It *was* Tobias.'

Moleglass came into the library. He looked like a plump, dishevelled crow: his hair sticking up in black feathers, his dark blue dressing gown rumpled and untied. Charlie had never seen him so distressed. Not even on the horrible night when he had seen the body of his dead wife. He stared at the four of them, his brown eyes dark with shock, and nodded his head. 'I have sent word to Topplesham and Blundell. The matter is out of our hands.'

'But Tobias!' cried Charlie.

Moleglass shook his head. 'I have given your instructions, Charlie. The boy is to be taken alive at all costs. But...there are never guarantees, child. We can only hope.'

Rose moaned. It was a low, hurtful sound and Charlie could hardly bear it. 'He'll be all right, Rose.' Her voice was fierce. 'If anyone hurts him, I'll...I'll...' She turned away from them and walked to the window. 'What about the fire?' she asked.

'A warehouse,' Moleglass answered. 'Near the river, thank goodness. The fire is contained. The City is not in danger.'

'Well that at least is a blessing,' the Dowager said with a sigh. 'There are little enough of them tonight. But, Charlie, I know of another one. A small blessing, but a blessing nonetheless.'

Charlie turned to look at her mother. The Dowager smiled. 'You are a persuasive young lady. Windlass may have most of the papers, my child, but he does not have all of them. I went to the safe last night, before I went to bed, and removed three pages. I committed treason, you know, for Topplesham had ordered me to leave all the papers in the safe.'

She shook her head. 'It will take a brilliant scientist months, Charlie, without those three pages. Months of hard work – and a great deal of luck. Windlass hasn't won. You and I will see to it that he doesn't. You have bought us time.

'I think,' her mother continued, 'that the whereabouts of those three pages will remain our secret. No need to tell Topplesham any of it. Do you agree?'

Charlie nodded.

'And you, Ancel?'

The butler smiled. 'Oh, I quite agree, ma'am.'

'I don't understand,' Nell said quietly. 'Why would Toby do such a thing? He hates Windlass. He hates him worse than anyone in the world.'

'Alistair has a talent for persuasion,' the Dowager said drily. 'If it was Tobias, and I hope sincerely it wasn't—'

'It was, Mother.' Charlie looked over at Rose, huddled on the sofa, her head in her hands. She walked over and sat down beside her, touching her gently on the shoulder. 'Rose,' she said. 'I'm sorry. I haven't been kind to you. I promise – I'll do everything I can to help him and keep him safe. I know that he loves you more than anyone in the world. He'll come back to you.'

Rose lifted her head. 'Bless you, child,' she said. 'But even a queen can't save him now. Only one man can do that. And I greatly fear he won't. You were right all along. I should have left him to hang!' And Rose Petch's eyes darkened with something Charlie had never seen in them before: hatred.

Thirty-three

'We're nearly there.'

Tobias blinked; he'd been staring without seeing, but now he realised that they had reached the docks.

'Tobias, look at me.' Unwillingly, he turned his head. Windlass was leaning forward, watching him intently. 'You're coming with me,' his father said. 'Will it be cuffed or uncuffed?'

'Unlock them.'

'You give me your word that you won't try to escape?'

Tobias just looked at him. 'Where would I go?' he asked.

He climbed out of the cab after the others and stood shivering in the early dawn light as Windlass paid the cabbie. Two carpet bags thudded into the mud, and the cabbie clicked to his horse and drove off in a clatter of harness, wheels and hooves.

Windlass had the portfolio tucked beneath one arm. He swept up one of the bags and threw the other to Tobias, who caught it clumsily. 'This way,' Windlass said and led off towards a shabby clapboard warehouse fronting the wharf.

It was even shabbier inside: sawdust floor, raw board

walls grey with cobwebs and dust, bales, boxes and parcels piled in a heap to one side of the room. At the back was a barrel stove with a rusty stovepipe climbing to the ceiling, a bare wooden table with a ledger, and a man. The man matched the room. His long grey hair hung in limp strands from a balding pate, his clothes were grey with dust and his long nose had a round red bulge at the end of it, like a rotting strawberry.

At the sight of them, he lifted a small, earthenware jug to his lips, and Tobias saw his Adam's apple jog up and down seven times in rapid succession. He lowered the jug, wiped his mouth, and said: 'Who're you, then?'

'Passengers for the *Lady of Ryme*. The name is Benson,' said Windlass. 'I want a boat to take us out to the ship at once.'

'Benson's two passengers. There's four of you.'

'Two,' said Windlass.

'What?' cried Molly. 'We're coming with you!'

Windlass turned to her, setting down the carpet bag. 'That was not the arrangement. I am not a nursemaid, Miss Petch. Here are the funds I promised Ambrose.' He pulled a wallet out of his breast pocket and handed it to her. 'Bearer bonds. Small denominations so that the banks will not give you any difficulty. There should be more than enough to fund his education and keep you both comfortably, if modestly.'

'B-but...Dad—'

'Is not my problem,' Windlass said. 'Keep out of his

way or leave the City. Your decision, and I wish you well. Goodbye.'

She stood looking down at the wallet in her hand. Ambrose ran to Tobias and tugged at his arm, his eyes round with alarm. 'I want to stay with you, Tobe. Please!'

Tobias looked into the bright blue eyes with their thick bronze lashes, and his heart felt frozen. He shook his head. 'It's not good with us, Ambrose. You'd be better off with your dad than us. Windlass is right. Take the money and get out of town. Molly'll look after you.'

She raised her eyes and glared at him, her lips in a thin line. 'Come on, Ambrose,' she said. 'Let's get out of here.'

'I don't think so.' Windlass's voice was soft and cold. Tobias turned, startled, and saw his father reach into his jacket and slide the revolver out of its holster.

'What?!'

'Someone's missing,' said Windlass, 'which can only mean unwelcome visitors. Come here, Molly.' He pointed the revolver at her.

'What're you doing?!' shouted Tobias. He lunged at Windlass, who swung his arm and knocked Tobias flying into the sawdust. He scrabbled up to see his father reach out, grab Molly and hold her against him, the pistol resting against her head. Ambrose began to scream, but he wasn't looking at Molly and Windlass, he was facing the door. Tobias suddenly understood. His eyes raked the warehouse. The man had gone. The shipping man had disappeared.

313

'I have your daughter here, Petch. There is a pistol at her head. Show yourself.' Windlass's voice echoed across the warehouse. Nothing happened and Tobias began to hope that it was all a mistake. Then the door opened and Zebediah Petch stalked into the room.

He was a blackened, soot-encrusted giant. His clothes were singed, his black beard and hair frizzled with great raw patches. His face was red and blistered, the whites of his eyes were yellow and the seaweed irises shone like glass. Behind him came Ezra, looking as though he'd been toasted over a bonfire, his face, clothes and ginger hair black with soot. At the sight of them, Ambrose stopped screaming and ran to cower behind Tobias.

Tobias stood, too shocked to move or speak. Petch's eyes swivelled from Windlass, and Tobias found himself staring into them. 'Wh-hat...?' he stammered.

'Your daddy wasn't content to steal my children,' Zebediah said, his voice cracked and harsh. 'He indulged himself in a spot of arson. The warehouse is burning. Years of work up in smoke. If the fire hadn't been spotted early, and we hadn't been on the river with plenty of water to hand, it would have taken the house as well, and no doubt half of Flearside. The whole family might have died in their beds.'

'Mum,' moaned Molly.

'She's fine. Don't fret, Moll,' said Ezra. 'They'll put it out.'

'You set the warehouse on fire? Why?' Tobias stared at Windlass in disbelief.

'To keep Mr Petch and his numerous relatives occupied while we escaped,' Windlass said. 'I guessed he had informants on the docks. And it worked, to a certain extent, or our welcoming party would be considerably larger. However,' he smiled grimly, 'I think we are still at least one person short. The back entrance, Mr Petch. Now, would that be Mr Sorrell, by any chance? Please ask him to join us. And any others. Molly is a pretty and intelligent girl. It would be a shame for her life to end prematurely.'

Zebediah glared at Windlass, his teeth glinting in a fierce grimace, and Tobias could feel his rage and frustration like a sheet of fire beating against them. 'Get in here, Perce!' The shout erupted like a volcano. 'Gentle-like, mind! He's got Molly!'

There was movement behind them and Perce edged into sight. He had a pistol in his hand and it was trained at Windlass's back. Ice gripped Tobias's bowels and he realised, in amazement, that he was afraid for his father.

'Put that away, Perce!' roared Zebediah.

'I suggest you do as your uncle tells you, Mr Sorrell.' Windlass's voice was calm. 'This pistol is cocked. If you shoot me in the back, it will go off.'

'Put it away, Perce, or I'll kill you myself!' Zebediah said, his voice deadly.

Reluctantly, Perce lowered his pistol. His hand was

shaking. 'Join your uncle and cousin, Mr Sorrell,' said Windlass. 'Slowly. And stay well away from the boys, please.' Perce circled Windlass and went to stand beside Ezra. 'Now, all of you, drop your firearms on the floor in front of you.'

There was a long moment as Zebediah and Windlass eyed each other, and then, slowly, Zebediah put his hand inside his coat and pulled out a revolver. It fell with a dull thud onto the sawdust floor. Ezra and Perce followed suit.

'Gentlemen, step back three paces,' said Windlass. 'Ambrose, go and gather up the pistols. Put them on the ground in front of me one by one, and be careful not to point them at anyone, including yourself.'

Without hesitation, Ambrose darted out from behind Tobias and began scurrying back and forth, until all three pistols lay at Windlass's feet. 'Thank you, Ambrose. Now I would like you to check the front and back entrances, just to make sure that we have no more unexpected visitors waiting outside.'

Ambrose nodded and disappeared out of the front door. A few minutes later he popped into the room from the back entrance. 'There's nobody,' he said. 'The brougham's outside, but there's no other Petches.'

Zebediah watched his youngest son with glittering eyes, and Tobias realised that he had guessed which of his family had played traitor. 'We've got to take him with us,' he said.

'It begins to look like it,' Windlass agreed.

'Let go of Molly.'

'In a moment,' Windlass said. 'But first, you need to secure our guests. The handcuffs are in my coat pocket. Take rope off those bundles.'

With trembling fingers, Tobias fished the handcuffs from his father's pocket. He could feel Molly shaking. 'It's all right, Molly,' he said. 'I promise, it'll be all right.'

'Get on, son,' Windlass said.

He raced to the pile of cargo, pulled a canvas bundle out and twisted the rope from it. He salvaged another piece and turned to look at his father. 'I've got it.'

'Start with your uncle,' said Windlass. 'The handcuffs are for him, I think. Mr Sorrell and Mr Petch, the younger, kindly back away from Zebediah five paces, turn around and sit with your hands on your heads. Now!'

'Do it!' growled Zebediah, his mouth twisting into a sneer.

'Petch, arms out to your sides. Try anything and Molly's dead. Remember that. Tobias, cuff him. Right hand first, then left.'

His heart began to hammer as he approached Zebediah Petch. His uncle's eyes stared into his, sparking green and brown and red. His arms were stretched out on either side. He was motionless, absolutely still, as though made of carved and painted stone. Only his eyes were alive. It was a shock when Tobias clipped the handcuff around his uncle's right wrist and felt warm flesh.

The next instant, Zebediah's hand clamped on his arm

317

and yanked Tobias in front of him. One of Petch's enormous forearms pinned him by the throat and lifted him off his feet. Zebediah was crushing his windpipe. He was choking, strangling. His vision faded and stars exploded in his head. He was aware that he was dying and that it hurt. His feet flailed and his hands scrabbled at the arm strangling him. It lowered slightly and his toes found the floor, pushed against it and lifted him up a fraction of an inch so that he could breathe. Air gurgled down his gullet, burning like fire, and death retreated.

Windlass was yelling: 'Let go of him!'

'I don't think so,' Zebediah snarled. 'Because if you shoot Molly, I'll break this boy's neck before you can shoot me. That's a promise, Mr Prime Minister. Drop the gun or your son dies.'

In the silence, Tobias's eyes sought his father's face. Windlass was pale above his beard, his eyes glittering as they stared at Zebediah. 'We have a stand-off, Mr Petch,' Windlass said, his voice cold as ice. 'Because if the boy dies, I will most certainly shoot first your daughter, then yourself.'

'Ah,' said Zebediah. 'But here's the difference.' He grabbed Tobias's left hand, twisted it sideways and levered his massive thumb beneath Tobias's little finger. Then he pushed. Tobias screamed as the finger snapped. His legs buckled, but his uncle kept him from falling, held him tight with one arm, kept his injured hand stretched out despite his frantic efforts to free it.

'Such a shame,' Zebediah said, over Tobias's moans. 'Clever hands, your son's got. But they're no use to me now. I'll break his fingers one by one, Mr Prime Minister, and then I'll break his arms. When I'm done, your boy'll be a cripple, fit for begging and naught else.'

Tobias was shuddering with pain and fear. He swallowed convulsively to keep from vomiting, and looked at Windlass. His father's face was bleached bone-white, his eyes staring at Zebediah with a look Tobias had never before seen in them. With a shock, he recognised it: defeat.

'No!' he shouted. 'Don't do it! He'll kill you!' Tears were streaming down his face. Then he screamed, as Petch set his thumb behind the next finger and snapped it like a twig.

'Stop!' roared Windlass. 'Promise me the boy goes free. Give me your word as a thief, Zebediah Petch. He goes back to his mother at the Castle.'

'Done,' said Petch. 'I won't kill him; you've my word on it. He can go to his mother and welcome.'

'Ambrose?' said Windlass.

There was a long pause. Tobias was shaking and sick, tears clouding his vision, but he looked for his cousin and saw him crouched in the sawdust near Windlass, staring at Zebediah with eyes large with terror, the blue nearly dissolved in the black of the pupils. 'That's none of your business,' growled Petch. 'I'll deal with my son as I see fit. He's betrayed me and the Family, and he'll pay for it.

Now, drop your gun, Prime Minister, or it's another finger. Consider I'm doing you a favour. A bullet's cleaner than the rope.'

Windlass looked at Tobias. He was whiter than ever and Tobias saw a flicker of fear deep within the pale blue eyes. 'No, Dad!' he cried, all hope gone.

'Sorry, son,' Windlass said, a smile twisting his mouth. 'Give my love to your mother.' He lifted his pistol to point at the ceiling and stepped back from Molly. She collapsed on the ground, weeping. Windlass uncocked the pistol and let it fall from his hand.

'Back off,' growled Petch. 'All the way to the wall.'

Windlass turned without a word and walked to the back of the warehouse.

'Now lean on that wall and don't move.'

Tobias heard his own strangled sobs. Watched his father lean forward onto his hands. The next second Zebediah's arm was gone from his neck and he was flying through the air and crashing onto the floor. He lay motionless, stunned, one thought in his mind: Zebediah was about to shoot his father in the back. Alistair Windlass was about to die for him. He scrabbled to his knees, but before he could stand up, the warehouse exploded with the roar of a pistol.

Tobias leapt to his feet and ran forward. Zebediah Petch stood with his back to him, blocking his view. As he watched, Petch staggered, stepped sideways and toppled over, slowly, like an oak tree struck by lightning. He hit the ground with a thud that shook the building and sent a shower of sawdust swirling into the air. Tobias froze, staring at his uncle, stretched face down on the floor. Sawdust drifted out of the air and settled on him like snow. Molly began to scream, and he lifted his head and saw Ambrose, holding Windlass's pistol in a shaking hand and pointing it at the spot where his father had been standing a moment before.

The next second, Windlass was beside the boy, had taken the pistol from his hand and turned it on Perce, who was lurching forward. 'See to your uncle, Mr Sorrell.' Windlass said coldly. 'He's not dead yet.' Ezra was already kneeling beside Zebediah tearing at his father's coat and shirt to get to the wound. Windlass's eyes flicked to Tobias, assessing, paused for a moment on his face, then returned to the two men kneeling beside Petch.

'He'll bleed to death!' moaned Ezra. Molly gave a strangled cry and jumped up.

'Molly,' Windlass said. 'Take clean shirts out of our luggage to use for bandages. You'll have to stay behind and help Ezra. Ambrose is coming with us.' Molly turned a tearstained face towards Windlass, then moved to look at Ambrose, who was staring at Zebediah, his eyes large and unseeing. She nodded and ran for the carpet bags.

Windlass turned, scooped up the pistols with his free hand and broke them open, scattered the bullets, then flung the guns away. He picked up the wallet of banknotes and handed it to Ambrose. 'Keep it safe, Mr Petch. You're holding your future.' Then he walked to the carpet bags, shoved the tumbled contents back and fastened them. 'Can you manage one, Tobias?'

'Please.' Tobias stepped forward on legs that seemed disconnected with his body. His fingers were swollen and throbbing; he was shaking and felt like he might fall over at any moment, but he hardly noticed. There was a chance. He had seen it in his father's eyes. Surely, he couldn't be mistaken. 'Please,' he said. 'Let me have the papers. Let me take them back to Charlie.'

Windlass stood, tall and elegant despite his filthy clothes, and looked down at him without expression. After a moment, his mouth curved in a wry smile. 'I see,' he said. 'I suppose I shouldn't be surprised.' The smile faded and his father gazed down at him, his mouth grim. His eyes were the colour of a northern sky in midsummer.

'No, son. The papers are coming with me. That is not negotiable.' He grimaced. 'I nearly lost you just now. It wasn't a pleasant feeling. I'm asking you to come with me, but I won't force you.' He paused. 'It's your decision.'

'I can't go back without the papers,' Tobias said. He clenched his good fist and swiped at the tears on his face.

'I think, perhaps, you misjudge your friends.' Windlass raised a sardonic eyebrow. 'If you explain the circumstances they'll be only too happy to put the blame where it belongs: on me.'

'You don't believe in blame,' Tobias snapped.

Windlass smiled his crooked smile. 'Decision time.' The smile faded again and he reached out a tentative hand, rested it on Tobias's shoulder. 'Son, I'm asking you to come with me. One year, Tobias. I only ask for one year of your life.'

Two pairs of pale blue eyes studied each other and Tobias nodded, once.

Windlass squeezed his shoulder in a brief, fierce grip. Then released him and stepped back. 'Can you bear the pain in your hand for a while longer?'

'Yes.'

'And are you able to carry a bag?'

'Yes.' Tobias dropped his eyes. He went to the remaining bag and picked it up in his good hand; turned, saw Molly kneeling beside her father tearing strips of cloth and handing them to Ezra, who was binding them round his father's naked shoulder. Perce stood some distance away, glaring at Windlass. Tobias glanced at his father, who had gathered Ambrose and was waiting by the door, then walked over to the group huddled in the centre of the warehouse and looked down at Zebediah Petch. His uncle was breathing harshly, his eyes half shut. Tobias looked at the man who had terrorised him and felt nothing. He felt nothing at all.

'He'll live,' said Molly breathlessly. 'The bullet's gone clean through.' She turned and looked up at him, her face white and strained. 'Look after Ambrose for me, Toby, please. He didn't mean it.'

323

'I reckon he did,' Tobias said slowly. 'But I'll look after him, Molly. And will you do one thing for me?' She nodded. 'Go to the Castle, as soon as you can. Tell them...tell them what I did and that I'm sorry, and I'll put it right. Tell them that especially: I'll put it right. Mr Moleglass, the butler, he's a good man. You can trust him. And, Molly, tell my mother...tell her...' His voice faltered.

Molly's sapphire eyes shone into his, bright with tears. 'I will,' she said. 'I promise. Goodbye, Toby.'

He turned and followed his father out into the morning.

Thirty-four

Charlie jerked awake. Moleglass was standing beside the sofa with a trolley of coffee and bread rolls. 'What time is it?' she asked, sitting up and rubbing her neck.

'Eight o'clock.' Moleglass handed her a cup of coffee. 'You need to eat something.'

'Why didn't you wake me?' Charlie shouted, splattering coffee as she thumped the cup down on the nearest table.

'There was nothing to tell you, Charlie. You needed sleep. Be reasonable.'

She glared up at him. 'I don't want to be reasonable.'

Mr Moleglass groaned. He looked exhausted. 'That, my child, is something of which I have long been aware.'

Charlie picked up the cup and frowned at him as she sipped the coffee. It tasted glorious. 'News?' she growled.

'Yes,' he said. We've only just heard: they have got away.'

'What?!'

'Windlass and Tobias have left the country on a ship called the *Lady of Ryme* and are making, by all accounts, for Esceania. The Navy is pursuing them, but Windlass has hired a fast ship, as you would expect. A privateer, with no loyalties to any flag. And his luck holds – the wind is in their favour. They will not be caught.'

Charlie sat, numb, not sure how she was feeling or how she ought to feel. 'He took Tobias with him?' It had been her greatest hope that Windlass would abandon his son, as he had abandoned his wife.

'Yes. I'm sorry. But there is more.'

Charlie lifted her head. She felt oddly hollow inside. She hadn't realised how much she had been hoping that Tobias would be found.

'We have Zebediah Petch.'

She stared at Moleglass.

'There was an altercation at the docks. Apparently, it was one of Petch's warehouses that was on fire. Arson. I think we can guess who was behind that. In any case, Petch caught up with Windlass at the docks and tried to kill him. Unfortunately, he didn't succeed. Instead, Petch is lying in prison with a bullet hole in his shoulder. His daughter wishes to speak with you. She has, I believe, information about Tobias which may be of use.'

Charlie's mouth fell open. 'Send for Nell,' she said. 'I want her here.'

Charlie stared at Molly Petch and decided she did not like her. She thought the feeling was probably mutual. She stood as straight as she could and glared at the older girl.

'You may tell me your message.'

''Tain't for you.' Molly stared back at her, seemingly

unimpressed at meeting her queen. 'Toby asked me to tell his mum, and I'll tell no one but her.'

'She's being fetched,' Charlie said, controlling her temper with difficulty.

'Well, we'll just wait a while then, won't we?' Molly said. Her face was pale and her eyes red from crying. Charlie could see the other girl was tired and upset, but she disliked her too much to care. This was Zebediah Petch's daughter. One of the people who had kidnapped Tobias, and she was not inclined to feel sorry for any of them.

'How is Uncle Zebediah?' Nell asked. The three of them were standing awkwardly in the middle of the library. Charlie was too agitated to sit and too angry to allow the others to do so.

'Do you care?' Molly asked coolly, staring at Nell.

'Not much,' Nell said. 'I reckon most folks would be better off with Zebediah dead, but I guess we ain't that lucky.'

'No,' Molly said. 'He'll live.'

'At least,' Nell said, her eyes narrowing, 'he's in prison. Which is where I hope he'll stay for many a day!'

Molly glared at her, but before she could speak the door opened and Moleglass came in with Rose. She looked pale and tired, but when she saw Molly she rushed forward, her eyes alight. 'Molly Petch?' Molly nodded. 'I'm your aunt Rose, child. Tobias's mum. Mr Moleglass said you had a message from him?' Her face was so anxious with hope and fear that Charlie's throat ached.

'Yes.' For the first time, Molly's face softened. The girl reached out and put her arms around Rose and hugged her tight. 'Your boy's a grand lad, Rose Petch,' Molly said. 'But I guess you know that. He asked me to tell you that he loves you. And that he'll be back as soon as he can.'

She glanced at Moleglass. 'This part of the message is for you, Mr Moleglass. Toby thinks a deal of you, so I'll tell you the straight truth. He stole them papers to save my little brother. Windlass is as slippery and twisty as an eel. He had Ambrose wound round his little finger with his lies and promises, and my brother would have broke into the Castle grounds and got himself killed for that man. Toby nicked them papers but he wants you to know he's sorry. He said to tell you – he'll put it right. I reckon he'll try. But I also reckon he'll never get the better of his dad. That man ain't natural.'

She sighed and turned to go.

'Wait!' Charlie cried. 'Why did Windlass take him? Why didn't he just leave him behind?'

Molly turned and stared at her. 'Toby didn't give me no message for you, Your Majesty,' she said bluntly. 'If you want that information you'll have to pay for it.'

Charlie's eyes blazed and she stepped forward, but Nell put a hand on her arm. 'What's your price, Moll?' she asked her cousin.

'I want my dad,' Molly said. 'I want him home where Mum can look after him. We lost the warehouse tonight, and we lost Ambrose. I don't reckon Mum can stand much more.'

'Your father is guilty of kidnapping and thievery and attempted murder and no doubt hundreds of other crimes blacker than I care to think of,' Charlie hissed. 'He'll hang!'

'If you hang my dad,' Molly said softly, her sapphire eyes shooting sparks at Charlie, 'you won't never know about Windlass and Toby. And I think you'd pay a lot for this information. If you want to beat that man, you need to know this. It ain't a big price. Dad'll never be the same. Doctor says he won't never use that arm again. His own son shot him, and he won't never get over that neither. Your decision: hang a cripple, or find out Alistair Windlass's weakness.'

Charlie glared at her. She hated this girl. 'All right,' she said. 'Your father goes free. Now tell me.'

'He loves his son.' Molly stared back at her, eyes bright with dislike. 'That's why he took him along with him. He loves the boy. Enough to die for him. Which is what he would have done if Ambrose hadn't shot Dad. So now you know…ma'am.' And, with a curtsey so brief it was almost an insult, she turned and walked out of the room.

Charlie climbed the highest roof ridge of Quale Castle, pressed her back into the great stone chimney and stared towards the sea. The wind tore at her clothes and hair in snarling gusts, gaining strength with the approach of night.

It was a week now since Windlass and Tobias had taken

the papers and sailed for Esceania. Her mother was busy synthesising crystal for the weapon they would now have to build. Her secretary had disappeared the morning of the theft, and Nell was working as the Dowager's assistant. Lord Topplesham was so horrified that the papers had been stolen that he was doing everything he was told.

Windlass might be gone, but she felt his presence like a shadow on her soul. She watched the sun sink towards the sea and shivered. Summer was here. It would soon be autumn. The first rook appeared, wheeling over the Castle, screeching its loneliness, its voice harsh and demanding. Others drifted through the sky like dark leaves, gathering overhead until a whirlwind of rooks spiralled above her, their rasping cries welcoming the night or shrieking defiance – she could never decide which.

War was coming. She could smell it on the wind. A war with the power to crush her City into dust and pound the ancient stones of Quale Castle to powder. Unless she and Tobias stopped it.

She was the Queen, and she was frightened. The fear of every man, woman and child in her Kingdom belonged to her. She stared across the sea towards Esceania. The wind lifted her hair, and it flew about her head like a flame.

Acknowledgements

This book exists because of the support and assistance of many people. I would especially like to thank:

My agent, Rosemary Canter; and Jodie Marsh and Jane Willis at United Agents.

My brilliant editor, Sarah Lilly, and the entire team at Orchard Books.

Lee Weatherly, for her friendship, support and guidance.

William and Kit.

My fencing coach, George Felletar, and everyone at Wellington Swords, for their friendship and encouragement, and for providing distraction, stress relief, and the perfect antidote to the sedentary life of a writer.

DON'T MISS
THE THRILLING

CASTLE
of
SHADOWS

Turn the page to read an extract!

They climbed the rickety stairs, opened the door onto the corridor and turned back the way they had come. A piece of wall near Charlie's head exploded. Watch lunged out from behind the corner. He had been lying in wait! Tobias cursed as they ran. Charlie thought: *two bullets. Four left. Unless he has more on his holster*.

There was only one way now. And it was almost as deadly as Watch. She grabbed Tobias's hand and tore up the twisting stairs to her attic. They had gained a fraction of time: Watch was slower on stairs.

Charlie ran to her bedroom, flung open the door and tore across it. Bashed open the window. 'Out!' she screamed at Tobias.

He stood frozen. His face white. 'I can't—'

'Out!' she shrieked. She pulled him to the window, pushed him through and scrambled after him. They stood on the parapet. The wind howled and shoved, making them stagger. Charlie grabbed Tobias's hand and began to climb.

She had spent five years playing on these rooftops. She knew every inch of them. Every slope and slide, gully and drain. But she never went on the roofs in winter. In the dark. Over the ice.

The first part was easy. A low-pitched roof to scramble over, then a lead gutter. Tobias slipped and fell to one knee. 'No!' he shouted. 'You're gonna kill us.'

Golden light spun out of the sky and pinned them against the roof. Another metal mosquito whined past, exploded into the slates behind them, shattering one, sending chips of slate flying. 'Ow!' Tobias clapped a hand to his cheek. Blood oozed between his fingers.

'That's what'll kill us,' Charlie screamed. 'Now come on!' She grabbed his hand and pulled. He followed.

Her mind was full of pictures. Pictures clear and sharp as crystal. She found a fragment of a second to be surprised by this and then concentrated on the image she needed. She knew the way they had to go. It was possible. Even with ice. There was only one place… *Think about it when we get there. Concentrate.*

They slithered and slid out of the gutter, free falling down a slide of roof to a lower level. *Now climb*, thought Charlie. Watch surely couldn't still be following them. But he was. She turned her head and saw the lantern dancing behind them, will o' the wisp light, death in its eye.

Tobias followed. She had let go of him now. He seemed to be over his first terror, if the solid stream of curses was anything to go by. 'Slow down here,' she called. 'Take your time. Feel for it.' They were drawing away, little by little, from the deadly gleam of the lantern. Just one last bit. The bad bit. She stopped. Put out her arm to steady him. They crouched at the top of a slope, and she saw that the cut on his cheek was still bleeding. Tobias didn't seem to notice. He looked over her shoulder at what lay before them, and his face went rigid with shock. 'Oh my God!'

It was the ridge. The one where the wind had nearly murdered her weeks before. Part of her mind wondered if she had always been meant to die here, and fate had just postponed it, as a sort of joke.

'We can't cross that!' Tobias reached out and grabbed her shoulder. 'I can't do it, Charlie. I'm terrified of heights. Always have been. I can't do this!'

'Remember what you told me about the dark?' she shouted back to him over the roar of the wind. 'The dark can't kill you.'

'Yeah? Well, the dark *can't* kill you. This can!'